continued . . .

"Jodi Thomas writes with a true love of Texas and her characters. What makes *Two Texas Hearts* special is the unique twist on the marriage of convenience plot created by her special brand of humor and characters who stay in her heart."

—*Romantic Times*

"This is a wonderful book, destined for my keeper shelf simply because I felt happy while I read it."

—*The Romance Reader*

"*Two Texas Hearts* is a provocative, sensual story of a man and a woman trying to do the best they can in an awkward situation . . . clever and captivating. Author Jodi Thomas offers a tale that keeps you riveted from start to finish. Her characters are the kind of folks you'd want to have in your own family tree."

—*Times Record News* (Wichita Falls, Texas)

TEXAS LOVE SONG

"*Texas Love Song* is a warm and touching read full of intrigue and suspense that will keep the reader on the edge of her seat."

—*Rendezvous*

FOREVER IN TEXAS

"A winner from an author who knows how to make the west tough but tender. Jodi Thomas's earthy characters, feisty dialogue, and sweet love story will steal your heart."

—*Romantic Times*

"A great western romance filled with suspense and plenty of action. It is the two tremendous lead characters, especially the pragmatic yet romantic Hannah, who will have the audience forever reading *Forever in Texas*."

—*Affaire de Coeur*

To Kiss a Texan

JODI THOMAS

JOVE BOOKS, NEW YORK

TO KISS A TEXAN

A Jove Book / published by arrangement
with the author

PRINTING HISTORY
Jove edition / May 1999

The Penguin Putnam Inc. World Wide Web site address is
http://www.penguinputnam. com

ISBN: 0-515-12503-2

A JOVE BOOK®
Jove Books are published by The Berkley Publishing Group,
a division of Penguin Putnam Inc.,
375 Hudson Street, New York, New York 10014.
JOVE and the "J" design
are trademarks belonging to Penguin Putnam Inc.

PRINTED IN THE UNITED STATES OF AMERICA

10 9 8 7 6 5 4 3 2 1

This book is dedicated to
Pam Wilson
If bravery were a jewel
you'd be covered in diamonds.

Also, a special thanks to the Mary E. Bivins Library and
to all the libraries of Texas.

To Kiss A

Texan

ONE

1868
Texas during Reconstruction

THE AIR HELD THE HEAVY STILLNESS OF AUGUST,
warning of a late summer storm. The kind of storm that
leaves a simmering dampness over the land. Weather
that reminded Weston McLain of battlefields hot with
gunfire and wet with blood and sweat.

A thin scar on his left cheek was another reminder.
Along with nightmares that still stole his sleep and kept
his Colt never far from his grip.

As the sun melted away, Wes rolled his wide shoulders along the rough brick building. His lean form
straightened from the shadows of the alley and took a
step toward the street. Without crossing into the lamplight, he watched in darkness while the good folks of
Denton, Texas, filed into the church across the road. The
A-frame building looked peaceful amid a town and state
primed to explode.

But tonight, Wes wasn't concerned about the town, or
the state. The explosion would erupt between him and a
lovely lady he hadn't seen in two months. Angela Montago. She'd promised to marry him after a few moonlight
kisses, though neither had spoken of love. He no longer
believed in love anyway. He guessed she saw the mar-

riage as a bargain, just as he did. Wes wanted a family, and she wanted a man as wealthy as her father.

He'd had no chance to tell her about his sudden loss of funds or how he planned to rebuild. The news of his poverty reached her before he could, and now the Montago gates were closed to him. He needed to explain how he would be back on his feet in a matter of weeks. She wouldn't see him, but he knew he wouldn't have long to wait, for Angela Montago was predictable.

She would attend church tonight. This time, she'd talk to him. There'd be no servants or family barring the door. If she had ended their plans of marriage after hearing of his loss, she could tell him to his face. He deserved that, at least, if her belief in him was so shallow. He'd never tell her of the map and the fortune in gold waiting for him if she refused to stand beside him now.

Angela and her older sister, Maria, never missed a traveling preacher—though tonight's bill seemed to belong more in a circus than a revival. Some circuit minister from Austin planned to exhibit a wild woman who'd lived with the Indians so long he claimed even her soul was savage. Wes had no doubt the benediction would ask for prayers and money to save her.

As he waited, a wagon rattled to a stop in the alley just behind him. Rough boards framed a cage in the wagon bed. A tiny creature could be seen between the slats' shadows. She was almost too small to be a full-grown woman, huddling in the center with her hands chained to a ring. She wore a filthy, ragged dress several sizes too big. Her mud-colored hair was long and matted wildly about her. Wes couldn't tell if the smudges he saw along her bare arms were bruises or dirt. He wasn't sure he wanted to know.

"Get back!" the crusty driver yelled. "You'll see her at the service."

Wes ignored the warning and leaned toward the cage. There had been hundreds of accounts of kidnapping of settlers and their children. Most of the men and women didn't survive, but every few months children would be ransomed in trade or brought back by a friendly tribe. Wes had seen more than once, over the three years he'd been in Texas, children who'd grown up Indian and saw their rescue as a kidnapping from their tribe.

The man atop the wagon waved a withered hand and shouted again, "She's crazy wild and she'll kill you without blinking if she gets the chance." The driver lowered his voice when Wes didn't cower away. "So step back, mister." His tone grew more conversational. "I was told to wait here in the alley until time for the meeting to start. Nobody's s'posed to notice her till then."

Wes folded his arms and widened his stance as he glanced toward the street. No one looked in the direction of the alley. Most hurried toward the church.

The driver climbed down and tied the horses to the same railing Wes had used for his own mount. He pulled a bottle from beneath the seat and took a long draw as he eyed the street to see if anyone besides Wes witnessed.

The evening shadows hid his actions from any passerby, but the driver nodded toward Wes before leaning over and taking another drink.

In that glance, Wes met his stare in the moonlight and what he saw chilled the air. The man's eyes were tombstone gray, void of all kindness. Wes had seen men in the war with hate-fevered eyes and a few with a lust to kill reflected in their stare. But Wes would bet his last twenty-dollar gold piece that this man didn't hate, he simply didn't care about anything or anyone in life.

Wes didn't take his gaze off the girl in the cage as he asked the driver, "You the preacher talking about her tonight?"

"Naw." The man rested his withered arm against the wagon. "I'm just hired to get her here. The Rangers who found her gave her over to the reverend I work for part-time. No family would claim her. Can't say as I blame them. A woman who's caught like that living out in the wild. . . . She'd be better off dead."

He took another drink. "She fights us like a wildcat

when we pull her through the crowds. Preacher's even tried to beat the devil out of her while a whole congregation watched, but there just ain't no helping her.''

He slammed his fist against the slats as if to keep back a wild animal. "She's a lot of trouble. I liked it better when the preacher did a traveling magic show. You wouldn't believe the act he had. He could disappear with you standing right beside him." The driver finished off the bottle. " 'Course, it don't pay like preaching does.''

The man lifted his empty bottle, then moved onto the boarded walk. "Get near her at your own risk," he warned. "I'll be right back.''

Wes glanced at the woman huddled like a wounded animal. She might be acting as part of the scam, or she might be insane. Either way, she'd fill the offering baskets.

An open carriage, flanked by well-armed guards, pulled to a stop between Wes and the street lamp. In sharp contrast to the chained creature in the alley's shadows, a young woman dressed in white stepped from the carriage. She was tall and walked like a queen. Her every movement spoke of breeding and wealth.

For a moment Wes could only stare. Angela was a woman who expected the world to stop and notice her entrance. Individually, none of her features were outstanding, but combined, they created an air about her. He hardly noticed her older sister and mother move from the carriage and flank her like twin generals.

"Evening, Angela." Wes crossed in front of her, guessing she would be angry at him. But his pride wouldn't allow him to start with an apology. "I was hoping I'd find you here. We need to talk.''

She looked straight ahead. One gloved hand pushed back a wayward strand of velvet black hair. Wes had thought she'd be upset about his sudden poverty, but he never thought she'd lose faith in him. All his promises to her would still come true, they'd just take a little longer.

But she wouldn't look in his direction. She obviously

thought her denial of attention would be a punishment worse than death for any man.

Her older sister, Maria, was the only one who faced him. "She doesn't wish to speak to you, Weston McLain, so step aside. You no longer exist in her world."

Wes glared past Maria to their mother. "I need to talk to Angela alone for a moment." He tried to keep the anger from his voice as he turned back to Angela. "I need to explain." He had to tell this stately woman who had never wanted for anything in her life that he'd lost a fortune and had only himself to offer. He might have barely enough cattle left to feed them through the winter, but they'd make it. They could still start the family he'd planned and, in time, the ranch would grow. "Nothing's changed." Surely the strength he saw in her carriage was equaled in her character. She'd given her word and she'd take him as is now without knowing about his plan to be wealthy again in a few weeks.

Maria took a step forward, blocking Wes's view of the woman he'd hoped to marry. "You are wrong. Everything has changed, Mr. McLain."

"But we—"

Maria's anger snapped, sharpening her already angular features. "You are no longer engaged to my sister. As a former cavalry officer, I assume you will be gentlemen enough not to bother her again."

Wes advanced. "I'll hear that from her!"

He was so lost in the hardness of Maria's words and the coldness of Angela's stare, he didn't notice the Montago guards.

The riders were off their mounts and at his side. As he took another step toward Angela, their shoulders closed like a gate, blocking him from passing. He felt the cold press of a gun barrel against his ribs.

Maria smiled as Angela and her mother moved toward the church. "We have nothing else to say to you tonight—or ever."

Wes struggled against the guards. "But we agreed.

She promised we'd be married as soon as I returned. You'll not stop me—"

A sudden blow into his midsection ended Wes's threat.

Moving a step closer, Maria whispered, "As a rich man, that scar across your face added character; but poor, Angela cannot stand the sight of you. Do not muddy her world with your presence again, or my father will have you killed."

Wes jerked against his bonds.

Another blow slammed into his rib cage.

Maria made a motion with her hand as though sweeping away trash toward the alley.

The Montago guards dragged Wes the few feet into the shadows. He fought wildly, angry more at Angela and life than at the men surrounding him. As others advanced, he downed several before two caught him from behind. While they held him, the others took turns plowing blows into his midsection.

Wes took the pounding without a sound. No one in Denton would help him if he called for aid. No one would go against the Montago family. Most would think he deserved such a beating. After all, he, an outsider, had courted a rich rancher's daughter. He dared to think he could step into the closed circle of ranchers with only his hard work to stake him.

Finally, a blow knocked him against the cage. He crumbled to the ground.

"Stay away from the Montago ranch, Yank," a Southern voice ordered. "Or the next time you won't be treated so kindly."

Wes tasted blood and felt along his ribs. "This isn't over."

The guard laughed and kicked Wes hard, folding him over in the dirt. "Yes, it is."

When Wes raised his head again, they were gone.

With great effort, he wrapped his fingers around one board of the cage and pulled himself up. Fighting not to cry out in pain, he held his side and stood in the darkness, knowing no one could see him from the street.

The pain in his body was nothing compared to the wound to his pride. Angela had been part of his dream . . . the only part that hadn't died at the Red River when he'd watched two years of work vanish in one stormy stampede. He'd loved the ideal of her, a proper wife and family, though he hadn't loved her. They would have made a good match. But he'd never have that chance now, for the dream or the woman.

He gripped the slat tighter, his pride forcing him to straighten despite the pain.

Timid fingers moved from within the darkened cage and closed over his.

Wes raised his gaze to the woman on the other side of the boards. Kneeling inside her prison, she faced him. Her chains pulled tight against her wrists so she could touch his hand.

All the anger and hurt left him as she raised her hand and gently traced the scar along his face.

A tear bubbled in her eye and fell, cleaning a streak down her cheek.

Wes opened his hand and let her thin fingers lace through his. The world shifted as her cool palm pressed against his. The broken engagement didn't matter, or the beating, or even his lost wealth. All that mattered as he looked into dark blue eyes was this creature dressed in rags.

If it cost him his life, this woman would not be pulled through a crowd tonight!

TWO

WES SHOVED AN IRON STAKE BETWEEN THE CHAIN and the cage and twisted. Even hurt, his powerful strength rocked the wagon with his effort. There was no time to pick the lock. He knew it would only be moments before someone noticed him and he not only had to get the cage open, he had to convince the poor creature inside to come with him.

Wes glanced at her. She backed as far away from him as she could.

"Now wait a minute!" a familiar slurred voice shouted from the entrance to the alley. "Don't break that lock. Louis won't like it."

Wes straightened, his right hand an inch from his Colt, his left gripping the iron tool. He turned slowly as the driver ran toward him with a full bottle of whiskey in his good hand.

Without warning, the man's drunken laughter polluted the night air in a breathless hiccuping sound. "I know you want her, mister." He raised his bottle as if in salute. "Some men have the taste for a little wild seasoning in their women. I guessed you was one of them by the way you stared at her. She'll give you a fight for what you take, if that's what you like. But don't break my lock. The reverend will make me pay to have it fixed."

Wes stepped back, knotting his fists to keep from clobbering the drunk. "Open the cage," he whispered between clenched teeth.

The driver hesitated. "I don't like to do this kind of business till after the service. Last crazy woman we had killed herself one night after the boys from the saloon took turns dancing a few rounds with her. How about you wait until later? Then I'll give you this throwaway."

When Wes didn't answer, the man raised one eyebrow as if weighing Wes's worth. "I'll only charge you five dollars for the night. I won't ask no questions, long as she's back in the cage by dawn." He winked at Wes. "Ain't none of my concern what you do with her."

"Open the door." Wes fought down the bile in his throat. He felt like he was bargaining with the devil, but he knew time was running out for her. The church bell stopped ringing. It would only be a matter of minutes before she'd be pulled across the street. "I'll give you a twenty-dollar gold piece."

Wes pulled the last of his money from his pocket and shoved it into the driver's withered hand. "I want her unchained. Now!"

"All right." The driver tested the weight of the coin. "I got to get her out anyway. It's almost time." He glanced in the direction of the church and slipped the double eagle into his vest pocket. "You can feel of her while I remove the ring from her chains. But you'll have to wait until after the show to have her. She'll be all tired by then and not so hard to handle. She's tiny, but she's got big, ripe . . ."

The cage door swung open, and Wes felt his heart stop in midbeat. Suddenly there was no air, no town, no drunk beside him. All he saw were her eyes staring at him with total hate. The blue depths that had been filled with kindness only minutes ago now were wide with panic and fear. The terror of a child blended with the hatred of a woman as she watched him.

For a moment he hesitated, wondering if she truly was insane and if he'd do her any good by setting her free.

Maybe this life, as terrible as it seemed, was better than her dying if left on her own.

She backed away as he and the driver stepped into the cage. Her dress caught in her movements, pulling the material from one shoulder. Bruises were plain even in the shadowy light. Wes closed his eyes. With all he'd seen in the war and since, he wasn't sure he could bear to know how completely she'd been harmed.

The drunk knelt and began unlocking the ring that held her wrist chains. "Go ahead, get yourself a good feel. She ain't going to do nothing but scream and that'll let them know we're coming. It don't matter if you bruise her. She don't talk none. She ain't going to tell anyone. Grab you a good handful."

Wes took a step toward her.

The creature looked as if she might bolt and run the moment her chained wrists were free. She raised her hands and shook her head wildly.

The driver laughed. "Go ahead. Slap her a good one to let her know you mean business. There ain't nothing feels better then getting a tight hold on a ripe woman. Since you paid twenty, I'll even hold her if you like. That way you can slip your hands up her dress."

Without thought Wes swung toward the man. With one blow, he knocked the drunk out the open cage door and onto the ground.

The woman let out a soft cry and covered her face as though she thought she would be his next victim.

Wes backed out of the cage and tapped the driver with the toe of his boot. The man was out cold. Unswallowed whiskey blended with blood and dripped from his open mouth, but his withered fingers still held the bottle tightly.

Glancing into the cage, Wes met her stare once more. She still shook, but no longer looked at him with hate. The fear was there, the panic—but he'd won an ounce of respect in her eyes.

"Come on," he whispered as he raised his hand slowly to her. "I'll get you out of this mess."

Wes had no idea where he would take her, or how he would handle her if she truly were crazy. Only one fact remained certain: he couldn't leave her here. Not alone. Not with this man. Not as a curiosity for the town.

"I won't hurt you." He tried to make his voice calm. "I'm only trying to set you free."

She hesitated a second then bolted toward him. In a heartbeat, she'd jumped into his arms, holding him so tightly Wes wasn't sure if she was hugging him or trying to choke him.

"It's all right." Through his rage at her captors, he forced out the words. "It's all right." Awkwardly, he patted her back and felt her tense beneath his touch. He didn't have to look to know there would be whelps beneath her dress.

"I'll get you out of here." He wrapped one arm about her waist and lifted her a few inches off the ground as he moved around the wagon. "Do you understand?"

She didn't answer or lessen her hold on him.

As he felt her tears on his throat, someone from the street yelled, "Hey you! Turn loose of that woman!"

Wes swung around. A huge man in black was running toward him. The bearded man waved a long staff over his head like a weapon. His great coat flew around him, reminding Wes of the wings of a bat flying through the darkness.

"Let her go! She's my ward."

Wes wrapped his arms around her legs and lifted her as he turned away. He felt her fear pounding against his heart and couldn't help but wonder how many times the long stick had been used across her back. She shook with terror, telling Wes plainly that this man in black was the preacher who planned to put her on stage tonight.

"Let her go!" The minister reached the alley entrance with several men only a few feet behind him. "Stop him! He's kidnapping her!"

The creature's weight did little to slow Wes down. She clung so tightly, he knew she wouldn't leave his arms if he let go of her. She was far more afraid of the huge man with the stick than of him.

Years of battles during the war served him well. He'd stayed alive by never hesitating. His movements now were swift and purposeful.

Just as he reached his horse, the preacher ran past the wagon. "Shoot him! He's stealing my property!"

Wes swung onto his saddle with the sound of metal clearing leather. He kicked his mount into action as bullets danced past his head and ricocheted off the brick wall in front of him.

The powerful animal beneath him jerked wildly in panic. Shots echoed down the alley and back. With one hand around the woman's waist and the other twisted firmly in the reins, Wes leaned forward, protecting her as he kicked the horse into a run.

Ride! he screamed in his mind as the voices faded in the background. *Ride!* he commanded himself as hot fiery pain shot through his back. Ride!

The night loomed black and silent, with no sign of civilization in sight. Allie felt as if her arms might fall off at any moment. She'd held the tall man in the saddle for hours. Judging from the sky, it would be dawn soon. But she wasn't sure he had enough life left in him to see its coming.

Somehow he'd managed to stay in control of the half-wild horse until they were well away from the town. But she felt the blood, warm and thick along his back, and knew with each pounding of hooves his life passed.

With all her strength, she pulled on the reins. To her surprise, the horse obeyed, stopping in a wooded area with tall undergrowth all around. It didn't matter where they were; they had to rest.

Allie slipped from the saddle and tried to catch the man who had taken her from the cage.

But his body weighed too much for her, and they both fell to the ground as he toppled over. With sudden panic, she shoved him from her and rolled away.

He didn't move.

Run, she thought. Now might be her only chance to get away. She could survive off the land. She'd done it before. This might be her only chance at freedom. She would live once more without cages or chains.

The man has passed to the next life, she told herself. He doesn't move. She could take his horse and be into the hills by nightfall. He would have no use for a horse. If he lived, the preacher's men would catch up to them soon. If she kept running, maybe the posse would be satisfied with catching him and leave her to her hills.

Allie moved toward the horse, forcing herself not to look back. She didn't even know if he was a good man or a bad one. After all, the Rangers who'd captured her had said they were good and treated her kindly. But they gave her over to the reverend. The women at the first fort had given her this dress, then laughed at how she looked in it. She couldn't tell good from bad anymore. It was safer to be alone.

He's dead, she thought, without looking at him. *He must be dead. He won't mind my taking the horse and supplies.*

Running her hand along the leather of the saddle, she felt where he'd worn down the design. It was a fine quality saddle, she guessed. And a fine horse. The gun he wore strapped to his leg looked worth a fine bargaining also.

She glanced at him. If he didn't need the horse, he wouldn't need the gun.

Slowly, she retraced her steps. He was so still he might already have stopped breathing. She moved to his side and knelt. If she had anything to give him, she'd trade. Even if he were already dead, she would leave a trade if she had something.

As Allie touched the cool handle of the weapon, he moved slightly. She jumped back.

For a long moment she watched him. He still breathed, she decided. Watching closely, she saw the slight rise and fall of his chest. He might live. If he'd been planning to hurt her last night, he deserved to die. But if he'd been helping her, if his whispered words to her were true, she owed him her life.

She had to take the chance. She must help him . . . at least until she knew.

THREE

WES FOUGHT THROUGH THE PAIN AS HE SLOWLY opened his eyes. He tried to remember what he'd done this time in his endless efforts to get himself killed, but too many scars, from battlefields to barrooms, clouded his memory.

The words of an old sergeant he'd known back in '63 drifted through his mind. "If you can hear yourself breathing and don't see your brains splattered beside you, there's a good chance you'll make it to fight another day."

Wes took a deep breath. *That's half the test*, he thought. Slowly, he forced himself to focus and look around.

The air seemed thick, foggy, as though a cloud were resting on the ground. And colors, from the dark green of late summer to the blue-brown of aging foliage, surrounded him in varying hues of clarity. Wes guessed it was evening or just before sunset. He couldn't be sure. The trees distorted the light, and his mind blocked out a sharpening of his senses.

He felt along his side. First order, check his Colt. Still in place. Then his ribs. Painful to the touch.

Slowly, he forced his hand to his back as he closed his eyes in dread. He hated the feel of his own blood.

The memory of the fiery pain returned, and the night ride, and the woman.

Wes glanced up. The woman! He opened his mouth to call out, but to who? He couldn't very well yell, "Hey, crazy lady!" or "creature" or "wild woman." The best he could think of was "blue eyes." He doubted she'd answer to that.

She was probably long gone anyway, he figured as he swore aloud and fought to stand. Judging from the pain in his back, the bullet was still lodged just above his waist. If he didn't get to a doctor fast, it wouldn't matter about his loss of blood—the bullet's poison would kill him.

The forest became a merry-go-round as he stood. Wes staggered from one tree to another. Corrected and stumbled again.

From nowhere, an arm moved about his waist and straightened his path. Gentle hands guided him as she made her body his crutch.

When he looked down at the tiny creature helping him, blue eyes met his gaze. She was still dirty, with hair flying around her and a face that seemed made of more mud than skin. But her eyes were filled with a kindness that touched his soul.

"Where are we?" he asked, not expecting an answer.

Silently she helped him to his horse. He guessed that she'd taken care of the animal while he'd slept. The mane looked freshly brushed. Maybe he could cross off crazy from her names. She was smart enough to take care of the animal, knowing that the horse would very likely be the difference between life and death.

"I have to get to Fort Worth, Blue Eyes," he mumbled, hoping she'd prove even smarter. Fog fought to overtake his mind. "I have a brother there who's a doctor. I have to get to him."

She pushed Wes into the saddle.

"Do you understand?" he asked through teeth gritted from the agony of moving. He'd climbed into a saddle a million times, and reasoned he'd be able to hold on even if he passed out. After all, he'd spent months sleeping atop a horse during the cattle drives.

The tiny woman jumped up behind him without showing a sign of understanding anything he said.

"Find Doctor McLain." Wes fought for a few more moments of clear thought. "Find him. If I don't make it, make sure he gets my saddlebags."

"There's a map he must see even if I die." Wes knew he was mumbling, but he had to fight the darkness closing in. "Doctor in Fort Worth named McLain."

Allie heard his words, but she didn't answer. She wasn't sure she knew how. It had been so many years since she'd spoken the language of her people, she wasn't sure she remembered. When she'd been captured by the Rangers, none of the words had made sense, but now she understood many of them. She liked the low voice of this stranger and wished he'd talk more to her.

She'd thought the man would be dead by the time she watered the horse. Then she could have given him a burial in exchange for his supplies. But he hadn't known her plan, for when she returned, he'd been stumbling worse than the man with the crippled hand who drove her cage.

He was still alive, still bleeding. This stranger would not be buried here in the quiet of the woods tonight.

She'd have to think of a new plan, for planning what she would do had been the only thing that had kept her alive these past few weeks.

Much as she hated to go toward a town, the only way she could be rid of him was to drop him in Fort Worth, as he apparently wished. Then she would vanish back into the hills. He had saved her from the preacher and she owed him for that.

She knew the way to the place called Fort Worth. She'd crossed the road many times. If the man had family there, it would be only right to take him home to die. Once he was with them he wouldn't need his horse or gun. He'd probably give them to her if she asked. In fact, she was sure he would, so there was really no need to ask. She'd just take him to his family and vanish with his unspoken gifts to her. With a horse and a gun the Rangers would never capture her again and call it "a saving."

Allie worked on her plan all the way to Fort Worth, fighting down the fear that grew with each mile. She'd go back to the hill country where she'd lived alone for the past five winters. She had no tribe, no people. If she wanted to stay alive, she must stay away from everyone.

In the darkness before the stars appeared she rode into Fort Worth. The man was mumbling out of his head about a map and a treasure hidden long ago. He managed to hold himself in the saddle. Sometimes he'd call out names of people or yell orders as though he were in battle.

Keeping her arm around him, she leaned against his back more for warmth now than need to hold him upright. The day had turned from cloudy to rainy. Her cotton dress did nothing to keep her warm. She could no longer tell if the dampness against her abdomen was from rain or the stranger's blood. It no longer mattered, for their journey would soon end.

Turning the horse down a main street, Allie wondered how she would ever find his kin. She could hear music and the sounds of voices, but very few people walked the street. She was afraid to ride close to the lamplight for fear someone would recapture her and put her back in a cage. They would see that she was a wild creature.

But if she didn't get someone to assist them, the man would be dead before he saw his family.

Allie nudged the exhausted horse forward, hoping to find a way. Men stumbled out of the bars, but she didn't ask for help. People rode by in wagons, without slowing enough to notice her. She'd gone from being the center of attention to being invisible. The few folks who crossed in front of them looked at Allie in disgust and quickened their pace. They didn't take the time to see his blood, or her exhausted tears.

Allie was alone in this town full of people with a dying man no one would help. Maybe it would be better to lower him to the street and leave him among his kind. Maybe it was she no one wanted to look upon. Except for this one stranger in her arms, no man or woman had ever offered to help her. Even the stranger would call her a creature in time. For all she knew he'd been taking her to put in another cage. The preacher had told the Rangers he'd help her; an hour later she'd felt his staff across her back.

But the memory of this stranger's low voice close to her ear when they'd run from the cage returned. He'd whispered that everything would be all right. He'd spoken the words to her, not at her. For once in her life, Allie wanted to believe it could be true.

Moving through the streets, she searched the faces, hoping to find someone who would meet her gaze and show enough kindness to assist a dying man. But the light rain kept heads bowed as people rushed by.

Stars spotted the partly cloudy sky as time passed and Allie fought to keep from falling asleep as she crossed back and forth through the town. Finally, they passed a big two-story building full of activity. People inside ate at tables covered with white cloths. Allie stared at the sight. It didn't matter that she hadn't eaten a meal in two days, she couldn't take her eyes off how grand everyone looked. All dressed up like visions she sometimes saw in her dreams. Women in dresses of every color with their hair piled high atop their heads, and men in black jackets and shirts as white as new fallen snow.

Moving the horse closer, she held to her charge as she watched the people through the tall windows. They all smiled as if they didn't have to worry about the weather or where they would eat tomorrow.

Allie could never remember smiling. Not in her entire life. Not in the long-ago time before her people all lay dead. Not when she was traded from tribe to tribe and tied with the dogs each night. Not when she'd finally run away and lived alone. She was not sure she could make her mouth do such a strange thing.

Just as she nudged the horse to move on, she saw him. A man inside by the window. He was all dressed up. His hair, though combed, was warm brown like the man with her, only there was no scar along his cheek. His eyes, his height, his jawline were the same. They had to be kin.

As she watched, the man inside stood and moved toward the door with a tall woman at his arm.

Allie knew this might be her only chance. She slid from the saddle and hoped her stranger could hold on a few minutes without her. Before she had time to change her mind, she darted across the street and climbed up the railing. She reached the steps just as the couple came out.

Without hesitation, she grabbed the man's arm and pulled him toward the shadows where her horse waited.

He stumbled down a few steps, straightened and looked at her. "What's this?" He appeared surprised, but not angry. "Who are you?"

Allie didn't answer. Pulling on his arm didn't seem to budge him. Frustrated, she pointed into the rain. But he couldn't see the horse or the dying man and she couldn't find any words to tell him.

"What is it?" The man's voice was kind, not loud and demanding. He had the same low sound in his words as her stranger had. "Do you need a doctor?"

Allie pulled again, now panicking that he might turn her over to the Rangers at any moment. After all, she was in a town, the very last place in the world she ever wanted to be. They might leave her stranger in the rain to die while they took her somewhere. She'd heard what folks said about her. She'd heard one say that she belonged in a cage.

Before she could turn and run, the woman stepped from behind the man. She was very tall with a dress and cape of deep blue.

"Help her, Adam," the woman said, her voice laced

with understanding. "Can't you see she needs you to follow her?"

Then the woman did the strangest thing Allie had ever seen anyone do. She pulled her long cape from her shoulders and placed it over Allie's. This lady, all clean and stately, tied her cape closed over Allie's cold shoulders and stroked her hair back until the hood covered her wild, muddy hair.

"We'll come," she whispered and smiled, as though giving away her clothing was of no concern. "My husband is a doctor. He'll make everything better. But you're soaked to the bone. You must cover up."

They followed Allie without asking any more questions. But when they were still several feet away, the doctor called Adam saw the dying man. Suddenly he was running, shouting orders as if a tornado were aground.

Then the tall woman did another strange thing. She took Allie's blood-covered hand in her white-gloved hand and motioned with her head for Allie to follow her. Suddenly, they were rushing through the streets.

Allie glanced back. Adam was lowering the dying man to the ground. He had none of the trouble that Allie had had getting people to help. Men stepped forward to carry the wounded stranger and to hold the horse. Everyone seemed to want to help the doctor.

"Hurry!" the lady shouted as they ran. "We have to get home and get everything ready."

Allie wanted to pull away. She'd done what she came to do. She'd delivered the stranger to his family. But the woman's grip was tight around her fingers, pulling her along.

They ran past several houses then crossed through an opening between buildings to another, much quieter street.

The lady let out a long breath as she climbed the back steps to a huge house. "We're home." She held the door for Allie.

As Allie crossed into the house, the woman called,

"Rose! Adam's bringing Wes and he's hurt. We'll need water and all the supplies ready fast."

The lady pulled Allie through the house before Allie had a moment to look around and swung her into a huge chair beside a fireplace.

"Sit and warm yourself," the woman said as she placed a blanket over Allie's legs. "I have to get things ready, then we'll talk." She smiled again. "I'm Nichole, Adam's wife, and of course that makes me Wes's sister-in-law."

Her words made little sense to Allie. And what she did next made no sense at all.

The lovely woman leaned forward and kissed Allie on the cheek. "Thank you," she whispered, tears in her eyes. "Thank you for bringing Wes to us."

Allie touched her cheek and leaned back into the cape as the woman moved away. She thought of all the names she'd been called in the past. Savage, wild, crazy, worthless. But none of them fit her now. This beautiful woman treated her like a treasure. Somehow in the act, Allie had gained value.

The large room came alive like a forest does when one stands perfectly still. The one called Nichole and others passed back and forth carrying water, supplies, and lamps. Allie closed around herself, making herself small inside the folds of the chair. As she'd done all her life, she shut the world out.

Closing her eyes, she let her mind wander to her dreams. In them, she was inside a room like she'd seen tonight. Her clothes were rich and flowing, with warm colors. In the dream, there was music also. Not the clangy music from the bars she'd passed riding through town, or the church music pounded from an organ, but soft music, lighter than air, floating around her. And tables of food, all kinds of food with their rich aromas blending together. And candlelight twinkling like diamonds over fine crystal and shiny table settings.

In her dream world Allie was no longer a "throwaway woman." She was a treasure. As she'd been for a moment tonight in one person's eyes.

FOUR

"I SAY WE ALL GRAB HER AT ONCE AND THROW HER in the tub. She's dirtier than any human I've ever come across and most animals."

Allie slowly opened her eyes at the sound of a high-pitched woman's voice behind her. The room before her had emptied of most people, so she felt brave enough to look around. The huge space seemed packed with items of all sizes and colors. All the lamps except the one on a desk had been turned down. Fireplace flickers danced off tall windows black with night, making the room seem alive.

She guessed the room to be the doctor's office, but this place bore little resemblance to the tiny room the Rangers had taken her to that they'd called a doctor's office.

"You'll do no such thing, Rose," another answered from behind Allie's chair, reminding Allie she wasn't alone. "She may very well have saved Wes's life. If she wants to dress in mud, it doesn't matter to me. We'll offer her a bath after you see if she wants anything to eat."

Allie gripped the cape tighter about her and peered through the small opening. She wished the room were not all in shadows, for she wasn't sure which were spaces between bookshelves and which were doors.

She couldn't see the opening where they'd entered hours ago. The man called Adam sat several feet away at his desk. He looked far too interested in the book in his hands to even hear the women's voices behind Allie.

The wounded stranger, who'd helped her from the cage, lay on a high bed under one set of windows. She could see white wrappings across his ribs and the slow rise and fall of his chest. He was still alive.

"Miss?" The high-pitched voice grew closer. "I've cooked you up something in case you're hungry before your bath."

A woman, not much taller than Allie, appeared before the fireplace. She looked a few years older than the one called Nichole. Her cheeks had odd red full moons painted on them and her breasts seemed to form from the top of her shoulders to her waist.

"Rose!" the woman called Nichole said softly from somewhere behind Allie. "Don't bother our guest. Allow her to eat in peace."

Letting the slit in the cape widen slightly, Allie watched a tiny woman move across her line of vision. The painted lady carried a tray loaded down with a week's supply of food. All kinds of food. Not just meat, or bread, or roots.

"Here you go, sweetie." The woman smiled with dark red lips as she set the tray on a footstool and stepped back. She folded her arms over her ample breasts and waited for Allie to make the next move.

For a moment, all Allie could see was the piece of meat, bread layered in butter, a baked apple still steamy from the oven. From somewhere far in her past came the memory of such foods. Then she saw it—the knife placed beside the plate.

In one lightning lunge, she raised from her coverings, grabbed the weapon, and folded back into the cave of covers.

The woman called Rose jumped back as though someone had punched her. "Did you see that?" she yelled toward the doctor.

"See what?" Adam answered without lifting his stare from the book.

Rose pointed toward Allie with a shaking hand. "She stole the knife!"

"Then get her another one," Adam answered without giving the matter a glance.

Rose huffed and stormed out of the room. "Well, I never in all my born days seen . . ." Words trailed after her.

Allie closed her eyes and let the knife turn over in her hand. The food looked good and the room felt wonderfully warm, but nothing compared to the feel of a weapon in her hand. She was no longer defenseless.

"There!" Rose appeared in front of Allie once more. "I brought you another fork, too." She clanked the gift down next to the plate.

When Allie grabbed the second knife Rose screamed again, this time drawing Adam's full attention.

"She did it again, Doc. She took the knife." Rose waved her finger in a whipping motion. "Land's sake to goodness, she'll kill us all in our sleep."

"I doubt anyone in the house is asleep, thanks to your screaming." Adam stood and moved slowly toward Allie. "Get another knife, Rose," he said calmly. "In fact, bring all we have."

"What!" Rose shifted her startled gaze to the doctor.

"You heard me. Bring all the knives from your kitchen."

Rose stormed off, her hands at full-blown mast above her head and words following her like smoke does from a train.

Adam knelt in front of Allie. Very slowly, he lifted the bread and offered it to her.

Allie didn't move. She'd been offered food before only to find it a trap. If she didn't take the bread, maybe he wouldn't hurt her or demand something in return.

"You've no call to be afraid," Adam said calmly. "We owe you a great debt for bringing Wes to us." He put the bread on the tray and picked up the glass of milk.

She didn't reach for it.

"I'm sorry if Rose frightened you. She's a great cook. Won't you try her meal?"

Allie knew his words, but somehow all the meaning didn't come through. She'd been tricked too often to trust now.

Rose returned with her starched apron loaded down with weapons.

Adam reached in her stash and offered Allie a small knife. "If you want these, you are welcome to them," he said. "We've nothing to fear from such a brave one as you. I don't know how my brother found his way into your care, but I'm glad you brought him to us. We are all in your debt."

Allie could never remember being called brave. She'd always thought of herself as a coward. All her life it seemed she'd been running. First from the raid that killed her family, then from tribes that warred against one another, then from the men who captured her and called it a saving.

"I'll just put a few of them here." Adam stood, taking the knives, apron and all, from Rose. He placed two on the bookshelf beside the door he opened. "The rest will be in the room across the hallway. Nichole prepared you a bath, and Rose will take your food in there so you can have some privacy."

Rose looked at the doctor as if he'd lost his mind and this wasn't the first time she'd noticed. She let out a loud sigh and shook her head toward heaven. "Lord, Lord, protect us all tonight so we don't get knifed in our sleep." She lifted the tray and followed the doctor without ceasing in her prayer. "Lord, please send Sister Cel and the others safely back home, and Lord, please don't let them be the ones that finds us all dead in our own blood from the knife wounds, and Lord, I'm truly sorry for my life of sin. It was an evil life, and I don't have time to list everything one by one, but I don't deserve to be stabbed like a hog neither and Lord—"

"That will be enough, Rose," the doctor interrupted. "You'll frighten our guest."

She opened one eye to glare at him as she continued silently mouthing her prayer while following Adam out of the room.

Allie waited.

Silence.

She could still smell the baked apple. Slowly, she shifted the weapons in her hands. Could it be possible no one was going to fight her for them?

Letting the blanket slip away, she looked around the room.

No one. Only the stranger, who Adam had called Wes. He lay on the bed asleep.

With a tight grip on the largest knife, Allie stood. She turned a full circle twice.

No one.

Without a sound, she moved toward the door where Adam and Rose had disappeared. They could be just beyond the opening, waiting to jump at her. Waiting to take her weapon away. Waiting to hurt her.

But as she inched past the door, she saw no one. Only the light from across the hall. The knives Adam had carried from the room were spread out on the bed like an offering. The tray of food sat on a table.

Hunger drove Allie closer. Every inch of her was alive, ready to bolt at any sound or hint of danger. She moved into the hallway.

Nothing.

She entered the small room and, once again, turned a circle with her knife drawn. The room was too small to hide a person. There was only space enough for a bed, a small table, a chair, and a huge tub of water.

As she finished the rotation, Allie caught sight of Nichole in the doorway. Allie's knuckles turned white with her tight grip on the weapon, but she didn't advance. She waited. She had no desire to harm the lady, but Allie had made up her mind she wouldn't let anyone hurt her again.

Nichole stepped to the bed and laid down a pile of clothing. "I thought you could use these for tonight," she said as she backed from the room. "I'll leave you to your privacy, but if you need anything, you've only to ask."

She closed the door.

Allie bolted, dropping one of the knives in her hurry to grab the door.

But the knob turned easily in her hand. It wasn't locked. She jerked it open to make sure.

Nichole stood a few feet away. She smiled as if she'd read Allie's mind. "The key's on the inside of the door. You can lock it if you wish. But no one will bother you. You're safe here."

Allie closed the door quickly and looked down. The key. She knew about locks. She'd been locked in many rooms over the past weeks. Again and again, she'd seen the preacher take the key, then the lock would turn and she'd be imprisoned once more.

Hesitantly, she placed the knife on the table and let her fingers close around the key. When she pulled, it came away in her hand.

She put the key back in the lock and twisted it as she'd seen the preacher do. Next, she tried the door. Locked. Then she twisted the key again and opened the door.

The hall was quiet.

Allie slowly closed the door and turned the key once more. She wasn't being locked in. This time she locked the world out.

Without taking her eyes away from the door for more than a moment, she sat on the floor and lowered the tray of food to her lap. For the first few bites, she scooped the food with her fingers. When the hunger grew more under control, she picked up the fork. Deliberately she stabbed for each bite. The fork felt strange in her hand, but not totally foreign. Halfway through the meal, she slowed enough to taste. *Good*, she thought. *Very good.* The tiny loud woman might wear war paint, but Adam had been right: Rose was a cook.

When the food was gone, she drank the milk. Wiping her mouth on the back of her arm, she pushed the tray aside and returned to the door, testing the lock once more.

Satisfied she was safe, Allie removed the cape Nichole had given her. She laid it next to the garments. Her hand reached for the white clothing then paused.

Allie pulled her fingers back, not allowing herself to touch the gift of clothing. It was spotless. She couldn't bare to dirty it with her touch.

Moving away from the bed, she noticed the tub once more. Timidly, she lowered her fingers into the warm water, washing away the crumbs of her meal and weeks of grime.

An inch at a time, she lowered her arms. It felt so good. Suddenly the filth covering her was suffocating. She'd had to use all her energy to stay alive. There had been so much more to think about besides getting enough water to bathe. But now she could wait no longer.

She pulled off her dress and slipped into the tub, lowering until water covered her. She stayed beneath the surface for as long as she could. When she finally came up for air, mud dripped off her hair.

With a war cry, Allie grabbed the soap beside the tub and began to scrub. An hour later, she stood and stepped from the now cold water. She'd used all the soap and only hoped the people of this place had more. Full and clean, she wasn't nearly as frightened as she had been.

Proudly, she crossed to the clothing on the bed and touched it. Her fingers left no stain. She pulled the cotton over her shoulders and fought with the buttons at her throat. Then, she lifted a brush from the table and began pulling it through her hair. By the time she'd finished the brush was full of hair and her scalp hurt, but her long hair hung in a ripple of waves down her back.

She examined her clothing. Night clothing, she guessed. Allie wished she had something more to leave in, but this had been a gift. If she took anything else it would be wrong. Besides, she had clothes hidden in the cave deep in the hill country and this night clothing would be far better than the thin dress she'd been living in for weeks. The cape would keep her warm enough. With Wes's horse, she could be back at her cave in three, maybe four days. The cotton would last until then.

Carefully, she lifted the dirty dress and moved to the stove in the corner of the room. The iron fireplace was small, probably putting out only enough warmth for the room on cold nights. She stuffed her ragged clothing into the opening. The dress would be fuel. She would not save it, or any memory of wearing it. The days of being trapped in the cage must be pushed away.

It was time to go.

Looking over the knives, she selected two and placed them in a bag she made from Rose's apron. They were all a gift from Adam, but she'd take only what she needed. She had done what she'd planned to do; there was no need to stay. She'd brought Wes to his people. And they'd paid her back most kindly. But if she didn't leave soon, the preacher would find her, or the Rangers. They'd put her back in a cage.

Allie turned the key and unlocked the door. Then she pulled the key from the lock and placed it in her bag. The key had been the greatest gift.

She silently moved through the house. It would be dawn in a few hours. Everyone slept. She thought through a plan as she crept along the hallway.

Maybe it was being around these people, hearing their way of talking, or maybe it was the food or even the bath, but the memories of a time long ago flickered in her mind as she picked her way carefully.

She remembered a boy, only slightly taller than her, pulling her through the fields as he'd screamed the words that ran through her mind now. "You've got to have a plan, Allie, if you're going to stay alive."

Well, she had a plan now.

As she slipped into the room where she'd sat by the fireplace, memories flooded back from a time long buried. She and the boy had run until she'd tasted blood as she breathed. Shots shattered the morning air and black billowing smoke rose from the barn and screams seemed to come from all directions. The boy had been trying to make it to the trees, which grew too thick together for horses to follow them.

Allie forced herself into the present as she moved silently past the doctor, who slept soundly in a chair by the fire. She tiptoed to Wes's side and looked down at him. He slept on his side, facing away from the fire so that only the part of his face without the scar showed.

In sleep, he didn't look nearly as frightening. With his face relaxed, he looked younger. His jawline was strong and true. She'd done right, she thought. He had been helping her when he'd opened the cage. Now, by bringing him here, she'd helped him.

Carefully, she swept the dark brown hair from his forehead. It was really too bad he was dying, for he must be a good man. She wondered why the woman back in Denton had turned her face away and had her men beat him. If Allie ever had such a man, she would not turn away. He had the strong features of a warrior.

She moved her fingers through his hair, knowing she'd never have a man look at her the way this one had looked at the lady in Denton. His eyes told everyone that all his hopes and dreams were riding on her. He looked at the woman as though he valued nothing higher.

Allie blinked away a tear. No one would ever look at her like that. She knew what she was. She'd heard it said in more than one language. She was a "throwaway woman." Of no value. Of no worth.

She fought down the tears. Not worth feeding when the winters are hard, she thought. Not worth saving when her mother ran with a baby in her arms and left Allie. Not worth loving and protecting by anyone. She'd fought with the dogs enough times for scraps to know what she was.

The days and nights of no sleep suddenly caught up with her. She leaned close against the stranger and rested her head on his pillow.

His warm breath brushed her wet cheek.

The memories of the boy who'd run with her returned. He'd fallen before they reached the trees. Allie remembered being afraid to go on without him. He'd told her to have a plan, but she'd been too small and frightened to think of one. She'd curled beside him and smelled the blood dripping from his body. He hadn't moved, not even when a Comanche yanked her up by one arm and draped her over his horse. The boy hadn't helped her or even cried out when the brave rode away with her as a prize.

Allie rubbed her eyes on her sleeve and lifted the blanket covering Wes. She was too tired to plan now. All she wanted to do was sleep. No one would ever know if she lay beside this man called Wes. For a few hours, she could pretend she had someone looking out for her. Someone valuing her. Someone caring for her as she slept.

She slipped in beside him. The heat of his body took away the chill of the night. She lay an inch away, not touching, but close enough to feel his breath on her cheek once more.

Allie closed her eyes. No one would see her here between this man and the windows. She'd sleep next to his warmth until first light, then disappear.

Tomorrow she'd follow her plan.

FIVE

WES BECAME AWARE OF HER SOMEWHERE DEEP IN
sleep, more on a primal level than on a conscious one.
A feeling born basic into the soul of a man, even though
layers of civilization concealed it. A need to protect, to
shelter, to hold, reacted in his dreams as strongly as reality.

Ignoring the pain from his wound, he moved his arm
over her, curling her into the protective length of his
lean body as he pulled her close. When her back rested
against his chest, he felt a heartbeat that matched his
own, and the pain passed, allowing him a deeper sleep.
Her nearness began to heal him.

With the first light of dawn, she stretched. Half asleep,
Wes opened his eyes to find a stranger curled beside
him.

"Good morning," he mumbled for lack of anything
better to say. Dreams and consciousness battled in his
mind, for he had no idea who she was. Yet she seemed
a part of him. "Did you sleep well?" He didn't want to
admit that this wasn't the first time he'd awakened without remembering a lady's name who slept next to him.

Her hair covered the pillow in waves of golden brown.
He couldn't resist rolling his head slightly so that it
brushed his cheek. The smell was fresh and clean. The
feel, soft and warm.

She twisted slightly to face him. In so doing, her breasts brushed against his outstretched arm. Full, rounded breasts. Not so large to be bothersome, but big enough to enjoy caressing, he thought.

Wes closed his eyes in the pure joy of feeling her against his skin with only a light cotton gown to cover her. If she felt so good just touching his arm, he wasn't sure he could endure the pleasure he might have closing his hand over her flesh. And nothing would have made him forget such an enjoyment. Whoever this woman was, she wasn't someone he'd made love to.

"I must be dead," he whispered as he moved his face against her hair once more. "I remember thinking I'd die last night. Now it's happened. I can't reason why I dreaded passing so, if you are my heaven."

She didn't answer but placed her fingers lightly against his throat, as if testing his theory.

Wes laughed and opened his eyes once more. The makeshift bed they shared was hard as a table and had been placed in front of tall windows. Her hair caught the first gold of the sun. It took Wes several seconds to force his gaze to her face.

Bright blue eyes met his stare. Blue eyes!

Slowly, as if rising through water to the surface, he saw her. Her small shoulders, hardly big enough to be a full-grown woman's. A bruise beneath her eye and another running along her throat. The white lace of her gown stood in sharp contrast to the deep purple mark at her collar.

He gently moved his fingers from her elbow to her hand at his throat and raised her arm slightly. Then he knew who she was, for the bruises of her chains were deep along her wrists.

As he put the pieces together in his mind, he knew she realized his memory of her had returned, for she pulled away. The beautiful woman whom he'd awakened with now lowered her head and raised her arms in defense as she slipped from his side.

Though he wanted her to stay, Wes didn't try to stop

her. The dirt might have been removed, but the poor creature he'd tried to save had returned. She moved into the cornered space between his bed and the bay window. Her wild blue eyes darted for an escape. He hadn't the heart to reach for her against her will. Her stare was once more layered in fear and panic. She reached for a cape and pulled it about her shoulders as though the material would somehow make her vanish.

"Wait!" He wondered if she could understand anything he said. "I'm not going to hurt you." How could this woman who looked like pure paradise at dawn be watching him as though she thought him from the depths of hell?

With trembling hands, she fished into the knot of cloth she carried and drew a knife. The blade blinked bright in the morning light. She pointed it toward him with the butt of the weapon against her middle, as though she'd use the force of her entire body to run him through if she must.

He swung his legs to the floor on the far side of the bed. He knew he still penned her in, but hoped that by increasing the distance between them, she'd feel less threatened.

Slowly, he reached for a shirt at the end of his bed as he glanced around. Somehow this creature had managed to get him to Adam, which told Wes that there was a good chance she understood at least part of what he'd said last night. Judging from his bandaging, Adam had done the usual grand job of patching him up.

"Thank you," he whispered, "for bringing me here. You saved my life."

She nodded slightly. A quick, tiny nod he would have missed if he were not studying her so closely.

"I'm in your debt." He meant his words to be kind, but he'd had little practice being gentle. He could see her shaking beneath the cape as if fearing he'd murder her at any moment.

"Do you have a name I can call you?" Wes tried to ease the tension.

She stared at him, her knuckles still white around the knife.

A noise sounded from somewhere beyond the hallway and he watched her panic grow.

Wes reached for his holster and strapped on his Colt. "Don't worry. You're safe here." He only hoped he spoke the truth. If the preacher had asked before trailing him, a few of the folks in Denton could have told him where Wes's brothers lived. If Wes had had any other choice, he'd have stayed clear of Adam and Daniel. But last night he'd been out of options.

He could tell by the way she watched him arm himself that she didn't believe him. He couldn't help but wonder if she'd ever had the luxury of feeling safe in her life.

"Adam!" a man's voice shouted from the hallway. "Adam. Nick. Anybody here?"

Wes relaxed. "In here, Daniel," he answered as Adam jerked awake with the sudden noise and unfolded from the chair by the fireplace.

A huge man suddenly framed the doorway, and Wes thought he could feel the woman's fear as thick as smoke between them. Her gaze darted from the doorway to Adam's sudden rise from sleep, to Wes, as though now her problems had tripled.

"Wes, I was hoping you'd be here." Daniel took a step into the room, then froze when he saw the woman. "Then it's true? You did kidnap a girl from Denton?"

Wes shrugged, unwilling to deny the truth. "News travels fast." He motioned from the woman to Daniel. "Kidnapped woman, I'd like you to meet my younger brother, Daniel McLain. He's a blacksmith on weekdays and a preacher on Sundays."

She took the news with a shudder as though Wes had said Daniel was a killer on Sundays.

Wes quickly nodded toward Adam, who was still rooted by the chair. He had never lived fearing enemy attack as Wes had, so he woke up more slowly.

"I assume you met Dr. McLain last night, since you got me safely here, so you know the whole family now.

Seems like whenever trouble's around, we McLains always manage to find one another.''

Daniel took a few steps toward her, then stopped when the glint from the knife she held blinked in his eyes. He raised a questioning eyebrow to Wes.

"She doesn't talk," Wes answered the unasked question. "I don't know if she can. The man in Denton seemed to think she couldn't. Despite the knife, she hasn't hurt anyone that I know of."

He looked toward Adam for more news, but Adam only shrugged. Then the doctor straightened his clothing and added, "You really shouldn't be up, Wes. As your doctor, I must insist—"

"I'm fine," Wes snapped, always resenting his brother's advice. Adam was the only doctor Wes would let touch him. But as soon as he could stand on his own, stand he would. No younger brother would treat him like a frail old maid.

Daniel slung his blond hair from his eyes and looked at the woman behind Wes with his head tilted slightly. "She doesn't seem all that friendly toward you, Wes. Did she come willingly?"

Wes rubbed his forehead as if trying to remember. "She came willingly enough from the cage they had her in. They were using her as the savage for a revival. You know the kind of service. I couldn't stand the thought of her being paraded around to fill the preacher's pockets. So I took her out of the cage. I was shot as we rode out. She managed to get me to Adam."

Daniel raised both eyebrows as he glanced once more at the knife in her hand.

Wes shrugged. "She just doesn't face mornings well, I guess." He moved a step away, allowing her more space, but still close enough to stop her if she tried to bolt. "How'd you know about us?"

Daniel ran his fingers through his sandy-colored hair in need of cutting. "Riders came by last night at the settlement. A preacher with the last name of Louis seemed to be the leader of the group. A Ranger rode with him and several hands from the Montago spread, by the markings on their mounts. As soon as they left, I headed here, knowing this is where you'd come if you were wounded.''

Daniel looked worried. ''The preacher said he has the law for a hundred miles around searching for you. Most have orders to shoot first and not be overly worried if the woman gets in the way. He was ranting and raving as if volume alone could make everything he said true. He even claimed you'll do her harm if she doesn't kill you first.''

''All the harm was his doing,'' Wes said. ''I'm not sure I'd lay a hand on her even to stop her from running. She's had enough, judging from the pain in her eyes and the bruises on her arms.''

Adam approached the woman. ''The bruises along her neck are too deep to be new, but the law won't take the time to notice that. Do you think she'd let me examine her?''

''I don't think so,'' Wes answered. ''But I felt whelps on her back that probably need tending.''

Adam crossed to one of the white cabinets and began pulling supplies. ''If she won't let me touch her, maybe she'll at least use the medicine herself. If any of the wounds are open, she could be in real danger.''

Wes leaned back against the bed, feeling the full load of what he'd done. No one would believe him against the preacher and, in truth, he *did* kidnap her. Four years as an officer in the Union army would probably do him more harm than good here in the South. Every cowhand who knew him to be a man of honor had died at the Red River. Vincent Edward had been his only friend who grew up in Texas, and he'd disappeared during the stampede. No one would probably ever find his body or be able to identify it.

''What'll we do?'' Daniel paced. The worry reflecting in his face made him look almost as old as his brothers. ''It's only a matter of time before they get here. I only made it first because I know the trail.''

"I'll handle it." Wes hardened his jaw.

"No." Adam did the same. "We'll handle it. We're your brothers. We stand together."

"It she wants to run, she can take my horse," Daniel offered. "It's tied out back. We can't keep her here against her will or we'd be no better than the one called Louis. But if she goes, so does your proof that she came with you willingly last night."

"If we let her run, we'll all be dead before they figure out she isn't here," Wes answered. "I got myself into this. You're a doctor, Adam, and you're a man of God, Daniel. The two of you have responsibilities. When they come, they'll only be looking for me. I don't want you two getting in the line of fire."

Both brothers seemed to have gone as deaf as the wild woman.

"If she stays, she's still Louis's ward." Daniel glanced from her to Wes. "And in this state that means he can do whatever he wants with her, including beat her half to death."

"But she's a woman, fully grown." Wes reached for his rifle by the window. The sound of horses arriving drifted across the morning air. "He'll put her back in a cage and treat her worse than an animal."

"She's his ward until she marries," Daniel explained as he grabbed Adam's rifle from above the wardrobe. Though he might be a man of the cloth by profession, he was a McLain by blood.

Horses thundered to a halt at the porch out front. All three brothers straightened, preparing, hardening to face whatever came through the door.

Adam slid his Colt into the band of his trousers at his spine and straightened the string tie at his throat. He moved toward the front door of his home. "Then marry her," he whispered as he passed his brothers. "I'll stall them for as long as I can." He disappeared into the hallway.

"That's insane!" Wes made no effort to keep his voice down. He glanced at the woman, who still held her weapon. For a moment he remembered the soft creature who had lain next to him before dawn. Where had that woman gone?

"Adam's right." Daniel nodded. "If you're married, they'll have no right to take her back. I can perform the ceremony right now. But I'll not marry a woman who's not willing."

Wes saw the idea as hopeless. "How are we going to know if she's willing? She hasn't spoken a word."

Daniel leaned his rifle against the desk and took a few steps toward the woman. She backed up against the wood between the windows—the knife still tight in her hand.

Daniel leaned over the bed and opened the window. "Crawl out if you like. My horse is tied to the back porch." He pointed, showing her the way. "If they catch you, they will probably force you to go back to the man who calls himself a preacher or put you away. Or you can run toward the front to find Louis if you want to go back to him."

She didn't move as he straightened.

He pulled a thin gold band from his little finger. "Or put on this band and be married to my brother. No one can force you to go back then." Daniel glanced at Wes. "He's not much of an option. To be honest, he's broke, drinks more than most, short-tempered, and generally hard to get along with. But I'd swear on my life that he'd never hurt you."

"Thanks for the glowing recommendation." Wes watched, but she didn't move. "What makes you think I want a wife? Even one this willing and friendly. The idea of marrying me seems a fate worse than death for most women, judging from my track record. I doubt this one would see it any different, even if she did understand a word you're saying."

Daniel frowned. They could hear the men yelling from the doorway. "You don't have a choice. They hang men in this state for kidnapping."

A shot rang out. Both brothers grabbed their weapons and moved toward the door.

Shouts echoed from the hallway as they took positions by the door and waited.

Daniel glanced back. The woman was still there.

"Do you?" he asked as she lifted the ring that had once belonged to his wife.

She nodded slightly.

"What about me?" Wes snapped. "Don't I get a vote?"

Daniel shook his head. "She's willing and you're breathing. I pronounce you man and wife."

SIX

ALLIE CROUCHED BESIDE THE BED UNTIL SHE could just see over the tossed sheets. There was no doubt in her mind that everyone in the room was crazy. She'd heard old folks tell stories about how an entire tribe would go mad from eating strange roots or drinking bad water. This McLain tribe was worse than she first thought.

The huge, blond one they called Daniel said he was a man of the cloth, but he didn't look like any preacher she'd ever seen. His arms and legs were thick as tree trunks, and he swung a rifle like a man who was used to having it fit his hand. He was younger and less talkative than his brothers but no less stubborn.

The doctor had kind eyes and a gentle way about him that made her want to believe him. But he'd walked out of the room with only a pistol, so he couldn't be overly blessed with brains. Allie guessed, from the sound of the many horses, that Adam faced more trouble than a six-shooter would solve.

And then there was Wes, the man with the scar. He talked rough and acted angry most of the time. But he'd saved her from the cage and held her so gently before dawn that the memory of his arms still lingered against her skin. Now he stood beside the doorway, listening to all the shouting as if he were strong enough to rush out and help his brother. He tried to steady himself along the wall and held in the pain at his side with his free hand. Allie knew he was too weak to fight.

She glanced down at the ring on her finger. Her mother had worn such a band of gold. She'd told Allie once that when a woman puts such a ring on she never takes it off—not ever. Allie knew what it meant. She and Wes were married. Daniel had said so. She knew it wouldn't be for long. A fight was coming and when it did Wes would die early in the battle. He was a warrior weakened by his injury.

Her gaze fixed on Wes, really looking at him for the first time. He was a good man, she decided. Honored by his brothers, who came to fight at his side. She'd gladly help him if she could, but two knives would do little in a war with guns. So she made up her mind that when the time came, she'd hold him as he died, and when the battle was over, she'd stand proud to be his widow. There was great dignity in being such a man's wife and honor in being his widow. She'd wear the ring forever in honor of his bravery.

Shouts rang from the hallway. The sound of stomping boots echoed, making the intruders seem legions more. She lowered slightly, awaiting the storm.

"Weston McLain, we know you're in there!" someone yelled from beyond the door.

Allie heard Wes swear beneath his breath. She didn't have to understand every word to know how he felt. They'd come for him.

"Let the wild girl go, and give yourself up!" an angry voice echoed off the hallway walls.

"Come and get her!" Wes answered as he straightened. "I've never backed down or given up. I'll not come out without a fight."

"Stop stalling!" another yelled. "You haven't got a chance."

Allie moved past the bed to a few inches behind Wes. If he was going to fight, the least she could do was cover his back. She drew the other knife.

Mumblings came from the crowd as Adam retreated into the room like a man avoiding the ever-rising wash of a wave. Only this wave was a line of well-armed, dust-covered men.

Adam's hands were held high, to make peace, but no one was listening to his reasoning. Wes and Daniel flanked him with their guns at gut level. The brothers moved to the center of the room.

"You're not taking the woman," Adam said in a controlled voice. He lowered his hands slowly and pulled the pistol from the band of his trousers, showing the men how fully he meant his statement.

Allie jumped back to keep from being stepped on as the McLains formed a wall around her. She stayed just behind Wes, waiting for the time when she'd be needed. If any man in the crowd fired at her husband, the shooter would have a knife in his heart as fast as she could raise her arm.

She guessed that since Adam, the gentle brother, had pulled his weapon, the time to fight was near. She twisted one knife until she held the blade in her fingers, ready to throw.

The crowd tumbled into the room like a noisy pot boiling over. Allie fought to keep from shaking as she recognized the tall preacher in his flowing black great-coat. A few of the cowhands who'd beaten Wes in the alley stood beside him.

She didn't miss the fire in Preacher Louis's eyes. She'd seen it more than once after a sermon when he was full of the spirit and himself. She knew what was to come. He'd rant and rave for sometimes hours, then he'd grab whatever was near and hit her. If she yelled, he'd beat her for screaming; if she didn't, he'd think he wasn't hitting her hard enough. He'd continue the beating until he grew tired, or she no longer responded to the pain.

Allie moved closer to her new husband. She wouldn't go back to the preacher. She'd die with Wes and his brothers first. Maybe a bullet would pass through Wes's body and kill her. Maybe the crowd would shoot her when she threw the knife. She didn't care. All she knew was that she wasn't going back to the cage. She was no longer a throwaway woman. She was a wife. The wife of a brave man. Somehow, that made her brave also.

Tension thick as sap hung in the air as Allie fought to draw in a breath. The McLains stood their ground and so did the men behind the preacher. She could see the madness in Louis's eyes and knew he was in a hurry for the fight to begin even though he moved to the side of the crowd.

She didn't know if he did so to encourage more men into the room, or to be in line as the first to run if the battle should turn against him.

"This man interfered with my work! He's Satan's handyman!" Louis's voice could be heard above all the others as though sheer volume gave him heaven's ear. "He's walked off the straight and narrow onto the wide road of sin. And he's taken this poor lost child with him. A soul so wild she doesn't even know she's human."

Allie moved closer to Wes. Louis was building, letting his words bubble across the crowd. Soon he'd boil over into full rage.

She wished she could warn Wes, for he seemed to face the preacher without fear. He'd never be able to fight and win against such a man. The McLains were greatly outnumbered. If she had any sense, she'd step away from them now, before the firing started.

But she needed Wes's strength in this last hour, and somehow she sensed he knew she was near. Weak as he was from loss of blood, his rifle was steady and pointed directly at Louis.

Just as the preacher raised his hand to point a condemning finger at Wes, Nichole walked into the room as casually as if she were greeting guests in her home. The tall, beautiful woman drew everyone's attention. She was striking in her starched white high-collared blouse and deep blue skirt, thick with pleats at the front.

The insanity of her action didn't surprise Allie, but

the gunbelt high on Nichole's waist did. This fine lady
had come to fight, and there seemed no doubt in the
room that she'd be able to use her weapons. The
matched set of pearl-handled Colts fit into a finely tooled
gunbelt that looked to have been made for her.

"Gentlemen." She smiled toward everyone except
the preacher. "If you came to kill a McLain, you'll have
to kill us all. For I am one, just as is the woman you
seek."

"Nichole," Adam whispered. "You should have
stayed safe, darling."

Allie saw worry in the doctor's eyes but no reproach.
He was not a man who'd practiced ordering a woman
and had no skill to do so now.

"No. I belong here with the father of the child I carry.
Honor should be doubled with him inside me, not lessened." Nichole joined the line of McLains, her hands
only an inch from her Colts. "If you gentlemen intend
to take my brother-in-law or new sister-in-law, it may
not be as easy as you think."

The men in the crowd were mean and primed by the
preacher for blood, but not one doubted he was in the
presence of a lady. They lowered their weapons and
slowly took off their hats as their own mothers had
taught them to do long ago. Not only was she a fine
lady, she was with child, and no one wanted to show
anger in front of her.

A man with a badge pinned to his duster stepped forward. "We don't come to kill nobody." He gulped out
the words. "And we didn't mean to frighten you,
ma'am. But Wes McLain stole a ward of the preacher.
Almost killed a man in doing so. We come to get the
lost creature back." He put his rifle behind him, as
though embarrassed to have it out in Nichole's presence.
"The preacher says she'll kill somebody if we don't get
her back caged."

Adam winked at his wife, realizing she had done what
he'd been unable to. She'd tamed the mob.

"She's not his ward." Adam's low voice could now

be heard. "The woman the preacher calls wild is my brother's wife." He looked at Nichole. "Just as this brave lady is mine."

Anger turned to confusion in the crowd.

Allie slipped her knives into the cape's pockets. In all the tension, she'd been the only one watching Wes. He'd fought a gallant fight to keep from slumping or showing his pain, but she knew he was losing the battle. Just as he crumbled, she moved beneath his shoulder, offering him the support he needed to remain standing. One arm crossed behind his back while the other braced him in front. As his arm came around her shoulders, her head rested on the bandage covering his chest.

He was her brave husband, she thought. He would stand and face death just as she would.

"Look!" someone said as Allie moved into view. "That's her."

"She doesn't look like a wild woman to me!" another cowhand shouted. "I wish my wife looked that good in the morning."

"She's got a wedding band on. Ain't no wild woman gonna wear a band."

"It don't appear to me she's been kidnapped."

"She ain't no unwilling wife, that's for sure. Look at the way she cuddles to him!"

"Stop yelling, Phil, you're scaring her!"

"I ain't the one with the bright idea to storm this place!"

"Who said this little woman was wild? She looks more worried about her husband than dangerous."

Allie couldn't listen anymore. All her energy channeled into holding Wes on his feet. She was vaguely aware the mob left the room yelling at and chasing the man they'd followed in. Suddenly Louis looked the villain for trying to take another man's wife.

Louis screamed to Wes that it wasn't over, but Wes wasn't listening.

Adam's calm voice drifted through Allie's panic. "Get him to the bed, Dan. Nick, bring more bandages.

I think he's broken the stitches. He should have listened to me and stayed down.''

Dan's massive arm moved beneath Allie's and took the load of his brother. "I've got him now," he said. "You can let go."

She didn't want to. All her bravery would vanish if she wasn't close to him. He and his family had saved her once more from Louis. He'd made her his wife, and she decided she didn't want to be his widow.

Unlike last night when they'd placed her in a chair to rest, this time she was a part of it all. Adam asked her to help. She held the water pitcher and poured a little out when he turned to her. Allie moved the lamp closer as he stitched the skin back in place. She covered Wes again and again to keep him warm as he thrashed.

It seemed they worked for hours. Finally, Adam and Daniel folded into the chairs by the fire. Nichole brought them a basket of breads, but no one ate. Allie stood by Wes as Rose pulled the curtains closed behind his bed.

"Maybe he'll rest better if it's dark," the little cook offered. "It's turning cold outside, fixing to storm."

Adam leaned his head against the chair. "I doubt he'll rest. But if he doesn't, he'll pull those stitches again, and I'm not sure he's got enough blood left for another round of stitching."

"We could take turns holding him down," Daniel offered.

Adam let out a long breath, showing his exhaustion for the first time. "He'd just fight us. Look at the way he fights the pillows we used to keep him from rolling over. It might have helped if we'd been able to pour down more whiskey. I don't know."

Allie watched her new husband. Each time she moved the covers to keep him warm, he twisted in his sleep, battling in a war long over—except in his dreams.

She thought of her plan to run, but she couldn't be sure Louis had given up waiting for her. The preacher's threats to return haunted any peace she might have felt. Besides, Wes had saved her life. She had promised herself to stay with him until he died, which, from the looks of him, couldn't be much longer.

Carefully, she crawled up on the bed and positioned her body against his back. Now if he tried to roll onto his wound, he'd only press against her.

Wes settled in his sleep with her warmth near. Allie closed her eyes and let the tension pass. She was vaguely aware of Nichole pulling a blanket over them and of rain tapping lightly against the windows. She would stay a while, until she thought it safe, until Wes was better or he died. She couldn't leave without knowing.

It seemed long after dark when she awoke. The room was in shadows and empty. The fire was low, but blankets kept their warmth beneath the covers.

Allie slipped from the bed and tiptoed to the desk, where someone had left a tray of food. She took a piece of bread and the glass of milk then crossed to the windows once more.

Fall's first storm had blown in while she slept. Even if she'd planned to leave tonight, it wouldn't be a good time. The rain could turn to ice by morning. Without warm robes, she'd freeze before she could reach her caves in the hill country.

She felt the chill of the night move across her. Winter in the hills would be cold, with endless days of looking for food and checking over her shoulder. She would only be able to risk a fire once a week to cook. The rest of the time she'd have to live on roots and sleep in a cave colder than the outside. On rainy days like this one, she'd be trapped in the darkness without a fire to warm her. In the rain or snow, she'd be easy to track, and Allie knew she'd have to move over the land like the wind if she planned to stay free.

She shivered more from the glimpse of the future than from the present. Almost running, she crossed to Wes and slid beneath the covers on the other side of him from where she'd been sleeping. For a second, she feared he might turn away from her and roll onto his wound, but he didn't.

After a few minutes, she drew closer to him for warmth. She was only a hair's-width away when she looked up and saw him watching her. His brown eyes told her he was still too much in sleep to question her nearness.

"Allie," she whispered. "My name is Allie." It was the first time she'd spoken words in any language for more than five winters and the first time she'd said her real name since the day she'd run with the boy toward the trees. Since the day she'd seen her mother's body, all bloody and twisted, piled with others. Since the day she no longer had a home.

"Allie," Wes mumbled. He closed his eyes and placed his arm over her, pulling her near as he drifted back into sleep.

SEVEN

WES MCLAIN PULLED HIMSELF TO A SITTING POSI-
tion. He fought back a groan of pain in favor of a few
swear words. Tugging his trousers on slowly, he stood.

As the fog inside his head cleared, he glanced around
the tiny space that had once been his brother's rented
bedroom in this huge house. After Adam and Nichole
married, they bought the place from a widow who was
in a hurry to get back East. They moved their living
quarters upstairs and used the downstairs rooms for
Adam's medical practice and study. But they'd left this
little room between the kitchen and the office as a spare
bedroom.

The floor was cold. Wes had no idea where his boots
were ... or his shirt, for that matter. Nor did he much
care. He needed a drink, maybe two, to kill the throbbing
in his side and back. Only thing worse than getting shot
was having a doc pull the bullet out. At least Adam
knew what he was doing, even if it did feel like Adam
had made what felt like a cannonball-sized hole in his
back.

But the pain didn't erase the memory of Vincent's
map or what Wes had to do as soon as he was able.
Time was ticking away.

Wes stumbled to the dresser. The compass he'd carried through the war lay next to his saddlebags. He

shoved the compass in his pocket and unbuckled one side of his bag. The map was still there, folded in a square of oilcloth just as it had been before the stampede. Waiting.

A wealth buried in gold, Wes reminded himself. Gold enough to make a fresh start.

Wes rebuckled the bag. The map's secret had waited over thirty years; it would have to wait a few days more. He wasn't sure he could sit a horse in his condition, much less ride. Vincent Edward had known the land; if he'd lived, finding the treasure would have been much easier. But Vince was dead, and Wes would have to trust the map.

Moving to the door, he shoved his hair from his eyes and felt a week's growth of a beard along his jaw. A beard he'd shave as soon as he had the energy. Without looking, he knew the whiskers didn't grow along the scar across his cheek. His almost-black brown hair would only make the thin lightning bolt an inch above his jaw look whiter.

He pushed away from the door frame without looking in the mirror. He was across the hall and two steps into the kitchen before anyone noticed him stumbling around.

When Nichole let out a little cry of joy, Adam stood from beside her at the table. The easy smile that always came to Adam brushed his face at the sight of Wes. Adam took a step toward him then halted.

Wes couldn't help but grin. His younger brother knew him well. If he could stand on his own, he wanted no help or coddling.

"I see you're up," Adam stated the obvious.

Wes fell into more than sat in the chair across from them. "I could use a drink." He glanced toward Rose, the cook, who was openly crying with relief. "Whiskey, Rose."

"Coffee," Adam corrected. "Or better yet hot cocoa."

Wes frowned at him, but didn't argue. He'd never admit it out loud, but he respected Adam more than any man. All through the War Between the States, Adam had been Wes's only touch with family. Now, he was still Wes's only link to what he thought living should be like. For Wes, life was an endless swing of highs and lows. He'd be rich one month and dead broke the next. Adam's life was stable. He had a home and a wife. Everything Wes once thought would be important. But Angela's coldness had finally convinced him. That kind of life would never be his.

Wes accepted the shirt Adam handed him. He wasn't jealous of Adam, he wished him the best. But Wes couldn't help but wonder from time to time why some men have to fight for every inch of ground they stand on and others don't.

Rose brought a coffee laced with whiskey. After setting it before Wes, she wiped her eyes on her apron. "I'm so glad you're gonna live." She sniffed loudly. "I made them apple turnovers you like every day, hoping you'd smell them and wanta wake up."

"That's what brought me from the grave." Wes winked at her. "How long was I out?"

"Four days," Adam answered. He returned to his seat next to Nichole.

Wes downed half the cup, enjoying the way it warmed his throat. "I'll eat a few turnovers if you got them ready now, Rose. It appears the knitting Adam did across my back didn't kill me this time."

Adam grinned. "If you're well enough to eat and complain, you're fine. But you cut it close, brother. If the woman hadn't got you here, McLain blood would have puddled a wide spot of prairie."

Nichole could be silent no longer. "Tell us about the girl, Wes."

For a moment, Wes wasn't sure who Nichole was talking about. Then he remembered. The woman from the cage. The one who'd slept beside him and kept him warm. From time to time while he slept, his mind registered her moving near. He remembered her holding his head, making him drink once when all he wanted to do was sleep.

"Where is she, kid?" he asked over his cup. Nichole might be one fine lady now, but Wes could still remember the Nick who rode like the wind and proved herself a friend.

Rose returned with two apple turnovers on a plate. The little cook leaned close to Wes and whispered, "That strange woman is in the laundry room taking a bath. She takes one every morning. 'Bout used the winter's supply of soap." Rose raised her nose. "It ain't healthy, a person being that clean in the winter. But I ain't saying a word, of course, 'cause I'm the last one on this earth to judge—"

"We'll buy more soap," Nichole interrupted with a warning glance at Rose to hold her tongue. "Except for when she bathes, she never leaves your side, Wes. We can't get her to say a word. Not even her name."

"Allie," Wes answered between bites. "Her name's Allie. I promised to get her to her family."

"Her family?" Adam leaned forward with interest.

Wes shook his head. "If there is any. She must have been picked up during the raids before the war. All her kin might have been killed, or decided the state was too wild and moved on. All I know is I have to try to find them."

Nichole leaned close and placed her hand on Wes's arm. "I'll help," she offered. "I'll use my connections at the marshal's office." She glanced toward the laundry room. "In the meantime, let the girl be. My guess is she's got wounds on the inside that may take longer to heal than those we see on the outside."

Three days later, to Wes's frustration, no one had been able to get the woman called Allie to talk. Texas was too big a state to search every settlement for her kin. Her name wasn't much help, and he'd begun to question that he'd heard her say that. Maybe he'd only dreamed it.

She seemed to be changing before his eyes. If he

hadn't seen it happen, he wouldn't have believed the creature in the cage and this shy girl were the same person. Nichole, with her limited skill as a seamstress, had managed to cut down two dresses for Allie. But the browns and dusty blues that looked so striking on Nichole faded Allie into the woodwork. She wouldn't allow anyone to touch her hair, and the brown mass of waves always seemed to cover her face. She moved like a whisper from room to room.

On the third evening, Wes was able to sit at the supper table without feeling like he might fall over at any moment. He decided he'd had enough of her silence. His mood, never sunny, was made even worse by his injuries. Allie refused to eat with anyone. In truth, he hardly saw her now that he was awake. She kept to the background.

"Allie!" he shouted when he entered Adam's office and saw her by the windows.

She jumped at the sound of her name and glanced around as if looking for a place to run.

"Don't be afraid to talk to me." Wes stumbled over his words as he neared. "How many times do I have to tell you, I'm not going to hurt you?"

She seemed to shrink before his eyes, melting into the dark cape she wore across her shoulders like armor.

Wes was determined not to back down. This couldn't go on. The woman had to talk sometime. "Nichole said the marshal thinks he can help you find your family . . . if you can remember your full name. He's already got the word out over most of Texas." Wes was within three feet of her now, but he wasn't sure she was listening. "Is Allie short for something? Allison? Alisha? Allene?"

She didn't raise her head.

"You probably have relatives worrying about you. Do you remember your home? Were you captured on a farm, or some little settlement? If you speak English, you must remember something. Give us something to go on."

Wes stared at the ceiling and swore. He felt like he'd asked these same questions a hundred times. He didn't have to look at her to know what was happening. She was shaking with fear and backing as far as she could into the corner. He'd seen her watching the rain and guessed she was just waiting for a break in the weather to run. But to where? To who?

"Allie," he tried again, not wanting to think of her dying out in the wild somewhere. Maybe she was just wanting to run from people. If so, a hundred deaths could be waiting for her. "Allie, listen to me!"

He reached for her wrist and pulled her toward him, determined to make her understand.

Like a sudden explosion of dry lightning across the sky, Allie came to life. She jerked the arm he held and fought wildly to pull away.

For a few seconds, Wes's grip tightened, pulling her closer as if to quiet the terror he saw in her eyes.

But he was the cause of the fear. Her struggle only intensified. She swung her free hand, frantically trying to hit his head. Her bare feet kicked at his legs. Her teeth bared like an animal preparing to bite.

Wes turned loose of her wrist and backed away. He felt like a fool. She was a wild creature, he could see it in her eyes. She would have killed him if she could have. And for what? For asking her full name. If he had any sense, he'd be worried about the wolves who might be unlucky enough to try to attack her. There was no reasoning with this woman. It would be better to allow her to go her own way.

Without turning his back to her, Wes walked to the center of the room. All the pain in his body was forgotten as he watched her slip back into the corner. "I know you understand me!" he shouted, as if somehow he could win a battle he'd already lost.

He tried to pull his nerves together. He'd never been afraid to face anything in his life. He'd always been one to ride headlong into danger, but how could he handle her? No matter what she did, he could never raise a hand against her. But he'd seen the fear in her eyes and knew she'd kill him if he ever tried to touch her again. That made him about the biggest fool on earth, because he knew he'd stand there and let her.

The memory of the woman who'd slept beside him played through his thoughts. He closed his eyes and remembered how she'd let him touch her hair and how soft and willing her body had felt against his.

"I'm not going to say I'm sorry." Wes opened his eyes. "I wasn't trying to hurt you, Allie, only get you to talk to me. I swear I'll help you find your family. But you're not making it easy. You have to tell me what you know about your past. Any little detail."

She turned to face the rain once more, as if she hadn't heard his words.

"Can't you even answer me?" He tried lowering his voice, but he'd never had much cause to sound gentle and kind.

Her head dropped slightly, and he thought he saw a tear. He didn't move to comfort her. He'd already gotten too close once tonight.

"You have nothing to fear from me. We'll stay married so you will be safe until I find your family, then you'll be free of me. I owe you that much for saving my life."

He could see her shoulders curl in as she pressed against the icy window. He had no idea where she wanted to be, but it definitely wasn't with him.

"All I ask is that you help me to help you. Nothing more." Wes set his jaw. Why should helping her come any easier than anything else he tried? "I want no wife in my life or my bed. You've no worry or fear there." He had to say the words out loud, even if he was the only one listening. "As soon as the weather clears, we'll start the search."

He never wanted to see the hatred in her eyes again. But the only way he'd be rid of her was to find her a safe place to stay. He'd have an easier job finding someone to adopt a porcupine.

She avoided him the rest of the evening, acting like he was the enemy. Since he'd been feeling better and moving around, Allie had taken to sitting in the sewing room upstairs with Nichole. She seemed to like Nichole, for Nichole was the only one in the house who accepted her on face value, never asking questions, never demanding answers. Also, unlike the cook, his sister-in-law felt little need to keep a conversation going when it was one-sided.

Wes undressed for bed and stretched out on top of the covers, not caring that the air chilled his skin. He'd felt lousy all day, but it had nothing to do with his wound. How could a woman who didn't speak or ask a blasted thing of him make him feel so angry?

Long after the house had grown quiet, the bedroom door slowly opened.

"Evening," Wes said, knowing she wouldn't answer.

Allie slipped into the room and placed clean clothes on the dresser.

"You still mad at me?" Wes waited a moment just in case there was an answer. "Not that I care one way or the other. A man can't go around apologizing for something he didn't do."

He watched her closely, wondering where she'd sleep tonight. Since he'd been able to stand on his feet, she'd curled into the chair in the corner every night. He was surprised she stayed in the same room with him if she feared him so much.

The thought occurred to him that maybe nowhere else felt safe either.

Allie wrapped her cape around her and tucked her bare feet up into the chair as she curled into a ball and closed her eyes.

Wes watched her for a while. She looked so tiny. She didn't stand tall enough to reach his shoulder, and her arms looked thin to the point of starvation.

Her hair was just curly enough to look like it grew wild around her. In the firelight, he thought he could see red streaks running through it. But at dawn, he would swear gold drifted through the strands.

Wes opened and closed his hands. How he wanted to touch it again. Which made no sense, he decided, because he didn't even like the girl. She was just one more barrier slowing him down in his quest for the Goliad treasure Vince had sworn was just waiting for them. If Wes hadn't seen her in the cage, he'd probably have the gold in his hands by now. Gold that reminded him of her hair at dawn.

He turned away from her and closed his eyes. She was a long ride from normal and she was driving him to the same destination. They were a fine match. No woman had ever loved him, and no man would ever get close enough to love her. He fell asleep listening to a wind that sounded almost as lonely as he was.

Deep into the night, the fire in the tiny corner fireplace burned itself out, and the temperature dropped so low that rain froze against the window. Wes rolled over and saw her still curled in the chair, hugging the cape around her to keep warm.

He could feel her chill as though it were his own. Slowly, he stood and lifted a blanket from his bed. As silently as he could, Wes crossed to her chair and draped the quilt over her.

The memory of how she'd fought him was thick in his mind, as he looked down at her huddled between the arms of a wooden chair. Carefully, he wrapped the blanket around her and lifted her. Ignoring the pain that shot through his back, he carried her to the bed and placed her where his body had already warmed a place. Then, very carefully, he stretched out beside her and pulled the remaining covers over them both.

Wes lay still, expecting her to bolt at any moment. But she didn't. After a few minutes, she stretched beneath the warmth and curled against him in sleep.

"I promise," he whispered as her hair brushed his cheek, "I promise I'll never hurt you, Allie."

EIGHT

ALLIE PRESSED HER BACK ALONG THE WALL BEHIND the door to the kitchen and listened. In the days since she'd been at the doctor's house, the rhythm of their words had become natural to her once more. She knew what they were talking about most of the time. Sometimes, when she knew no one could see her, she'd mouth the words, practicing the patterns.

She was still firmly convinced the entire McLain tribe was a full measure short of normal sense. Her best plan would be to escape as soon as possible. At first, she waited because of the weather, but now, a curiosity held her here.

"The telegrams went out to every lawman in the state," the doctor's wife was saying. "We may get answers for weeks as the word passes."

Allie leaned closer to the door, trying to see through the crack.

"We've had several replies." Nichole sounded pleased. "Some people are already on their way to see her."

Allie could see Wes at the end of the table. He held his coffee cup in both hands. As always his face looked like it was trying to mock a thunderstorm, all dark and angry. "I don't want people gawking at her like she's a freak. I'll not have people just dropping in to see her like she's a sideshow.''

"She's starting to matter to you." The woman's voice drifted to Allie.

"Nonsense," Wes answered. "I'm not the kind of man who knows how to make a woman care. Men like me were meant to be alone. I've learned that lesson plain enough. I'll never love a woman the way Daniel loved May or Adam loves you. I can't see myself settling down and forcing some poor woman to look across the table at me every morning.''

"Of course you will," Nichole started. "That scar—"

"No," he interrupted. "It's not meant to be. Daniel swore he'd never marry again after May died delivering the twins. And I know the closest I'll ever come to marriage is this farce we're playing to protect Allie." He sat his coffee mug down with a thud. "Or whoever she is.''

A knock at the door echoed the sound of his cup. Allie jumped and darted to Adam's study before anyone could come from the kitchen to answer the summons.

A few minutes later when the guests were ushered into the room, Allie tried to melt into the wall space between the curtains. Her dark brown dress and hair seemed to blend with the mahogany as she found herself in the presence of strangers.

"I'm Marvel Pickett," a stout woman announced. She walked straight to the fire and began warming herself as though the blaze were hot enough to penetrate her multiple layers of long clothing. "This is my husband, Harold Pickett. We've come all the way from Tyler to look the savage girl over.''

Allie watched Nichole stiffen and step between the new arrivals and the windows. "You think our Allie might be your relative?" Nichole's voice hardened slightly as the stocky woman helped herself to a muffin on a tray that had been set for Allie's breakfast.

Wes followed Harold into the room. As Harold joined

his wife, Wes leaned against the corner of the desk in the center of the room. Only a slight limp showed he favored his side. He pulled the top drawer of Adam's desk open a few inches. Between them, Nichole and Wes formed a blockade to Allie.

"We think we might be her kin," the woman mumbled as she chewed. "She's about the right age. My sister and her husband had a bushel of brats. When he died, she loaded them up and planned to come live off of us. Their wagon was ambushed about the Arkansas-Texas border. She never made it. An express rider found her dead, but not one body of a child. They must have all been taken to live with the savages."

"What were your nieces' names?" Nichole glanced at Wes and shook her head slightly.

The chubby woman frowned and wiped her mouth with the tips of her fingers for a duster. "I don't remember. Never having children of my own, I thought learning their names didn't seem all that important. All I know is if this girl is likely one of them, we'll take her off your hands. Me and Harold ain't getting any younger, and we could use the help around the place."

Allie saw Nichole's fingers open and close as she asked the woman, "Would you describe your sister and the girls? Hair color, eye color, general build?"

The large woman placed her hands on her side-shelf hips. "What does it matter? Just show me the girl. I'll tell you if she's the right one."

Harold crushed his hat with big work-worn hands. He didn't look directly at anyone as he asked, "She is in good condition, ain't she? Not sickly or anything?"

"Why?" Nichole glanced again at Wes. But Wes was stone silent.

Harold remolded his hat with greater speed. "We're worried since she's here at a doctor's house. Thought she might have some problems."

"If she's sickly, she ain't my niece," Marvel added. "I'm from sturdy stock. I ain't paying no bills for some sickly captive who can't remember who she is. Now if she's healthy, she might be my kin.''

"She's not the one you're looking for," Wes's voice was hard, with an edge Allie hadn't heard before. "See them to the door, Nichole. They're wasting our time and theirs.''

Marvel Pickett bristled like a wild hog and headed straight toward him. "And what makes you know that? I ain't saying the creature ain't mine until I see her with my own eyes. I figure I'll know my own.''

"Is she or is she not healthy?" Harold asked. "The sheriff said she was.''

"She is," Nichole answered. "But she doesn't talk. Do you have anything, a tintype, a drawing that might show us she could be your niece?''

"We don't have to prove nothing," Marvel puffed up. "We're her relatives if we says we are, and that's all you nosy do-gooders need to know. There is plenty of women and children left to starve on the streets since the war. We just want to do right by our kin and take her in. She'll have her three meals a day and a place to sleep if she earns her keep.''

As Marvel finished, she spotted Allie between the curtains and yelled, "There she is!''

Both the Picketts moved toward Allie like seasoned cowhands closing in on a mustang.

"She seems healthy enough!" Marvel pointed with her head for Harold to cover the other side of the girl and not let her get away.

"But wild," Harold held back a little, letting his wife take the lead. "Look at her eyes.''

"Don't worry about that." Marvel tried to step around Nichole. "After a few weeks on the farm, we'll settle her down—even if we have to keep a rope on her.''

Allie felt panic rise in her blood. Just before she tried to fight her way around the weak Mr. Pickett, Wes stepped in front of her. Only inches away, Wes blocked Allie's view of the advancing couple.

"Wait!" His voice was as hard as granite. "You'll not touch her."

"Who do you think you are?" Marvel huffed. "We is this girl's family."

"I don't think so. I'll not have Allie tied up and broken like an animal." Wes raised a gun he'd pulled from the desk drawer. "And if you take one more step toward her, you'll be showing little value for your own life."

Marvel glanced at Nichole but found no sympathy. "Who do you people think you are?" She almost spit the words. "We got as much right to take her as you do."

Allie moved beside Wes and slipped her hand into the fingers of his free hand.

He jerked slightly and looked down at her fingers resting in his. "She's staying here," Wes said calmly as he closed his hand over hers. "She's my wife."

Marvel started to argue, but saw that it was hopeless. "Hold on, Harold," she shouted as though she were afraid her shy husband might advance even against a gun. "There's another girl down at Fort Griffin that we might take a look at."

Harold nodded with relief.

Nichole ushered the Picketts to the door.

All at once, Allie was alone with Wes—and he was holding her hand. His fingers felt warm and protective around hers, not binding.

"You didn't want to go with them, did you?"

She shook her head slightly and pulled her hand away. He was still so near, she could feel the warmth of his body. He'd stood up for her once again. He had no idea what it meant to her. This strange man with the thin scar on his face didn't seem to know how worthless she was. He seemed to believe she was a person of some value. His insanity was flattering.

"You're more afraid of them than me." His voice was low, only for her ears. "I guess I should take comfort in that."

Allie raised her head and met his gaze. Despite the

hard set of his jaw, his brown eyes were warm when he wasn't angry.

"Don't worry, little wild one, I'll not turn you over to anyone but your real family. If they turn out to be like the Picketts, you don't have to go—no matter what proof they have. I promise."

There he went again, she thought, promising. Like he could hold to his word. Like she believed him.

In the days that followed, several people visited. Some were bereaved parents praying for the hope Allie might be theirs. Some were bounty hunters paid by a family back East to find survivors.

Always Allie watched them, a tiny part of her hoping that she would see the family she'd lost. But the memory of her parents' bodies piled high in a heap to be burned was still too real in her mind to let herself believe in a dream. She knew no matter how hard Nichole tried to help, no family would come.

Again and again, she moved close to Wes and slipped her hand in his, silently telling him that she would stay with him. And as always, he stood beside her, allowing no one close enough to touch her.

Each time, she left her fingers in his grip a moment longer. Each time, he silently accepted her gift.

NINE

WES FOLDED THE MAP HE'D SPENT AN HOUR STUDY-
ing and leaned back in the kitchen chair. "I have to go,"
he announced. "The Goliad treasure is real, I can feel
it."

Both his brothers, across the table from him, frowned.
Long past midnight, coffee and adrenaline had kept them
anchored in the conversation.

"It's a wild goose chase." Daniel folded his huge
arms over his chest. "I'd never thought you'd fall for
such a scheme. The map's barely readable and obviously
drawn with a hand shaking of age or drink. Texas is full
of buried treasure stories, a lost Confederate gold shipment, Indian burial grounds, miners after '49 who left
their fortunes here until the war was over. How many
others are you going to fall for after this one?"

Wes gave him the look all big brothers give their
younger siblings, the look that silently says, "I'll always
be older and wiser than you." He'd expected them to
be skeptical, cautious, logical. Even a little excited. But
not blatantly disbelieving.

"How much did you pay for this map?" Adam lifted
the oilcloth as if weighing its worth and finding it light.

Wes grabbed it out of Adam's hand, frustrated at them
both. They had what they wanted out of life. Adam had
Nichole, and Daniel had his daughters. Why couldn't

they allow him his dream? "I paid nothing. Vince gave this map to me for safekeeping a few nights before he died. He seemed skittish about someone trying to take it from him. He was always glancing over his shoulder as though a ghost followed him.

"Since he died, I guess that makes the map mine. Vince told me once that his only relative was his grandfather, and the old man passed on soon after drawing the map."

Daniel shook his head. "There's probably nothing there, or it was found twenty years ago."

Wes shrugged. "Maybe. But Vince said his grandfather rode with James Fannin at Goliad back in '35 when the war with Texas and Mexico began. He said they left the mission with every man they could round up to go help the men fighting at the Alamo. Over five hundred strong, some say, a mixture of Texans and several volunteers from the southern states. Within a few miles, one of the wagons broke down, and they stopped to make repairs. Santa Anna's army, still excited from their kill at the Alamo, caught up to Fannin and his men in an open field.

"The grandfather told how they fought for hours, but it was hopeless. They were surrounded and outnumbered. Fannin, a West Point dropout, decided to surrender with the understanding that they'd be marched to the border and told to leave Texas forever. But Santa Anna marched them back to Goliad and held them inside the old Spanish mission. There were so many, only a third of the men could lie down and sleep at one time. As the days passed, the men knew their chances of dying grew. They started digging a tunnel, hoping to reach the river. By Palm Sunday of 1836, with the tunnel only a third finished, they knew their luck had run out. Santa Anna began ordering the men out to face the firing squad.

"Frantically, the men pooled all their valuables and stuffed them into the tunnel. Then the last few to leave the mission collapsed the tunnel and placed stones across the opening so that no one would ever find it."

Daniel leaned forward with interest. "Then what happened?"

"They were all marched out and shot. Fannin was already wounded in the leg. He was carried from the mission in a chair, but insisted on standing for the execution. His last request was not to be shot in the head. The firing squad blindfolded him and twelve rifles were raised to his skull."

"What about Vince's grandfather?"

"Vince said he was with volunteers from South Carolina called the Rovers. They were told to march out as a unit, away from the others. At first they thought they might be taken to the border, but then they noticed the soldiers carried only rifles, not canteens.

"About a mile from the mission, the Rovers were ordered to stop and kneel in the grass. Vince's grandfather was toward the back of the company. He said the Rovers refused to kneel, and the army opened fire. In one round of blasting the first rows fell, screaming and crying in pain. Smoke from the old flintlock guns rose everywhere. Vince's ancestor saw his chance. He ducked low and ran as fast as he could toward the river. He took a ball in the leg but didn't stop.

"He tripped and rolled in mud until he landed among the roots of the trees that grow along the Guadalupe. He lay there all day listening to the army hunting down the runners and shooting them. Finally, long after dark, he slipped into the water and floated downstream to freedom. He drew the map from memory, but the bullet he took crippled him too badly to let him reclaim the treasure."

"But others escaped?" Daniel asked, suddenly allowing the boy to show through in the man not yet in his midtwenties.

"I'm sure a few did. If they were healthy, they went on to fight with Sam Houston. But maybe they weren't among the last to leave the mission and didn't know where the treasure was buried. Or maybe they were like

Vince's grandfather and never could go back and claim it.''

"It's a long shot." Daniel shook his head. He'd never been a risk taker.

"Yeah," Wes agreed, "but it's the only shot I've got left. That stampede at the Red River not only cost me the lives of most of my men, it took every dime I had. I've got a ranch with no cattle. When we first came here, after the war, I could have rounded up enough strays to start over, but not now. The treasure at Goliad—if it exists—will give me a fresh start."

Adam stood and moved to the stove to pour himself another cup of coffee. "It sounds too good to be true. All the valuables from hundreds of men just waiting to be found."

Wes laughed and held out his cup to be refilled. "That's what I thought, too. There's only one thing I forgot to mention. Vince gave me the map saying that his grandfather believed the treasure was cursed. I told him I didn't believe in curses or ghosts. It seems every man who ever had the map or looked for the treasure died. First Vince's grandfather, then his father and both his uncles, now Vince."

"Oh, fine." Daniel laughed. "We're all sitting about looking at a map that's killed everyone who ever got near it. Makes me want to go treasure hunting."

Wes shook his head. "No, I'll go alone. I only wanted you to know where I was headed. Since the night of the stampede, something's been bothering me. Two of the men on early watch reported seeing riders that night who asked about Vincent Edward. But no men came into camp, and Vince took his shift about an hour before the stampede."

"You think they were planning to do Vince harm?" Adam voiced his thoughts.

"Or take the map," Wes answered. "If they confronted him while he was on watch, I'd stake my life that Vince wouldn't tell them where the map was. But they may have guessed by now. Or, they may think the secret of the map died with Vince.''

"You think they might have killed him?''

"One shot would start a stampede,'' Wes answered. "We never found Vince's body to know one way or the other. Maybe they only meant to frighten him. Maybe they died along with him.''

"If they killed him for the map and lived, they'll be after you if they think you might have it.''

"That's why I need to get to Goliad as fast as possible. If the mission holds a treasure, I'll find it before this blasted curse catches up to me. And I'll telegraph back here every few days to keep in touch. If someone comes asking after me, they'll start with one of you.''

"We'll let you know if you're followed,'' Daniel promised. "But if you need help, send for us. Luckily, I still have Willow to look after the twins and every woman in the settlement thinks she's the assistant. I can be ready to ride within the hour.''

"What about Allie?'' Adam asked.

"I was thinking, she'd be better off staying with you.'' Wes set his jaw. "She gets along great with Nichole. Plus, I want her out of danger. I can't very well take her with me.''

"What about your promise to her?''

"It can wait a few weeks. I'll find her family, but first I have to find the treasure.''

Daniel frowned. "She may think her family is more important than the gold.''

Wes ignored his disapproval. Neither of his brothers seemed to understand that he was doing no good here. It might be weeks before a lead on her family came in. Time was running out on the treasure. He could feel it. The odds were against him already; every day lessened his chances.

Standing, he added, "I've made up my mind. I'll leave at first light.''

"You'd better tell Allie,'' Adam warned. "We'll be

glad to have her stay with us, but you can't just leave
her without telling her you're leaving.''

"All right." Wes didn't think it would do any good.
"I'll tell her now. Not that she'll understand or care."

As he walked out of the room he noticed Adam was
pouring Daniel another cup of coffee. He knew they
were planning to continue the conversation without him.
Neither of them understood the drive that pushed him.
Wes didn't want to settle down. Oh, he envied his brothers from time to time, but there was something in his
blood that didn't take to sameness day after day. He
needed the adventure, the unknown. The days spent re-
covering had been long and wearing on his nerves. He
wasn't a man who could be molded to routine. Angela
Montago did him a favor by refusing his offer of marriage. He'd only been dreaming when he'd asked her.
What was right for his brothers wasn't right for him.
The sooner he learned to live with that, the better off
he'd be.

Wes opened the door to his bedroom with a snap.
Might as well wake Allie up and tell her, he thought.
She'd probably breathe a long sigh of relief not to have
him around anymore.

As he'd expected, Allie was curled up in the hard
wood chair with her cape around her. She raised her
head when he entered and stared at him with those dark
blue eyes. Except for that cold night he'd carried her to
his bed, he hadn't slept beside her again.

"Evening," he mumbled, wondering how many years
would have to pass before he no longer saw the fear in
her eyes each time he entered a room. "Sorry to wake
you," he said without any sorrow in his tone or any
belief that she'd been asleep. "But we have to talk."

She straightened and pulled the cape tightly around
her.

Wes moved to the end of the bed and sat facing her.
He could have reached out and touched her, but he
didn't. "I have to leave tomorrow at dawn."

Her eyes widened slightly.

"You'll be safe here with Nichole and Adam. They'll stand beside you, should anyone come to see you." He hesitated, wanting to be honest. "Where I'm going may mean trouble, and you're better off here."

She didn't move. If he'd expected a reaction, he would have been disappointed.

"With luck, I'll be back in a few weeks. A month at the most. By then maybe we'll have a lead worth following on any family you might have left. I'm not forgetting my promise."

She didn't move.

Wes slapped his knee. "Well, good-bye." He wasn't going to get sentimental about leaving a woman who looked at him like he might kill her at any time.

But then he remembered the feel of her hand in his. Funny, he thought, he'd never considered himself the kind of man who'd hold a woman's hand. But he had to admit, he liked the way her fingers curled around his own. He liked the comfort of knowing that, for a few moments at least, she wanted him near.

On impulse, he stretched out his hand, palm up, toward her.

She stared at it a moment, then slowly lay her fingers on his.

Wes saw the ring and remembered that, as far as the world was concerned, this woman was his wife. The ring she wore had meant so much to May, Daniel's wife. And when she'd died, Daniel had slipped it on his little finger as if somehow he could keep the bond alive. He'd taken it off to save Allie. But the ring lost its meaning in the passing. Allie wasn't Wes's wife. No woman would ever be. She'd saved his life and, with the ring, he'd saved hers. That was all.

"I'll miss you, little blue eyes." Wes smiled. "I've grown used to our long talks." He placed his other hand over her fingers, warming them. "If I don't make it back, you'll be safe here. Adam will know what to do."

Her hand felt so tiny in his. Now that the bruises were healing, he could see she was really a pretty girl. Once he found her family, she'd probably fit right in with a circle of friends.

"Well. . . ." He stood without letting go of her hand. "I have to get some sleep if I'm going to leave at dawn. I've been out of the saddle too long."

As he turned loose of her hand and moved away, she watched him with those huge blue eyes he figured he'd see in his dreams for the rest of his life. She didn't really need to talk. Her stare told him much. She was still afraid of him, but she didn't want him to leave.

Wes undressed and climbed into bed. But sleep wouldn't come. He lay there staring at the darkness, wondering if she were doing the same thing. He thought about getting up and carrying her to bed, but the night wasn't all that cold and she might not understand.

Not that she was any company anyway. He wasn't even attracted to her in the way a man's attracted to a woman. He told himself it was more like how a man would feel about helping a child . . . well, not exactly. Maybe the way he'd feel about saving a wild animal . . . well, not just like that.

"Well, hell," he mumbled and rolled to face her. "Allie, are you awake?"

She didn't answer, but he sensed she was watching him from her perch on the chair.

"I . . ." Wes stopped. What could he say? I want you to come over here and crawl in bed with me? He didn't need her. He'd never needed anyone.

"I thought . . ." Wes closed his eyes tightly, trying to forget that she was a few feet away. He'd sound like a blasted fool if he said something like, I'd like to hold you tonight and smell your hair. The woman didn't like him, as far as he could tell. She'd probably knife him in his sleep for even asking such a thing. The only reason she remained in his room was because she was more afraid to be anywhere else.

He twisted in his covers, then threw them off him. If he told anyone what he was thinking they'd laugh him out of any bar in town. But he didn't plan on telling anyone, and it was a certainty that Allie wouldn't.

"Allie," he started, determined to finish. "I want you to come over here and sleep next to me." There, he'd said it plain and simple. "I'm not going to hurt you. I just don't want to be alone tonight."

The minute the words were out, he wished he could take them back. Never in his life had he said something so foolish, at least not stone sober. If she did understand a word he said, she was probably laughing at him over in her corner. Here he was, a war hero, a hard man, a loner, telling her he didn't want to be alone in the dark, like some child. Her silent company was all he asked her to give. Nothing more.

Wes jerked as he felt the cover being pulled away from his side. Without breathing, he remained still as she slipped in beside him, closing the blankets over them both with her movements.

Her back rested lightly against his side and her head on his arm.

It was several seconds before Wes could draw a full breath. He lay in the darkness feeling her against him. Her hair was soft and warm on his arm and shoulder. He could just make out the beating of her heart against his ribs. Her bottom pressed lightly against his leg.

He'd never been further from thoughts of sleep in his life. He listened as her breathing grew slow and regular. In her sleep, she snuggled closer for warmth. Her hand moved across his arm and came to rest at his elbow.

Dear God, she felt good. He never remembered a woman feeling so good.

Wes tried to think back over the years. In truth, he couldn't remember ever sleeping with a woman. He'd made love to a few and then left. He'd passed out in a few beds along the way when he'd been drinking between battles. But he could never remember just sleeping next to a woman except for Allie.

She wore no perfume, yet he closed his eyes and drank in the fresh smell of her.

Wes slowly rolled on his side and moved his hand

along her middle, just below her ribs. He pressed his face into the soft warmth of her curls and took a deep breath as he tugged her gently closer against him.

She relaxed in his arms. Responding to his encouragement without question. He tightened his grip around her, feeling her breasts resting just above his arm, enjoying the way she molded against him all soft and willing.

Carefully, he moved her hair away from her throat and lightly touched his lips to the spot where her pulse pounded so regular. He wasn't kissing her, but drinking in the nearness of her. He moved his mouth across her throat once more, only this time his lips opened slightly so that he could taste her flesh as well as feel the slow, steady pounding of her heart.

She moved in her sleep, unknowingly offering him more. But he knew if he tasted deeper, he'd awaken her and probably frighten her.

Wes closed his eyes and tried to sleep. What had he asked for? He'd said he only wanted her near. And she came believing him. He couldn't break his word.

This night was a hell and a paradise of his own making. She'd trusted him so near for the first time. He couldn't betray such a trust.

All through the night, Wes only dozed. When he'd move, she'd adjust beside him. When she moved, rolling first one way and then the other, he'd settle her with his touch. Molding her back against him so that he could feel her resting against the length of him. Drawing her close enough so that the rise and fall of her full chest pressed against his. Slowly, he pulled her into a world that was only theirs.

"Allie," he whispered, half asleep. "Allie, I don't want to leave you."

His words brought him full awake. He stared down in the dim light and saw her looking up at him. Hate still filled her eyes.

Wes brushed her cheek with his fingers, pushing back her hair. "Allie, don't be afraid."

He closed the few inches between their mouths and lightly kissed her lips. When she didn't pull away, he touched them again. They were warm and full . . . and unresponsive.

Wes leaned away and studied her. She hadn't moved, but her eyes were still wild with fear.

He rolled slightly and tasted her mouth more fully. When he pressed his thumb on her chin, she opened her lips. He kissed her deeper, but she didn't respond.

Wes raised to one elbow, trying to read her thoughts. He placed his hand on her waist and heard her sudden intake of breath, but she didn't stir. When he pressed harder, she turned her head away, but didn't move as she fought down a cry.

"Allie," he asked in panic. "What is it? What are you so afraid of?"

She didn't answer.

"Allie! Look at me." He twisted his hand into a fist. The material of her gown drew up in his fingers, pulling the cotton tight across her breasts.

"Look at me!"

Finally, she faced him. He couldn't miss the tears in her eyes.

His hand brushed across her waist, feeling of the cotton of her gown, trying to comfort her, erasing the wrinkles he'd caused with his grip.

She trembled but didn't twist away from his touch. She seemed frozen in place.

Wes lowered his mouth to her once more. For a few moments, he waited, a fraction from her. He could feel her rapid breathing against his lips. He decreased the distance between them until his mouth brushed hers. When she didn't move, he tasted her lips with his tongue as he inched closer. She was still, as before, while he kissed her, but he could taste the panic, feel the fear.

"Allie," he tried again, raising his hand so that he in no way held her in the bed. "Tell me! What frightens you so?"

She laid her hands on either side of her and gripped

the sheet. She looked like someone waiting to be shot.

Wes watched her closely. "Do you wish to leave? Do you want me to stop?"

She closed her eyes, spilling tears as she did. Shaking her head back and forth, she told him no with her action even though her entire body looked as if she were preparing to be sacrificed.

He fought down his anger at the world and kept his voice low. "Then unbutton your gown." He ordered a test. He had to know.

With eyes stinging in unshed tears, she raised trembling hands and unfastened the buttons of her gown as Wes watched.

Fighting tiny sobs, she fumbled with each button as first the lace of her collar, then the white cotton of her gown began to fall away.

Wes watched her throat appear, then her collarbone, then the rise and fall between her breasts.

She stopped.

He studied her. Her eyes were closed tightly now, as if the terror to come was too great to bear. The few inches of open gown showed the swell of her breasts.

He could do nothing but stare. The beauty of her, even in the near darkness, was overwhelming.

"Allie," he whispered finally.

She jerked as if she'd been slapped and unbuttoned another button. It was taking all her strength to do what he wanted.

The opening in her gown widened slightly, revealing more of her flesh. When she finished the last button at her waist, she placed her hands at her sides, once more gripping the sheet.

"Allie?" Wes felt like his insides were being ripped out. "You'll do anything I tell you, won't you?" The test was over. He knew the truth.

She nodded.

"But why?" He brushed the tears from her cheek. "Are you so afraid I'm going to hurt you? I told you I'd never raise a hand against you, Allie." He knew by the way she was acting that she'd been hurt before. He couldn't help but wonder how many men had demanded she remove her clothes and how many times she'd been beaten, so that now just the fear of it made her tremble and obey.

Carefully, as she lay beside him, he rebuttoned her gown all the way to her throat. Then he pulled her gently against him and let her cry softly on his shoulder.

Finally, when the tears had stopped, he whispered, "Talk to me, Allie. Tell me how I can help. Tell me that you believe I mean you no harm. Let me know what frightens you so."

Her fingers touched his lips, silencing his words.

He turned so that he could see her face as she raised above him.

"Don't—" She swallowed as if the words were stuck in her throat. "Don't leave me."

He understood then. She'd do anything, let him do anything, but she didn't want to be all alone again.

"I won't," he promised.

TEN

FOLLOWING WES DOWN THE HALLWAY AND ONTO the porch, Allie noticed Adam and Nichole waiting for them at the steps. Daniel brought the horses from the stables as the two couples stood silently watching the sun come up over an awakening town.

Allie closed her eyes and took a deep breath, knowing it would be a long time before she got the smell of Forth Worth from her lungs. She'd figured her life all out in this place. If she wanted to stay away from the kind of people who'd put her in a cage, she had to stay near Wes. For some unknown reason, he thought she had some value. By thinking so, he convinced folks around him.

What she couldn't fathom was his strange behavior last night. He looked liked all the males she'd ever seen. He was taller than most, and thin in a lean, powerful kind of way. He seemed a normal man. But he didn't act like the others.

An old Apache woman had told her about males and females of all tribes when Allie was no more than ten summers. She'd said that once Allie was old enough to breed, men would take her beneath their blankets. The old woman had been very plain, saying that the less Allie fought, the less she would get hurt.

But Allie hadn't listened. She'd fought wildly every

time, except last night. When Wes had told her to join him, she'd ventured closer without the fear that usually choked her throat. And she wasn't at all sure why.

He'd still frightened her, but he hadn't hurt her. She made up her mind that, the next time he lay with her, she'd try to understand what he wanted. For after last night, she knew it wasn't her.

Most girls in the tribes were chosen as a wife to one man. But the old woman had explained that Allie was worthless, that she would have no man to call hers. She was also not of their people, so any trader who came could take her without offending anyone.

The old woman, who had been the chief's mother, said those were the rules set for Allie and that Allie was to tell her when her time of womanhood had come. Until then, Allie would be fed if she worked hard. After that time arrived, she might be traded. The old woman seemed to think Allie might gain some value as she aged.

But Allie was small for her age and hid the fact that she was a woman for as long as she could. In what Allie thought to be her fourteenth winter, the tribe she lived with was raided.

For months, she'd already been planning for when a raid came, for raids were a part of her life. And she'd prepared, storing what she could in a cave nearby, searching for a path to run that would leave no sign, thinking about exactly what she'd do, depending on the time of day.

With the warmth of spring came the first raid. A sudden attack at dawn. Dog soldiers from the Comanches to the north swarmed down on their enemy, the Mescalaro Apache. With the thundering of horses, Allie was up and in action before she had time to think. As the first shots were fired, she slipped into her dark robes and rolled out the back of the old woman's tent. Then, focusing totally on her destination, she ran without looking at the chaos around her. She didn't stop when she heard the old woman cry out or when answering fire volleyed though the little canyon.

She made it to the cave and ran silently through the passages she'd learned by heart. Ten turns, ten choices. If she made any one wrong, she might never find her way out of the tunnels.

As the day passed, she heard men moving in the cave, yelling for one another. She hid on a ledge out of sight with a knife in her hand. But they never reached her hiding place. Finally, all was silent and she slept.

When she awoke, it was the afternoon of the next day. She was alone. The winter camp had been burned and scattered in the wind. No one remained.

"Allie?"

Someone pulled her from her thoughts. She looked up as Nichole slowly lowered herself down the few steps.

"I brought you these leather boots. They may be a little big, but thick socks will help them fit." Nichole handed her a fine pair of leather footwear that seemed an odd mixture between a boot and a moccasin.

Allie accepted the gift with a nod.

Nichole flipped over the top of one of the boots and slipped a knife from the leather at the calf. "I found them to be very good boots during the war when I was on the run. This might come in handy for you sometime."

Allie met her gaze. Silently, she thanked her for the weapon. The boots seemed a great gift, but the hidden weapon was priceless.

"I don't understand," Adam said as he followed Wes to the horses. "Why are you taking her with you? We talked about it last night. She'd be safe with us."

Winking at Allie, Wes explained, "She told me she wanted to go. We had a long talk last night."

"Are you sure?" Adam seemed worried. "You're not fully recovered."

Wes crossed between the horses, nodding his good morning to Daniel. He checked the cinch and stretched out his hand. Allie joined him, allowing him to lift her into the saddle and adjust the stirrups to her leg length.

"Thanks for finding the fresh mounts, Dan," Wes

said as he worked. "You got most of Papa's sense about horses."

Wes didn't look at his younger brother, or expect him to answer. Daniel had a way of never having anything to say when emotions ran high in him.

Adam was another story. He paced restlessly just as he had every time Wes had ridden off to battle during the war.

"Stop acting like I'm kidnapping the woman again." Wes grumbled at the doctor. "She wants to go with me. Since she's my wife right now, there is no reason she shouldn't."

"I thought the priority here was finding her family, not looking for a ghost treasure."

Wes frowned. "It is. But we have no leads on her people. I can't just sit around and wait. You know if I had a direction to go, finding her family would be first. But, until then, I have to do something."

Adam nodded his understanding of his wandering brother and moved to the other side of Allie's bay horse. He looked up at her as he touched her knee. "Take care of him, will you, Allie? He has a way of finding trouble."

Allie didn't answer.

"We're wasting daylight!" Wes swung into the saddle and kicked his horse into action.

Allie took one last look at the crazy people who'd been so kind to her, and reined her horse half quarter. She felt sure Nichole would be starving on the streets by the time she saw her again at the rate the woman gave away her clothes and food. As for the doctor, he seemed no less giving. He was a healer who didn't know his own power. And the big one they called "little" brother wore his heart reflected in his eyes.

Wes's brothers waved and Allie saw Wes give them a quick salute.

"Keep an angel on your shoulder," Daniel yelled suddenly.

"And your fist drawn," Adam added.

"Until my brother is there to cover my back," Wes finished as he kicked up dust.

She rode beside Wes away from town thinking of how hard she'd worked to get each of her possessions that were still hidden in the cave. She'd had to make ten of anything before she'd be allowed to keep one. And that one always had to look poorly done or someone would take it from her. In the tribe, everything she made belonged to the old woman.

But, slowly, she'd collected bits of clothing and furs. Once she was alone, no one stole her things. If Wes knew what a wealth she had in pelts, he'd think her a fine wife. Maybe.

All day, she thought of telling him as they rode south. Wes only slowed long enough to water the horses and hand her a bite to eat from a food pouch. He said little.

By nightfall Allie's bones were so tired she slid from the saddle when Wes finally stopped the horses.

He caught her and carried her to the stream's edge. Wrapping her in both blankets, he watered and brushed the horses and built a fire without her help. He took the time to boil coffee and make flat bread out of the flour mixture from his pack. When he served her supper, it looked like a feast.

Allie ate all he handed her and drank the warm brown liquid in her cup. It tasted terrible, but she could feel the warmth running through her body all the way to her toes.

"I've pushed you too hard," he finally said as he watched her from a few feet away. "Why didn't you say something?"

"Never mind," he answered his own question. "I know why. You're afraid I'd leave you somewhere along the trail if you complained."

Again, she didn't answer. She didn't see the need.

"I'm not going to do that, Allie. I've nothing to offer you but my word." He leaned back against a tree trunk. "Somewhere you have people, your people. I'll help you find them." He studied her closely. "Do you remember anything?"

Allie shook her head. She remembered the boy in the field telling her to have a plan. She remembered her mother's body in a pile of bodies. But they were dead. They could be of no help.

"Somewhere you've got someone worried about you." Wes yawned and set down his coffee cup. "I can feel it." His eyes closed in sleep.

Allie stood slowly with the blankets wrapped around her and moved to his side. She cuddled beneath his arm and spread the quilts over them both.

I have you here, she thought, relaxing next to him. He was as close to family as she needed. Slowly, an inch at a time, she was learning to trust him.

Just before sleep drifted over her, a twig snapped.

Allie didn't move.

Another snapped.

She stretched her hand to her boot and pulled out the knife.

A dark form slipped from one cottonwood to the other in the shadows by the water. The few remaining brown leaves on the trees seemed to smear his outline, concealing him as the wind shifted.

Straightening, she stiffened every muscle in preparation.

The intruder drew closer, shifting from trunk to bush as silently as moss spreading. With each passing moment, darkness played into his hand as the fire burned lower and the last rays of daylight faded.

Panic pumped through Allie. Should she wake Wes? Defend them both? Or run? If she made any sudden moves, the man would be aware she knew of his arrival. If he carried a gun, they'd both be dead before Wes could fire a shot.

Allie stood slowly as if wanting to warm herself by the fire. She circled until the smoke and flames danced between the intruder and her. In a blink, she was gone, vanishing into the blackness as if melting into the scenery.

Silently, she crossed between the trees. Watching

every movement. Listening to the slightest sound. She could feel the man's presence though she couldn't see him. She could sense his nearness, layered in danger. The cold breeze against her face barely registered. She lifted her bothersome skirt above her knees and bunched it in one hand. Ignoring the brush scratches against her legs, she slipped through the night toward the stranger.

Crossing the undergrowth without a sound, Allie watched as the shadow advanced toward the spot where Wes slept.

Wes didn't move. He had no idea of the danger he was in.

Allie circled behind the intruder and began to close the distance to his back. Raising the knife, she filled her lungs with air so that all her strength could go to the kill.

Just as the shadow stepped into the glow of firelight, Wes rolled to his knee, raising a Colt to point directly at the man. Allie lunged forward, her knife poised.

"Wes?" the stranger managed to say a fraction of a second before Allie hit him from behind.

Her skirts tripped her final step toward him, sending her plummeting at him without control. The knife struck his back, but the blade was not true. It veered off his leather coat without penetrating.

The stranger stumbled forward as her body pounded against his.

Wes fired as they tumbled. Allie felt the bullet pass close enough to move her hair.

The stranger hit the ground with a thud. She landed square on top of him, pushing the air from his lungs.

With all her strength, she pulled away from him and raised the knife for another try. But Wes's sudden movements startled her.

"Allie! No!" he yelled.

She held the knife with both hands high in the air, ready to plunge.

"Allie!" he yelled again. "Stop!"

The man didn't stir beneath her. If he had, she might

not have listened to Wes's words. Survival was so strong within her, it was hard to stop and listen to anyone.

Slowly she climbed off the stranger, keeping her knife ready.

"Allie," Wes said more calmly. "He's a friend."

Without taking her eyes off the intruder, she backed toward Wes. When she was safe at his side, she lowered the knife, but didn't return it to the hiding place in her boot.

"Vincent?" Wes moved in front of her. "Vince? I thought you were dead."

"Darn near made me so," Vince Edward grumbled as he stood and wiped the dirt off a hopelessly filthy pair of pants. "I came in slow to make sure you were alone. I never figured both you and this woman would try to kill me. A knife in the back and a bullet through the heart, nice reception."

Wes replaced his Colt in the holster. "You don't appear to be bleeding with that complaining, so no harm done. You should know better than to sneak up on a fire after dark."

"I don't know anything anymore. I thought I was safe riding watch before the stampede, but three men tried to kill me." He limped closer to the fire. "They thought they had when they searched my body and took all my gear. But I was still breathing and, thanks to the stampede, they didn't have time to finish the job."

"But I looked everywhere for you." Wes joined him. "I wouldn't think a wrangler as homely as you would be hard to find."

Allie stared closely at the tall stranger. He was built wide in the shoulders and stood as tall as Wes. He looked like he'd been on the trail for several days, but even with the covering of dirt, she'd guess him a handsome man. Wes must truly be his friend to be able to call him homely to his face and the man not take offense at the lie.

"I was hurting bad after they took turns beating me. They planned to kill me without a sound, but the fight

I put up stirred the cattle nearby.'' Vince rubbed his leg as if he could rub away the pain. ''While they were trying to quiet their mounts and stay out of the way of a few hundred longhorns, I followed my grandfather's plan of escape and hit the river. By dawn, I was miles south with a knife wound in my right leg that still gives me trouble.''

He looked toward Allie. ''Before I tell you more, don't you think you should introduce me to your body-guard?''

Wes pointed with his head. ''Vincent Edward, I'd like you to meet Allie. Allie, this is the friend who gave me the map for safekeeping.''

Vince raised an eyebrow, waiting for more of an introduction, but Wes didn't offer one and it would have been impolite to ask more. He tipped his hat to the woman who'd tried to kill him. ''Nice to meet you.''

Allie backed away.

''She doesn't talk much,'' Wes answered for her. ''I'm helping her find her family.''

Vince straightened suddenly. ''I almost forgot. When I missed you at your brother's by a few hours, he handed me a letter to bring you.'' Vince disappeared into the darkness, then reappeared, pulling his horse.

He flipped the cover on his saddlebag and handed Wes an envelope. ''Adam said this was one strange letter and maybe you should take a look at it before you head toward your treasure at Goliad.''

Wes turned the brown envelope over in his hand then leaned down to his saddlebags resting by the tree. ''I need to give you back the map. Now that you're alive, it's no longer my treasure.''

Vince raised his hands, unwilling to even touch it. ''No, thanks.'' He backed away. ''That treasure has caused me enough trouble. I promised myself that as soon as I found you, I was heading home. The map is all yours.''

Wes opened his mouth to argue, but Vince cut him off. ''Someone out there is still willing to kill for that map. If you're wise, you'll forget it, too. I've got a wife and kids waiting for me. I'll count my blessings if I get out of this treasure hunt with only a limp.''

''But your grandfather—''

''He died eaten up with a fever to find it. The fever cost him his son's life and almost mine. I told myself when I was floating down the Red River that night with my own blood coloring the water, that if I lived, I'd never touch that damn map again.''

''If I find something, I'll mail you half,'' Wes offered.

''No, thanks. I want no part of it.'' Vince turned and began unsaddling his horse as Wes put the map away. ''I'll bed down at your fire tonight, then I'm heading home tomorrow. I've been following you for three weeks. Wanted to let you know I was alive.''

Wes moved the pot near the fire to warm the brew, then sat down close to the flames to read the letter Vince had brought him from Adam.

Vince talked as he unloaded. ''By the way, I found out you're not engaged to the Montago girl anymore. She wouldn't even see me. 'Course, her sister had plenty to say.'' Vince glanced at Allie as if the pieces he'd heard about Wes's activities were starting to fit together. But Vince wasn't the kind of man to ask or repeat gossip, no matter how interesting it might have been.

''Angela Montago wasn't interested in a rancher without cattle,'' Wes answered as he examined the letter. ''I didn't have time to tell her about the map and how I might have enough money soon to buy at least a starter herd. All she saw was a no-good ranch with only a dugout to live in.''

''Picky woman.'' Vince laughed as he poured himself a cup of coffee. ''No matter how beautiful a lady is, if she doesn't have time to listen to a man's dreams, she starts uglying up.'' The letter drew his interest as he relaxed with his cup in hand.

Scribbled on the side of the envelope in Adam's scratching was a note saying, ''Thought you needed to see this as soon as possible.''

Wes unfolded the letter inside. The handwriting was worse than Adam's. Some words were large, some small, as if the author of the note was just learning to write or forgetting how.

"What's it say?" Vince never was long on patience.

Wes read: "Girl, born 1847, captured 1852. Name: Allyce Catlin. Called Allie. Parents and siblings died in attack. Only known relative: grandmother, Victoria Catlin. She was part of the original Austin colony. Last known address: near Brady, Texas." Wes took a deep breath. "It's signed Sheriff Maxwell Hardy, retired."

"You think that could be your Allie's kin?"

Wes didn't want to sound hopeful. "Could be, but we've been down a few dead ends already. At least this comes from a sheriff. The dates sound about right, and the name fits."

Vince leaned back and studied his friend closely. "Come morning, I'm heading north to home. Do you go to Brady or Goliad?"

Wes looked at Allie. She was doing her best to pretend to be asleep, but he had no doubt she heard every word they'd been saying. "Brady," he finally whispered. "We'll head to Brady and hope this Sheriff Hardy is right. It's on my way anyway."

Vince lowered his hat over his eyes. "We've both got a long ride tomorrow."

Wes returned to the tree and sat down beside Allie. "A long day." He leaned back and closed his eyes, smiling as she spread the blankets over them both.

Hours later, Wes rolled awake just before dawn. The air hung still with new birth and the fire burned low in dying warmth. He glanced around, sensing something was missing even before he could reason what.

Vince slept soundly on the other side of the fire. Two horses moved by the water's edge. Two horses! The bay was missing.

Allie was gone.

ELEVEN

Allie slid from her horse and held the reins with one hand and her skirt with the other as she crossed the shallow stream. The bay protested as they splashed through the cold water, but Allie didn't slow her march. She doubted Wes would follow her long. He'd probably be glad she was gone so that he could get on with his search for the Goliad treasure. She only slowed him down. He'd helped her along the way, and now she kept him from doing what he wanted to do.

He'd saved her from the cage, and she'd paid him back by taking him to his brother. They were even—if she didn't count the bay she'd taken with her.

But horses weren't all that valuable, she reminded herself. There were wild ones Wes could catch as a replacement.

And—if she didn't count the saddle, she thought.

Saddles were several times more valuable than a horse. Wes would probably be mad about the saddle. But there was no way she could send it back. If she'd thought before she left, she would have ridden out bareback.

She felt like a fool. To take a horse was a small crime, but to take a saddle was a far greater wrong. She hadn't been fair with him. He would have every right to call her an enemy from this day on. Her tribe and his would be at war. Only she didn't have a tribe.

The horse shied away from the uneven ground beneath the water. With one hand, Allie held the reins tighter, pulling the animal along, while she tried desperately to hold up the hem of her skirt with the other. She knew she'd have to stay in the water for several hundred feet if she were to make her trail disappear. The possibility that Wes would follow made her trip through the water necessary.

Allie thought of the chance that Louis might still be around, but decided he would never have been able to keep up with the way they rode yesterday. If he'd gotten in sight, Wes would have seen him, for Wes was a soldier trained to watch his back.

She plodded forward, picking her path. The bay followed fitfully. Several yards into the water, she saw the problem. The shadows of bare branches moved like thin black snakes across the shallow edges of the stream. The river's flow seemed to give them life.

Panic gripped Allie. The horse seemed to sense her terror. He jerked his head, pulling the reins free from her wet hand.

Allie jumped to recapture control of the leather, but the animal had tasted freedom. With a sudden bolt, he was away, running at full gallop toward the water's edge.

Allie followed. Her boots seemed to weigh a ton. She splashed through the stream like a seasoned trooper. By the time she'd reached the bank, the horse had found his footing on land and was out of sight.

Holding her chin high, she refused to mourn the loss. The horse was not hers to begin with. She could make it to the caves on foot. She didn't need anyone or anyone's things. She had her own belongings.

Plopping down on the grass, Allie pulled off her wet boots and thought of all the treasures she'd hidden in her cave. Not treasures like Wes's gold, but her treasures. A warm coat she'd made of rabbit pelts, a bed of the fine buffalo hide she'd taken from the tent when the raid started, leather dresses that would never wear out, and leggings to keep her warm in winter. She'd carved bowls last fall, after she'd gathered nuts like a squirrel, and she'd made baskets every spring when thin branches were limber.

She leaned back into the dry grass and thought of her cave. The cold and darkness seemed a small price to pay. In every other world, she had nothing. But in her world alone, she had all she needed. Allie closed her eyes and let the sun warm her. Somehow she'd find her cave once more. Somehow she'd get back home to her own private world. Then she'd stay alone, where no one would bother her.

She pulled the key taken from the McLains from her pocket. From now on she'd lock the world out. With her fingers clutching the key tightly, she relaxed in the warm dry grass.

Wes found her by the water, sound asleep. When she first came into sight, he couldn't believe his luck. He'd thought it'd take him hours to locate her, if he ever did. But it wasn't long past noon. Her efforts to cover her trail had been good, but not nearly good enough to evade a man who'd spent four years in a war, reading signs.

He crossed the water far enough upstream that she couldn't hear him. Then he tied his horse, walked over to her, and sat down in the grass. For a long while, he studied her. She really was a pretty woman in a wild kind of way. Some men might find her quite attractive. She had hair that was made to be touched and eyes that looked all the way into her soul. Yes, once she was settled with her family she'd have no trouble finding a man.

Not him, of course. She wasn't his ideal of beauty. He'd always admired women who emphasized their looks with makeup and padding. And tall. He liked a woman he could look directly in the eyes. But for a man who liked his women plain, simply dressed, and short, Allie would stand out as prime.

Wes smiled, realizing it didn't really matter to him if his women had been hookers or fine ladies; he liked a lady who wore her beauty as if it were a canvas, fully colored and fully framed. He'd always been attracted to women who were realer than real. Who wore their hair higher or more brightly colored than nature intended. Whose lips were blood red and breasts were powdered white.

He watched Allie sleeping. She was truly plain, he thought. Brown hair, small built, thin. If she'd been a fish, he'd have thrown her back for a better catch. But something about her made her not all that hard to look at. He'd thought it was her eyes and the way he could read her every thought in them. But that couldn't have been it, because her eyes were closed now and he was still looking.

Maybe she wasn't pretty, exactly, he thought. There was nothing wrong with her. She just wasn't his type of woman.

Wes groaned. He was wasting far too much time thinking about something that didn't matter at all. The only thing that should be on his mind was getting her to Brady, then finding the treasure as fast as he could. If Vincent was right and other men were looking for it, they might have given up trying to find the map and gone down there planning to rip every stone out of the floor. It would only be a matter of time before they found the tunnel.

His groan woke her.

Allie blinked and jumped at the sight of him beside her. Like an animal alert at the moment of waking, she was several feet away before he could react.

"Now hold on." Wes raised his hands. "Don't go running off again."

She moved a step back. "You're angry?"

"Because you ran?" Wes shook his head. "You got a right to go where you want. I don't own you, Allie." He had to smile—she'd finally decided to talk to him.

Allie watched him closely. Her eyes darted from her

shoes to him. She knew she couldn't grab them without him being able to reach her. "I lost your horse."

"There are other horses." He watched her closely.

"And your saddle."

"It was Adam's saddle." Wes smiled as though he'd told a joke.

Tilting her head, she studied him. "Then why did you follow me?"

Wes made no effort to reach for her. "Because," he began, "we have to talk."

"We are talking." She'd already said more to him in the past two minutes than she'd said to another human being in five years.

"We have to talk about you." Wes pulled the letter from his pocket. "I received this—"

"I know." She might be quiet, but she was not deaf. She'd heard everything Vincent and Wes had talked about last night.

Wes glanced up at her. "Don't you realize this could be your family?"

"I have no family."

"But—"

"They all died. I saw their bodies piled like wood to burn." Allie lowered her head. She didn't like to think about the way the camp had looked after the raid. When she brought the image to mind, she could still smell the odor of burning flesh.

Long-buried memories flooded back. The sounds of screams and gunfire. The taste of terror in her mouth as her mother pushed her away, telling her to run for the trees. Her mother then grabbed the baby and ran for the shelter. Black smoke billowed from the barn, as if a great storm was being born there and would spread over the whole world.

"There's a sheriff forty miles south of here who thinks you might still have a grandmother alive."

Allie remembered no grandmother.

"You've got to give it a try."

He said no more, but Allie heard the words as clear

as if he'd spoken them aloud. *I can't go on worrying about you.*

She lifted her chin. "I'll go," she said. "But I won't promise to stay."

"Fair enough." Wes stood. "I'll go round up your horse."

By nightfall, they were in the small settlement of Brady, Texas. The huddle of houses and stores could hardly be called a town. A mercantile, a six-table cafe with a chalkboard menu outside, a blacksmith with livery stable, a three-story hotel with a saloon in the back half of its first floor, and several houses.

Some people didn't consider a place a town until it had a courthouse or newspaper or bank, but Wes always thought the difference lay in the presence of a barbershop. Once a place had a shop, he knew folks were settling in. His reasoning wasn't based on the fact that the barbershop was a meeting place to exchange information, as well as take a bath, get a shave, or have a tooth pulled. He'd decided, by observation, that when men start shaving regularly, it's usually due to females. And once women are settled into a place, it's only a matter of time before there are schools and churches, banks and newspapers. A town.

Brady hadn't yet become a town, but from the looks of things, it was only a matter of time.

If he'd been alone, Wes would have stayed with the horses in the livery for a quarter, but he couldn't do that with Allie along. The little money he'd picked up from a stash he always left at Adam's would be gone fast with hotel prices and double meals.

He paid the two bits for the horses' care and walked across the street to the hotel with Allie at his heels. She hid behind him as he ordered a room and asked to have a bath brought up.

The hotel owner told him the only room fit for a lady was on the third floor and, due to its size, cost twice as much as any of the others.

Wes groaned and took the room. When he climbed the stairs, he was relieved to find the accommodations much nicer than expected.

"Not bad. At least we'll be comfortable tonight." He tossed his saddlebag on the nearest of two small beds and turned to face Allie.

She stood just inside the doorway, her face ghostly white. Her hands knotted the fabric of her dress on either side.

"What is it?" Wes reached out to touch her shoulder.

Allie jerked away, backing as far as she could into the corner.

"Allie, talk to me." He knew if he took a step toward her, he'd only frighten her more. She was in that private hell of hers where everything was threatening and everyone was an enemy.

Her huge blue eyes stared at him with a terror in them so deep he wasn't sure it wouldn't kill her.

Wes glanced around the room. There was nothing frightening. The room was almost totally white, from bed covers to curtains. The floors had been scrubbed recently, and the water in the pitcher looked fresh. Even the chamber pot beneath the first bed looked to have been cleaned.

Wes backed toward the windows and sat down in the room's only chair, a rocker made with most of the bark left on the wood. "I'm no good at this," he mumbled to himself.

He leaned back and rested his head, closing his eyes, blocking out her suffering. "Allie, I'm a hard man who's spent most of my life fighting one way or the other. You need a man like Daniel with faith enough to help you or Adam with his soft, easy way of healing."

He heard the movement of her dress and the slight swish of a blade clearing leather. She'd drawn her knife. After all the nights they'd spent together, she still didn't trust him. Did she think he'd traveled over half of Texas, waiting until he reached *this* hotel, to kill her?

Wes tried again. "Allie, there is nothing to be afraid

of here. We're just in a hotel. There's even a lock on the door, which is more than I can say for a few of the hotels I've been in since coming to Texas.''

He folded his hands. ''How about I leave you to take your bath? The desk clerk downstairs said I could probably find the sheriff who sent me the letter in the saloon.''

She didn't move or answer him. He really didn't expect her to.

A maid tapped on the door then entered with two pails of water. The woman was clean and neatly dressed, but there was a hardness about her. A hatred of life that ran bone deep. A boy of about twelve followed with a small hip tub. She glanced from Allie to Wes, but she'd seen far too much to comment.

The boy set the tub down with a thud. Before the noise stopped echoing around the room, the woman backhanded him hard. He didn't react, not a sound, as he turned and left the room. The woman followed him out without saying anything to Wes or Allie.

Wes glanced at Allie and saw a reaction to the cruelty in her eyes. He gave her time to speak, but, as always, she didn't say a word.

''Well.'' Wes stood, not knowing how to comfort her. ''I'll leave you. Enjoy your . . .''

The sudden panic in her eyes made him forget to finish his sentence.

''D-don't go!'' she stammered.

''But . . .'' Wes watched her closely, realizing her terror was not aimed at him. ''Do you want to go with me to meet the sheriff? Allie, what frightens you so?''

She gulped down her fear. ''I hate hotels.''

Wes took a deep breath and smiled. Fear of hotels seemed a much smaller problem than the thought that she might have suddenly gone insane and planned to kill him in his sleep. He relaxed. At least he wasn't the one who sparked her fears.

''You've nothing to fear here. I'll lock you in.''

He'd said the wrong thing. She was backing away

again. It took Wes a moment to realize what he'd said.

"No, I didn't mean what you think. I only meant we can lock the door so that no one will disturb you while you bathe."

"No." Allie shook her head violently, making her mass of hair fly around her. "I will not stay here. I hate this place."

Wes tried to reason. "But you love taking a bath. How about you take a bath and I'll wait for you? When you're finished, we'll go down and look for the sheriff together."

Allie nodded.

Wes moved toward the door. "I'll be right outside."

She darted, beating him to the opening. "No! Stay. I don't want to be in this place alone."

Wes didn't understand, but he was too tired to argue. He pulled the rocker to face the window and sat down with his back to the tub. "Let me know when you're finished."

To his surprise, he heard her knife slip back into her boot. He pulled the last thin cigar from the silver box in his breast pocket and lit it.

As he rocked back and forth, he thought he'd had some crazy things happen to him in his lifetime, but being forced at knifepoint to stay in a hotel room while a woman takes a bath had never been one of them. Until now.

He leaned back as he took a long draw on his last cigar, enjoying the sounds of her bathing just behind him.

Allie watched his back as she removed her clothes. He had been right about the bath. If she took a bath every day for the rest of her life, she'd never feel clean enough. But he'd been wrong to come to the hotel. Allie couldn't tell him, but she knew about hotels. They were places of evil where she'd been locked in a room. Deep into the night, the devil walked the hallways of hotels.

When the preacher had locked her up, she'd learned

to wait in the darkness. Between midnight and dawn, the devil would unlock her door. She'd fight for as long as she could, then she'd try to numb her mind to what he did. But even through the numbness, she'd known she'd gone to hell and back with him in the blackness. At dawn, she'd wake bruised and alone. The preacher would come to get her, angry, he said, because the devil visited her. Sometimes he'd be in a hurry and only rant and rave about how evil she was, but other times, he'd try to help her by whipping the evil out of her.

Allie remembered days passing when she'd sleep in the cage, knowing that as soon as they reached the next town there would be another hotel and another visit.

Wes must not know of the evil of this place, or he wouldn't have walked in without his guns drawn. Maybe if he were with her, the devil wouldn't come. She watched his back as she slipped into the water and washed. He was a strange man, but one thing she knew, he wasn't evil.

As soon as she was scrubbed, she pulled her clothes back on and moved to stand beside him.

"You ready?" he asked in a voice that told her he'd almost fallen asleep in the chair.

She nodded.

He stood slowly and pulled the thin ribbon used to tie back the curtains from the window.

"I thought I'd borrow this," he said smiling, "to tie back your hair. We can't very well go downstairs with it flying about."

Allie slid her hand to her knife but didn't pull it from her boot as he looped the lace beneath her hair and tied it.

"There." He stepped back and seemed pleased with his work. "Shall we go downstairs?"

He offered his hand.

Allie didn't take it but let him guide her out of the room and down the stairs.

The lobby was empty except for the clerk behind the

desk. He glanced up at Wes. "That old sheriff you're looking for is in the saloon."

Wes thanked him with a casual salute.

"If you want any supper, you'll have to order it in there. Nowhere else to get food this late." The clerk returned to his reading, not expecting an answer to his comments.

Wes slowly reached for Allie's hand and placed it on his arm. "Shall we?" he asked as though they were a normal couple.

As always, she didn't answer.

When they entered the saloon, Allie moved a little closer to Wes. He crossed to a lone man sitting at the back of an almost empty room.

"Sheriff Hardy?" Wes asked as Allie peeked around him to see the old man.

Hardy ignored Wes's outstretched hand as he stood slowly, staring wide-eyed at Allie.

"Victoria," he whispered. His eyes brimmed with tears. For a moment, he was somewhere far deep into the past and not with them. "Victoria," he said again, with a love and a sorrow too great to fathom.

TWELVE

ALLIE WATCHED THE OLD MAN CAREFULLY. GRAY hair hung past his collar, and his eyes were the color of the whiskey he drank. He raised a hand, weathered with age, and lightly brushed her cheek as reality of the present straightened his stance.

"I'm sorry." He tried to pull his emotions back into a body and mind too fragile to hold them in check. "There for a moment I thought I was looking at a woman I knew fifty years ago. You're her spittin' image, girl."

Wes tried again. "You are Sheriff Maxwell Hardy." The words were far more a statement than a question. "I'm Wes McLain."

The elderly man nodded. "I'm Max Hardy. Retired sheriff. I'm the one who sent you the letter. Thought it was a fool thing to do at the time. Never dreamed you'd answer so fast."

He paused and stared at Allie again. "We've been looking for a survivor of the Catlin clan for years. Everyone but me gave up long ago, but I still go over to the Rangers' office in Austin and check the reports now and again. Hoping."

"You found the message posted by my sister-in-law, Nichole McLain?" Wes pulled a chair out for Allie then motioned for her to sit down. He did the same as he waved the bartender for drinks.

"I've followed a dozen dead-end trails looking for one child." Hardy returned to his chair, but his gaze never left Allie's face. "I was one of the men who found the burned settlement back in '52. We'd had a skirmish with the Comanches near the Sabine River and figured they were still angry when they came across Catlin and his people. The bodies had been burned but, near as we could figure, one was missing. One child. We weren't even sure if it was a boy called Jimmy or a girl called Allie. The Catlins had a kid every spring, regular as clockwork. Near as I remember, Jimmy wasn't even a year older than Allie."

"Then, if she's a member of the Catlin family, her parents are dead?" Wes had hoped he'd find a parent still living who would take her in with loving arms.

"She's Allie Catlin," Hardy whispered. "Looks just like her grandma did when I first saw Victoria. I'd been hired as a scout back before the Republic. We brought part of Austin's original three hundred settlers from the San Marcos River to the lower part of the Lavaco. About a dozen families. They was all afraid of the Karankawas then, hadn't met up with the Apaches and Comanches. Most of them were upper-class, educated people. They didn't take to the hard life."

The old man leaned back in his chair as his mind slipped into the past. "I remember it being powerful hot that summer, with the river sluggish and trees so thick with Spanish moss you had to fight your way to the water. I was heading down for a drink when a little slip of a woman came running toward me yelling like she was about to be scalped by a war party."

Hardy laughed, a low rumbling kind of sound that comes from one who laughs little in life. "Well, with my gun in one hand and a knife in the other, I hurried to save her. But the little lady didn't need saving. She was so mad she grabbed my gun and disappeared into the moss.

"A minute later, I heard a shots. Then, before I could follow, she was out of the foliage trading my empty gun for my knife. This time, I followed only a few steps behind. The sight I saw when I reached the river is as clear in my mind as if it were yesterday. There sat Victoria Catlin, proclaimed as one of the fairest beauties in the South, straddling a gator. She was stabbing him with my knife like she was fighting for her life, but that old gator was already dead."

Hardy raised one bushy eyebrow and winked at Allie. "She was still swearing and steaming when I pulled her off the poor critter. It seems the alligators down by the river loved the settlers' hunting dogs for dinner. Only this one made the mistake of eating Miss Victoria's pet."

Wes smiled. "Sounds like she was quite a woman." He couldn't help but think of Allie sitting atop Vincent about to stab him.

Hardy shook his head. "Miss Victoria is quite a woman. Outlived so many husbands she had to enlarge the family plot. Never took a one of their names after the first. Always said it wasn't worth changing her monogram for something as temporary as marriage. Bore six children by Catlin, three boys and three girls.

"The girls all died before they were grown. James, her oldest, was killed in the raid in '52, like I said. Darron died at Shiloh. Michael, her baby, is in his forties now, but he doesn't cast much of a shadow as a man. I figured if I could ever find James's one survivor, Victoria's only grandchild, she might die thinking she'd done something worthwhile in this life. From the size of the bones, we figured either Allie or James Junior lived.

"James told me once that he ordered his wife to send the children to the woods if trouble came. So I spent the best part of a week looking, but no child. By the time we caught up with the war party, they'd traded off any captives."

Allie listened without expression to the old man's story, not allowing hope to grow within her. She'd lived through too much to believe anything good was about to happen. The man seemed to think she had a brother named James, but that didn't sound familiar to her. She remembered a boy, but James or even Jimmy didn't seem to fit as his name.

Hardy looked at her, his whiskey eyes liquid with unshed tears. "Will you go with me to see Miss Victoria tomorrow? I'd give half of the time I have left on earth to see her face when she looks at you."

She glanced at Wes, but he was staring down into the drink a bartender had brought him. Allie didn't know what to do, but it seemed to matter so much to the old man that she nodded.

"I'll call for you at nine." A touch of the manners he'd learned in youth laced through Maxwell Hardy's voice. "Thank you, Miss Allyce Meghan Catlin. After all these years, a simple letter brought you home."

"I'll be coming along," Wes interrupted. "Just to see that she's left in safe hands. She's been through a great deal. I promised her that much."

The old sheriff looked at Wes as if he were intruding. "All right, Mr. McLain. I'll call for you both. The ranch is about a two-hour ride from here. I assume you have horses, but a bullet I took in the leg a few years back prevents me from riding in anything but a buggy."

Hardy stood and gathered his gloves and hat to leave. He downed the last of his liquor. "Don't tell anyone else in town why you're here. There are those who might give quite a lot to see that no grandchild of Victoria's ever reaches her ranch."

He left without explaining.

Wes ordered two bowls of the new kind of stew, called chili, he'd learned to eat on trail drives. They didn't say a word as they waited. Wes drank another shot of whiskey and Allie stared at her hands. He didn't know what to say. He didn't want to get her hopes up. He'd heard stories of families rejecting captives who'd lived with the Indians. He'd even seen a father once turn his back on his two daughters after they'd been returned to civilization. They were better off dead and, as far as he was concerned, they were, the father had said. The girls had cried and clung to him, but he'd pulled away and left them without another word.

Wes didn't want to think about such a scene happening with Allie.

The boy who'd brought the tub to their room carried out two huge bowls of chili. He set them down in front of Wes and hurried away as if still embarrassed by the maid having struck him in front of Wes and Allie.

Breaking the silence, Wes mumbled, "Eat up," as he shoved the first bite in his mouth. "They say this stuff was invented because the meat turns bad on the trail drives. Put enough peppers and chili powder in with it and the hands don't notice."

Allie didn't look at him as she tasted the meal.

The boy returned with a glass of milk for her and another whiskey for Wes.

"Thanks, kid," Wes said.

The boy faced him with a man's measure of courage. "Not kid. My name's Jason."

Wes always allowed a man, even a young one, his due of respect unless he proved he didn't deserve it. "Thanks, Jason. Tell your mother this is mighty good chili."

Jason stood an inch taller as if bracing against the north wind. "I ain't got no ma or pa."

Allie looked up. "No tribe?"

He knew what she was asking. "No one, but I don't need them. I'm fine on my own."

He was on the edge of manhood, too old to ask for a handout and too young to earn his keep.

"Well." Wes chose his words carefully. "We're new in town and need a little advice. If you'd allow me to buy you supper, I've a heap of questions I need answering about the locals."

Jason brightened. "I know everyone in these parts." He hesitated, glancing at the bowls, then smiled. "I suppose I got a slow enough spell to help you out."

In less time than Wes thought possible, the boy had fetched his own bowl of chili and a glass of milk. But he waited to eat until he'd answered a few questions.

While the boy ate, Wes learned all about the people called Catlin. According to Jason, Maxwell Hardy was an old sheriff down on his luck. He might be too poor to afford a full bottle of whiskey, but he was still more gentleman than any man in town.

Jason had heard of Victoria Catlin, but never seen her. Folks said the last time she left her house was to bury her son from the war. Some said she was crazy, others thought she'd just got tired of living and was holed up waiting to die. She had a little mouse of a sister who came in for supplies now and then.

What he'd heard of Michael Catlin wasn't good. Folks still talked about the wild pranks he pulled in his youth. Sheriff Hardy kept him out of jail more than once and, talk was, Hardy went to Mexico about ten years back to keep Michael from swinging for murder.

Michael came back wilder than ever, and Hardy returned with a bullet still lodged in his leg. Brady was too quiet a place for the likes of Michael Catlin. This youngest, and only living, son of Victoria just passed through once in a while.

When they'd all finished their meal, Wes thanked the boy and walked out of the saloon with Allie only a step behind. He was halfway to the landing when he noticed she was no longer following.

Wes turned around to find her still in the lobby. She stared at the staircase as if it were on fire and he'd ordered her to climb.

"Come on up, Allie, unless you plan to sleep with the horses."

To his shock, she turned and vanished out the front door of the hotel.

She was almost to the stables before he caught up with her.

He was careful not to touch her. He'd learned that lesson the hard way. "Allie, where're you going?"

She stopped so suddenly he almost ran into her. "To sleep with the horses," she answered in a tone that let him know she thought his question a strange one.

Standing in the center of the muddy street, Wes watched her go. He didn't know what to say. He'd just spent far too much money making sure she had a nice room, and the woman preferred to sleep with the horses. She had to be related to Victoria Catlin. She was every bit as crazy as a woman who'd fight an alligator over a pet.

Wes walked back to the hotel for his things. He couldn't very well let her sleep in the livery alone. As he retrieved his gear and headed down the stairs, he realized this would probably be the last night he'd spend with her. Not that it mattered to him, but he'd grown used to having her near. She was a bushel of trouble, but she'd probably be as close to a wife as he'd ever have. If he didn't need money so badly, he might just stay around and make sure she was treated right.

But he had to find the treasure and buy enough cattle to restock. He'd wasted too much of his life waiting to get started. Now was his time. The treasure might be a long shot, but it was time for a long shot to come in.

Wes entered the barn, thinking about exactly what he'd do with the money from the sell of the gold. He planned to send half to Vince, no matter what the stubborn man told him. Then, with the rest of the money, he'd buy as many head as he could, wait out the winter, and start counting calves next spring.

One lantern, nailed to a barrel in the center of the room, cast light over the stable. A half loft hung over one corner for hay storage. Most of the stalls were empty.

"Allie?" Wes called as he walked the length of the barn. She didn't answer, but a dusting of hay rained down from the loft, telling him where she was. "I thought I'd stay with you since you won't go back to the hotel room." He tried to make his words sound casual. There was no use pestering her about her insanity. "If you don't mind."

He started up the ladder.

The lantern light reached only half the hayloft, but he could see her as he climbed. She didn't turn in his direction as she spread her blanket over the hay.

He looped his saddlebags over the railing.

"Now, don't be worried about tomorrow," he said, thinking she was probably planning to run again. "I know it seems a strong possibility that this old woman is your grandmother, but if she's crazy you don't have to stay." He didn't add that he had no idea what he'd do with her if this didn't work out. "There's bound to be another place for you if this doesn't work out."

He stepped from the ladder and passed the blanket he carried from one hand to the other. "I'll sleep by the door. That way, you'll have no reason to be afraid here in the barn." He flipped the blanket over his shoulder and put his foot back on the ladder.

She looked at him then with those huge blue eyes that always struck him with the intensity of their emotion. She appeared to be about a flea's-width away from crying.

"Or," he fumbled for words, "I could bed down next to you for warmth. It's not a cold night, but it might get that way before morning."

For a time, she watched him and he wasn't at all sure she cared. Hell, he didn't even know if he did. He was pretty sure they'd gotten past the point when she thought about killing him in his sleep, but he wasn't sure she wanted to cuddle.

Finally, she made her choice by taking the few steps to him and lifting the blanket from his shoulder. She turned and spread it over hers.

Wes needed a little conversation, even if it was his own. "Well, all right. I guess I could sleep up here and keep you warm. I've no objections. I mean, after all, in the eyes of the law, we are man and wife. There's nothing wrong. 'Course, some folks might think it strange that we have the best hotel room in town and choose to sleep with our horses. But I'm not saying a word about that.''

She glanced at him as she pulled off her boots and placed them by his saddlebags.

"No, not me," he added quickly. "The barn seems just fine. It's cleaner than most, and there aren't enough horses in here to keep us awake."

He removed his gun belt and laid it within reach, then took off his vest and boots. When he spread out on the makeshift bed, Allie was still standing near the railing. The light was behind her, turning her hair to warm colors of fall. She untied the ribbon and placed it carefully on the board. Then she removed her dress and folded it over the rough wood.

Wes watched her, thinking how gracefully she moved. He knew she didn't want to sleep in her clothes, but putting on a gown in a stable seemed strange. She must have thought so too, for she shoved the gown back in her bag and turned to face the bed.

He opened his mouth to tell her that skipping her gown was a wise idea since she might have to get dressed quickly in the morning. But no words came out as Wes watched her move toward him. He'd seen her in a dress and in Nichole's high-necked nightgown, but he'd never seen her in just her underclothes. In truth, he'd seen very few women in their underthings. At the moment, he could think of none.

The chemise and drawer were a plain cotton, but they fit her body like a glove, molding like a second skin. The straps were an inch wide on her shoulders and bordered in lace. Lace also ran over the top of her breasts. He hadn't given it all that much thought, but her waist was smaller than he'd guessed. Her hips nicely rounded and her breasts . . .

Wes looked away. He didn't even want to think about her breasts. He couldn't let his mind concentrate on those high, perfectly rounded breasts. "Maybe you should sleep in your dress,'' he mumbled. ''It won't matter if it's wrinkled.''

He wouldn't think of those breasts even if he thought he could barely see the outline of the darker tips.

He glanced back at her, just to check his memory. Sure enough, there was the outline of the tip of what he wasn't thinking about showing through the cotton.

Allie didn't answer him as she pulled the top blanket back and crawled in beside him.

Wes didn't move. He was too busy trying not to remember the way her body looked with only a layer of cotton over it. The cotton wasn't even covering all of her, he decided. Almost half of her was showing. When she breathed, maybe more. He closed his eyes and tried to calculate the percentage accurately.

Don't think about them . . . I mean her, he reminded himself. He took in a deep breath and doubled his efforts as he stared at the ceiling.

An hour later, when she rolled against him sound asleep, he was still wide awake trying to clear his mind. He put his arm out for her to use as a pillow, and she cuddled against him for warmth, pressing the very thing he wasn't thinking about against him.

Carefully, Wes placed his free hand at her waist, telling himself he was protecting her. He moved his face against her hair, loving the way it felt on his cheek.

''Allie?'' he whispered, not wanting to frighten her. ''Allie, are you awake?''

She rolled slightly and looked up at him. The look in her eyes was worry, not fear.

''Everything's all right.'' He decided he'd been a fool for waking her. ''Go back to sleep.''

She placed her hand over his heart and closed her eyes again.

''I was just thinking. . . .'' He tried to come up with something to tell her besides what had been on his mind. ''This may be our last night together.'' He was starting to hope so. Otherwise, he might never sleep again. ''And I don't want to frighten you, but I'd like to kiss you good-bye. You know, now, while it's just us.''

He'd expected her to use a few of the words she kept so miserly, but she didn't.

She raised to one elbow and slowly leaned over him. Her hair draped around his face as she lowered her lips to his in a timid kiss.

Wes was so surprised, he didn't react. Her lips lingered for a few moments on his, then she pulled away, cuddling back beneath his arm as if there was no more to say.

He lay wide awake as her breathing returned to normal. She was, without a doubt, the strangest creature he'd ever met. Here she was, all soft and feminine beside him, wearing nothing but her underwear that didn't cover all it should, to his way of thinking, and she was sleeping like she was safe. Maybe she was. He'd never taken a thing from a woman that she didn't willingly give. But at the rate his heart was pounding, his honor might kill him before dawn.

Moving his hand to her waist once more, he slid his fingers to her back and pulled her gently against him. She melted into his side. Her head moved from his arm to his chest so that now he could feel her slow intake of breath against his throat.

''Allie,'' he whispered against her hair, ''I thought I might kiss you good-bye.''

With sleepy eyes, she raised her head.

THIRTEEN

ALLIE WAS STILL HALF ASLEEP WHEN SHE FELT WES'S
warm mouth move over hers. His lips seemed hesitant,
unlike the man, who was always so sure of himself.
There was something warm and caring in his action. His
hesitancy made him human and somehow declared her
an equal.

She circled her arms around his neck as he pulled her
atop his chest with a mighty hug.

Slowly, one sense at a time, she came awake. The
smells of the barn blended with the warm protective
aroma of Wes so close. The wind rattled boards on the
roof, and the horses shifted in their stalls. Wes whispered
her name so low she wasn't sure she hadn't read his
thoughts. Widening shafts of pinwheel light reflected off
the walls from the lamp below, while she rode the gentle
rise and fall of his chest as he breathed. The kiss continued, a part of her, a part of him, a part of the night.

She'd seen people embrace and kiss, but she never
dreamed it would be such a pleasant sensation. His arms
encircled her with a sense of homecoming, making her
feel treasured. He'd always been protective and kind,
even when grumpy, but she would never have guessed
he wanted to give her such a gift.

He rolled to his side, moving her with him. "Don't
let me kiss you because you're afraid," he whispered.

"And you don't have to for any other reason besides you want to. Nothing will change between us. Just say 'no' and I'll stop if you don't want this between us. I just thought since you kissed me, I'd kiss you back."

He brushed her hair with his hand as he spoke, telling her he didn't want even a kiss out of fear or gratitude. He wanted it to be something they gave one another, not something he took.

Allie understood him better than he thought. She also had been alone and wondered what it would be like to have someone by her side. Someone she wasn't afraid would hurt her. Someone who could share the warmth of a blanket and a touch.

"But if you've no objections, kissing you did feel grand," he whispered.

She leaned against him, brushed her lips over his mouth once more, and felt him groan as he finished the kiss she started.

His hand moved through her hair to her shoulders with an awkwardness of need. If he were in pain from her kiss, he wasn't stopping the action. He moaned again as she opened her mouth.

Allie felt a warmth spread all the way to her toes, just as it had when she'd drank his coffee. Only this taste was sweet. His kiss made her feel like she was floating, with only the light brush of his hands keeping her from rising to the roof.

She'd never dreamed such a hard, scarred man would touch her so lightly, so warmly. Her skin warmed beneath his care as he moved his hands over her shoulders and along her arms. The lace strap of her undergarments followed his fingers to her arm. When he moved his hands back to her throat, he returned the thin strap to its place.

The simple action touched her deeply. She sensed a respect in his touch. He was not handling her, or feeling her, he was caressing her with the tips of his fingers. She relaxed, enjoying the feelings washing over her.

He pulled away, watching her in the dim light. "Are

you all right?'' he asked, a hint of worry in his low voice.

"Again," she answered, wanting to feel the warmth pass through her body.

He gently cupped her face in his hand. She liked the way his fingers, rough from work, brushed her skin so lightly.

Stretching, she rolled onto her back with her arms at her sides. Waiting. If this was to be their last night together, she would feel his lips again and remember.

But he didn't kiss her again. He let his thumb leave her cheek and pass lightly back and forth across her slightly swollen lips.

"You taste so good," he whispered without drawing nearer. "The fullness of your mouth . . ." He didn't finish. He didn't need to. The movement of his thumb told her of his pleasure.

Arching her head back, she parted her lips in invitation. It seemed madness for him to wait, but the waiting made her want the kiss more.

His thumb passed over her open mouth as he moved closer, pressing the length of his body against her side. When he glanced down, her gaze followed. The pressure of his chest resting against her ribs had increased the swell of her breast. Lace strained across her soft flesh.

When she looked back up, she felt the heat of his gaze and saw that his brown eyes were almost black.

She didn't move as he raised his hand and slipped two fingers beneath the thin strap of her undergarment. The fingers pulled the material slightly as he lifted the strap over her shoulder to hang at her arm.

She glanced down again, noticing the material had slipped a little so that now the cotton barely covered her breasts. Expecting him to push the material further, she waited. She felt his warm breath against her throat as he watched the rise and fall of lace with each of her rapid intakes of air.

Closing her eyes, she fought down the fear and the embarrassment of him looking at her so closely. Some-

thing deep inside her told her he'd stop if she asked.
He'd roll away and never touch her or look at her again.
But if she asked him to stop, she'd never feel the warmth
of his kiss again. And she wanted that heat once more
before they parted.

"Put it back," she whispered near his ear in a gentle
demand.

Wes studied her with one eyebrow raised. "What?"
he said as if he heard, but couldn't believe her words.

"Put it back," she repeated. If she were to live without fear of this man, it must start now. She had to set
the limits.

In slow motion he used the same two fingers to return
the strap to its place. He dragged his hand free of the
strap, letting his fingertips trail along the lace. "Are you
still waiting for me to kiss you again? Or have you
changed your mind?"

"Again," she answered with a sudden shiver as his
fingers moved across the lace at the top of one breast
and dipped slightly beneath the material in the valley.

He might allow her to set the limits of their closeness,
but he made it plain he planned to test the boundary.

When she didn't protest, he trailed lightly back up to
the lace and moved across the exposed flesh of the breast
closest to him. His touch caressed once more, cherished.

"Again," she whispered as his body leaned over her.
"Kiss me again."

He didn't lower his mouth to hers, but slid his hand
behind her neck and raised her head to meet his kiss
with a sudden urgency.

He'd made her ask twice. It was time to give her fully
what she wanted.

Her body jerked with the sudden contact of his mouth
on her lips, but she didn't pull away. His mouth covered
hers, and she felt the warmth begin to spread through
her once more. As he kissed her, the warmth turned to
fire, pulsing through her like heated blood. His mouth
was tender and demanding, fulfilling the promise she'd
hoped for. She was lost in the sensations flooding her

as he made the kiss far more than she'd expected. He was tasting her, drinking her in. And in return, giving her a perception of a passion within her she'd never known.

Then it was over, and he lowered her head back against the blanket. His hand brushed her hair into place.

Allie felt a sudden coldness in the barn that hadn't been there before. She'd been floating, and he'd brought her back to ground with a thud. Opening her eyes, she was surprised to find Wes sitting.

When she reached to touch his back, he moved so suddenly that hay flew around him. He was on his feet, pacing. His lean body reminded her of a wildcat caught in a confined space.

She watched him for a while, trying to understand. His breath was coming in rapid heaves, as if he'd been running for miles. He dug his fingers through his hair as though he could root out his own thoughts. Something bothered him deeply, but she couldn't imagine what, unless he'd disliked the kiss as much as she'd enjoyed it.

Allie sat up and tucked her knees up to her chin. At first she reasoned she might have hurt him, but she hadn't done anything. He'd been the one who kissed her. Then she decided that he must have hated kissing her. But that reasoning didn't hold water, because he sure took his time doing something he hated.

Finally he stopped pacing and looked at her. His tall shadow was a little frightening but she forced herself to remember he was the one showing all the signs of hurting.

"I . . ." He paced another crossing. "I didn't mean for . . ."

Allie put her elbows on her knees and held her chin. Trying to figure out this madman was giving her a headache. One moment he could make her feel all warm and wonderful, as if she were in a trance, and the next he tortured her with his pacing.

"Stand up!" he demanded. "I mean, would you

please stand up, Allie? I can't talk to you while you're on that blanket."

She followed his order.

Wes faced her. "You're no bigger than a half-grown pup." His words were gruff but more mumbled to himself than aimed at her.

She tilted her head slightly, hoping the angle might make him or his words appear clearer. He was definitely angry about something.

"You're too short to even dance with," he added. "Not that I do a lot of dancing. I mean a man likes a woman he can look in the eyes. Not at the top of her head."

He paced again, like a rope twisted too tightly in one direction and then the other. "I've never liked brown hair, either. Now blonde, or black, that's something. But brown. The color of dirt."

Allie took a deep breath. She saw no point to his words, for she could do nothing about her height, or hair. Her mind, however, was starting to circle to the beat of his pacing.

He was back suddenly, standing only a few inches from her. "I'm not promising you anything other than what I have. I want you to understand that. I'm leaving you with your grandmother tomorrow, if she is your grandmother. That kiss means nothing more than a kiss . . ."

His voice lowered. "But damn, Allie, that was the best kiss . . ."

Allie suddenly understood. She placed her hands on his face and pulled him to where she could see his eyes.

"Again," she whispered as she raised to her toes and touched his mouth. "If you don't mind too much, kiss me again."

Wes lifted her off the floor. She could feel his arms around her, holding her in the air while his heart pounded against her chest and his mouth moved over hers. She was no longer cold as once more the fire passed through her.

If the kiss was causing him pain, he showed no sign. When he finally lowered her feet to the floor, her head was spinning from rivers of sensations running in her blood.

His arm slid from her back to her knees, and he lifted her up. He carried her the few feet to the blankets and lowered her.

"Again," she whispered without opening her eyes.

Wes laughed. "Maybe one more time."

The creak of the door broke into his words. In one fluid motion, he pulled the blanket over her and reached for his gun, the kiss forgotten as instinct took over.

Allie wrapped the wool around her as he crawled to the edge of the loft.

After a few silent moments, the sound of someone sobbing drifted up to them.

She recognized the sound before Wes did and was halfway down the ladder when he thought to follow. As they reached the bottom, Wes put his gun away when he saw the boy from the hotel.

Jason was huddled in the darkness between two empty stalls. His head rested on his knees and his arms were wrapped tightly around him as if to shut out the world.

Allie knelt at his side and touched his shoulder.

The boy's head jerked up at her touch. For a moment, his face was filled with fear and anger.

"I wasn't crying!" he shouted. "I'm too old to cry. So don't go telling folks I was, or I'll call you a liar."

Wes squatted down in front of them. "I wouldn't want to be called a liar, son."

"I ain't your son." Black-and-blue swelling had almost completely closed his left eye.

"Who did that?" Wes pointed with his thumb to the boy's face.

"No one did nothing," Jason answered. "I'm just fine. I ain't complaining."

Wes didn't have to ask more. He knew the times all too well. After the war, there were kids like Jason in every town. Their dads probably died fighting and their mothers worked themselves to death or starved. The kids were left to fend for themselves.

"Do you have any folks anywhere?" Wes mentally figured up what it would cost to put Jason on a stage to his brother Daniel's place. Dan would find someone to take him in.

"No," Jason answered. "And I don't—"

He stopped as Allie reached out and took his hand in hers. "He is of my tribe," she said calmly. "He goes with me."

Wes opened his mouth to say that he was the one taking care of her. How could she take care of a boy? But the question seemed pointless.

He stood and paced. First he has a wife he didn't want and now she has a boy. The treasure was moving further and further away; he could feel it. Even if this Victoria Catlin was Allie's grandmother, there was no guarantee she would want Allie. Or that she was sane. Or that she was able to take care of herself, much less Allie and a boy.

He'd just have to "lay down the law" to Allie. That was it. She couldn't go telling him this boy was of her tribe. She didn't even have a tribe, and, for all he knew, she didn't even have a grandmother.

But when he turned to have his say, Allie was doctoring the boy's eye. She'd wrapped her blanket around him.

The boy looked up at Wes with a knowing look of what was to come. He was too old to believe in miracles. He knew Wes wouldn't take him along.

Wes drew in a long breath. "We leave at nine," he said, as if it had been his planned speech all along. "If you're going with us, be ready."

Jason watched them closely as Allie and Wes moved back up the ladder. The boy was too shocked to answer until they were in the loft.

"I'll be ready!" he called from below.

"Good," Wes answered as he circled his arm around

Allie's waist. But his mind was no longer on the boy or on leaving in the morning.

"One more kiss," Allie whispered.

"If you insist."

FOURTEEN

THE MORNING AIR HAD A DAMPNESS ABOUT IT THAT
promised rain. The proper little settlement awoke with
the efficiency of an old maid never having been bothered
in sleep. Wes heard civilization come alive just outside
the barn.

He'd just finished strapping on his gun belt when
Sheriff Hardy limped around the huge door. The elderly
man looked to be every day of a hundred, with the
night's drinking showing in his eyes. He wore a gray
duster and what appeared to be a new hat.

"Morning." Hardy signaled the blacksmith to get his
buggy ready. "You folks about ready to go?"

Wes climbed down the ladder, smiling. He'd had a
feeling Hardy would be early and the man hadn't disappointed him. "We have one more who's coming with
us, if you've no objections, Sheriff." He nodded toward
the boy standing in the shadows between stalls.

The sheriff glanced at Jason, then at the bundle of
clothes beside him.

"Allie says he's of her tribe." Wes figured the words
didn't make any sense, but they were as good a reason
to take the boy as anything he could think up. If there
was anyone in town who might object to Jason leaving,
Hardy would probably know it.

Before the sheriff could answer, Allie appeared at the

top of the ladder. She'd combed her hair and pulled it back with the ribbon Wes had taken from the hotel. Her brown dress hung a little long at the hem and sleeves. Other than that, she looked quite proper.

"Allyce." The sheriff bowed a greeting as the blacksmith brought his buggy to the barn door opening. "Would you like to ride with me this morning?"

Allie glanced at the boy, then to Wes.

Wes lifted Jason's bundle and tossed it in the back of the buggy. "You take the other horse, son. Allie can ride with the sheriff."

The boy stiffened. "I ain't your son. I told you." Fear shook his voice, but he stood his ground.

Wes handed him the bay's reins without taking offense.

From the moment the boy touched the leather, Wes knew he'd never been near a horse. It was hard to believe, but the kid didn't even know how to lead an animal. In a country where riding a horse was as much a necessity as breathing, somehow this child had been forgotten.

The bay seemed to sense inexperience and jerked her head.

"Easy now." Wes patted the animal's neck with one hand while his other grabbed the reins close to the bit and tugged the bay's head lower. Once the horse settled, Wes pulled his own mount in front of Jason, slowing each action, silently showing the boy what to do.

Jason learned quickly, following Wes's movements exactly, as he climbed into the saddle.

Wes grinned. The bay was a gentle animal. She'd give the boy time, and she'd follow Wes's horse without much guidance.

Allie stepped into the buggy with the sheriff. Hardy talked as they moved away from the barn. He didn't seem to notice that Allie never spoke. Her presence was all the encouragement he needed.

By the time they'd ridden two hours, Wes began to believe that Jason *was* of Allie's tribe, for the boy said nothing. He mirrored each of Wes's movements, learning as they traveled. Wes watched him closely out of the corner of his gaze. Jason's bruises were starting to heal, but he looked pale, like someone who never saw the sun. His body had just started the stretch to manhood, leaving him thin, with legs and arms that didn't match his body size. If Jason were given regular meals, he'd grow into a tall man, Wes thought.

As they rode along a path dusted with wagon tracks just clear enough to mark a trail, Wes couldn't help but admire the landscape. It was good land, flat enough in places for farming and rich enough with rain to hold a tall grass for pasture. In many ways it reminded him of his own land farther north. He'd bought his land with back pay from the war, but he hadn't had time to build on it. He'd spent one winter in a little dugout on the property and swore he'd finish a house before he married. But it hadn't happened.

Wes pulled his horse beside the wagon. "When do we hit the Catlin spread, Sheriff?"

"We've been on it for half an hour," the old man answered. "Victoria owns one of the largest ranches in these parts, but she hasn't worked it in years. You should be able to see the house just over the ridge."

Wes kicked his horse and galloped up the hill. A lone adobe ranch headquarters sat in the middle of a valley below. The earthy buildings at the core looked inviting, but a thick wall surrounded the estate like a fortress.

Sitting back in his saddle, Wes let out a low whistle. "Whoa," he mumbled. "That's quite a place."

The sheriff pulled the buggy to a stop beside him. "Victoria's first husband built it for her. He thought to keep his family safe from any attack. But her oldest, James, didn't get along with Victoria's second husband and moved farther north after she married. By the time he was killed and Allie captured, Victoria had married husband number four. Husbands came and went after that. Seemed like every year brought a wedding or a funeral but the ranch stayed pretty much the same. Her boys all hated the place. Called it 'Mom's jail.' ''

A sadness seeped into Hardy's eyes. ''I guess that's what it's become for her. It's been some time since I've seen her. She no longer leaves the place.''

Wes didn't ask any questions as they moved closer. In truth, the ranch headquarters was massive but somehow lonely. They were within twenty yards before he even saw a guard. With a spread of this size a man should be posted at every side of the headquarters, making his presence known as soon as a stranger came into sight.

A stout man, dressed like a farmer, stepped from the small outer-wall door to greet them. He wore a gun belt strapped around his ample waist and carried an old single-shot rifle that would have been of little use if a band of outlaws came to rob the ranch. At first, he widened his stance and crossed his arms over the rifle as though he planned to stop them. But the moment he saw the sheriff, his posture changed.

''Sheriff Hardy!'' the large man yelled. ''Welcome.''

Hardy waved at the guard, and by the time his buggy had reached the main gate, the wooden doors were opened wide.

''It's been a long time, Sheriff.''

The stout man motioned for others to take care of the buggy as the sheriff helped Allie down.

''That it has, Gideon. That it has,'' Hardy answered. ''Too long, in my way of thinking.''

Wes stayed in the saddle for a few minutes, looking around as the two men talked. He liked the view he had from his horse. A man spends so much time in the saddle that when he steps to ground it seems like he's crawling for a while, Wes thought. The world looked more in balance from a few feet higher than a man stood.

The courtyard spread wide, but not very long. A main house loomed in front of them with what looked like a kitchen and laundry to the left and a bunkhouse to the right. Wes could see three men, besides the greeter Hardy had called Gideon, and two women. But the quarters on the right had been built to hold thirty hands or more. The main house looked to have at least a dozen rooms upstairs, each with a little terrace off full-length windows overlooking the courtyard. If the house was true to form for most of its kind, the back wall of the main quarters would be solid, with only tiny windows for observation. A freshly plowed garden stretched beside the kitchen. Wes also noticed a well, barns behind the bunkhouses, and a center courtyard with flowers.

It took Wes a minute to realize what was missing. Children. He'd never visited a ranch house so large that hadn't had a dozen children playing in the courtyard. The silence was almost pestering.

On closer observation he noticed all the people he saw were beyond childbearing years. The two women who stood by the kitchen door had been joined by a little round woman with an apron that must have used half a sheet's material to make. They stared for a while, then the round one pulled them all back inside.

"I'll tell Miss Victoria you're here." The stout man moved toward the main entrance of the huge two-story house.

"Thanks, Gideon." Sheriff Hardy tried to guide Allie up the steps.

Allie waited, rooted in place until Wes joined her. Then she followed the sheriff.

Wes glanced back at Jason and motioned with his head for the boy to join them, but Jason stayed several feet behind, testing the depth of invisible water with each step.

The house was cool and damp, holding the morning humidity. Wes thought he could hear the faint sound of whispering blowing in the breeze when he stepped inside the wide main hall.

Gideon ushered them to a large room with wide windows facing the sun, but the house still felt cold. Wes knew the others sensed it also, for Allie pressed close to him and Jason crossed his arms over his chest.

Allie stood like a statue in the center of the room, as

though afraid to look at anything. Wes guessed she didn't want to get her hopes up, but he could see a touch of excitement in her eyes.

Hardy moved around, handling first one item, then another, as if on some kind of investigation. The furnishings were fine quality, the lace neatly done, even the chairs had been stitched in a flower pattern that had long ago lost its color.

Wes, with his years of military training, checked each exit as though preparing for battle. He listened carefully, trying to figure out the whispering sound. It wasn't words exactly, more like years of lost conversations blending together, circling the room as though the past and present mixed somehow in this place.

With the door open wide, Wes could see both a wide staircase going up and the front door. Anyone sitting in the center of this room would know everything going on in the house.

Gideon brought in tea and hard white cookies, but no one ate. Wes noticed the china set looked yellowed with age and wear. The last plate in the set was chipped. For a fine house, he'd expected greater care.

The slow opening of a door and the slight rustle of skirts drew Wes's attention. He wasn't sure what he'd expected—a stately widow, a crazy woman, an older version of Allie.

The tiny woman in black who entered the room on the arm of another was none and all of those things wrapped together. She walked with the carriage of a woman who'd known of her beauty since birth. With hair combed high like a crown on her head, she was a queen in her world, a rare vision of perfection in aging, with pure white hair and thin skin feathered in wrinkles.

But first of all, and most of all, Victoria Catlin was blind.

Wes faced her as she held her head high and moved sightlessly through the room to what had to be her chair. The plainly dressed guide at her side stood next to her as Victoria, covered in black satin with layers of black lace, sat to hold court.

"Gideon tells me you've come to visit me, Maxwell." She spoke directly to the center of the room, unaware that the sheriff was to her right. "It has been far too long since I've had the pleasure of your company."

Max Hardy straightened, growing younger as he moved toward her without allowing his limp to show. "Hello, Victoria." His voice was warm with years of unspoken words. "It's good to see you again."

Victoria offered her hand, frail and blue-veined. Max's massive leathered hand embraced hers in more of a caress than a handshake. For a moment, no one moved or spoke. For a moment, Maxwell and Victoria were the only two in the room.

Victoria broke the spell by pulling her hand away. "Maxwell," she said, gesturing to her left, "you remember my sister, Katherine."

Max forced his gaze to leave Victoria and turned to the woman who'd acted as guide. Katherine seemed a too often washed, too heavily starched version of her sister. Her beauty had long ago faded to dull gray. Her face was smooth, void of both laugh lines and worry wrinkles. Void of having felt life at all. The thin lines that had once been lips didn't move to speak, but she nodded slightly at the sheriff.

"Katherine." Max cleared his throat as he spoke. "I hope you're doing well?" All emotions had vanished from his voice as he asked a question so dry it didn't seem to need a reply.

Katherine hardened, unwilling to lower herself to even speak to the sheriff.

If Wes were guessing, he'd guess she was a woman who died on the vine without ever being touched by love or even passion. In her old age, she'd found reason to her life with Victoria's blindness.

Max lowered to one knee beside Victoria's chair. "I've come with good news, Victoria."

She rested her hand on his shoulder as if needing to

feel where his voice was coming from. "I'm so glad. I was afraid something had happened to Michael. It's been so long since I've heard from him."

"Michael's fine," Maxwell answered. "I saw him in Austin less than a week ago."

Victoria raised her head slightly, showing no joy or pain at Maxwell's announcement.

"I've brought someone I think you will want to meet." Max nodded for Allie to come closer. "I've never stopped looking for the child of James who might have survived. I always go to the Rangers office and check on any recovered captives that might fit. Finally, I've found her."

Victoria's faced filled with hope.

"Allie Catlin, I'd like you to meet your grandmother, Victoria."

Wes watched Allie closely as she moved toward the old woman. He could see that she still doubted the sheriff's words, but he also saw an ounce of hope. She was shy, waiting for an invitation . . . outstretched hands, a welcoming word.

"Are you sure?" Victoria didn't even allow herself to breathe.

"I wasn't when I found the record. Thought it could just be coincidence that she was the right age and went by the name Allie. She was found hundreds of miles southwest of where she was captured. But when I saw her face, I knew. She's the image of you fifty years ago."

Victoria raised her hand, touching the air only inches in front of Allie. "I'd given up," she whispered. "Could it be true?"

Just as Allie moved within the old woman's reach, a sharp voice shattered the room.

"He's lying!" Katherine snapped.

Victoria pulled her hand away, drawing into her shell as if her sister were her eyes and she'd seen evil. Allie jumped back, reacting to the words like a slap.

"He's lying to you, sister. The girl looks nothing like

you. He's old and blind as you, if he sees a resemblance. I'd swear on our mother's grave there is not a drop of Catlin blood in this woman." Katherine's voice cracked like dry wood in a fire. "He's just another come to take your fortune."

Wes hardly noticed the anger that bubbled up in Maxwell, or the confusion in Victoria's blind stare, or the decades-old hatred laced into Katherine's words. All he cared about, all he saw, was Allie.

The flicker of hope she'd allowed herself to believe in now crumbled her from inside out. Allie had unlocked her heart, wanting to believe the sheriff, wanting a family again. She'd opened the armor to take a wound to a soul already fragile.

Wes ignored the sheriff's denial and Katherine's hateful words. Allie was shattering.

In one sudden movement, he swept her up and carried her from the room like a bandit stealing treasure. The others were so lost in their argument, they hardly noticed as he left and entered the hallway.

He glanced around, it didn't matter where he went. Away was the only objective. He hurried across the opening and into the first room he saw. Dusted in slits of light from closed shutters, the room paused, quiet as a tomb.

Wes closed the door and set Allie on her feet. He had no idea what he'd say to her, but he had to protect her from the others. Katherine's shrill voice still tightened his spine.

Allie erupted like gunpowder exploding in his face. All at once, she was crying and pounding on his chest with all the force she could gather.

He let her pound, ignoring the pain. She wasn't fighting him, she was fighting the world.

She shook her head so violently that the ribbon fell to the floor and her hair went wild around her, reminding him of the first time he'd seen her and thought her more animal than human.

Great sobs came and gulps for air, but not a word. The hurt was beyond words.

Wes closed his eyes, wondering what good he'd done her. He'd taken her from the cage only to deliver her to a place where they might not hurt her body, but they'd broken her heart.

Finally she grew tired, the last few blows barely touching him. Her fist rested against his chest as she lowered her head.

Wes pulled her to him then, ignoring her tired efforts to fight free. He held her tightly against him, feeling her sobs pass through his body.

A little at a time, she relaxed, letting him hold her. Her tears wet his shoulder, and her heart pounded against his side. He couldn't help but think of all she must have been through. How many times had she thought she'd be rescued, or dreamed of a family waiting somewhere to welcome her? How many times must hope die before tears were too deep to bear?

He rocked her in his arms. "Shhhh, Allie," he whispered. "They don't matter, none of them. They're fools for not wanting you."

Her crying lessened. He felt her arms move around his waist.

"You belong right here with me. I won't let them hurt you anymore."

She moved her face against his shirt, wiping away her tears as she looked up at him. "Take me away from here," she begged between gulps. "Now!"

Wes couldn't help but smile. She really had no idea how beautiful her eyes were when they sparkled with tears. She could probably talk any man in the world into doing her bidding if she looked at him the way she gazed at Wes.

"We're on our way." He placed an arm at her waist and reached for the door. As the light wedged in from the hallway, Wes caught the image from a tintype. He stepped to the wall of portraits. Allie, her hair all curled over one shoulder, stared back at him. Same huge eyes, same uplifted chin. But the style of clothing was old, fifty years or more, when hooped skirts barred women from many doorways. And the setting behind showed century-old trees with moss hanging from them.

Allie tugged at his hand.

"Are you sure you want to go?" He knew she'd noticed the tintype.

She nodded.

He couldn't blame her. She'd been through enough. She didn't need to fight for her family as well. It didn't matter that she was the true granddaughter. What mattered was that she wasn't accepted.

When they entered the hallway, Jason jumped back from where he'd obviously been trying to listen. He didn't lower his gaze from Wes, silently challenging Wes to question his actions. The sounds of an argument were still coming from across the hallway.

Wes didn't question. In truth, if he'd been the boy, he would have been doing the same thing. "Jason, run tell Gideon that I want our horses now," Wes ordered. "We're leaving."

"All of us?" The boy was fighting down fear as he moved with Wes and Allie down the hallway.

"All three of us," Wes said. "Maxwell can take care of himself with those two."

Jason nodded and vanished. Wes walked slowly out of the house and across the yard to the barn with Allie at his side. By the time they'd reached the barn door, the horses were waiting and Jason was standing beside them with his bundle in hand.

Wes handed Jason the reins to the bay and swung onto his own mount. Then he offered his hand to Allie. "I'd be honored if you'd ride along with me, Allie."

His words said far more and, from the look in her eyes, she knew it. He wasn't just offering to get her away from this place. He was offering her a place with him. And he was very politely asking as if she had a hundred other options and might take any one.

Allie locked her hand at his elbow, and he pulled her up behind him.

"Let's ride, son." Wes kicked his horse into action. "There's nothing for any of us here."

As they rode through the open gate, the servants lined the wall. When Allie passed, the men removed their hats and the women curtsied. They knew, Wes thought, even if Victoria was too blind to see, or to believe.

FIFTEEN

JUST BEFORE NIGHTFALL, WES AND HIS SMALL BAND reached a little town deep in the hill country called New Braunfels. They were traveling farther south, where winter didn't settle so harshly across the land. This area of Texas was thick with German settlements, New Braunfels being one of the first. Though many of the Germans had settled the land two generations ago, in the 1830s, they'd kept to themselves with hard-working ways and little interest in learning English. Their love for the new land seemed great, but old ways clung to them like comfortable clothes.

Wes rode silently through the sleepy little town. Unlike many settlements its size, New Braunfels was clean, with wide streets and spotless storefronts. The churches, schools, and barbershops were already here.

As they reached the far end of town and headed out, Wes turned and whispered to Allie, "I know a place we can stay tonight since you hate hotels."

She nodded and eased her grip around his waist.

Wes patted her arm, understanding her if not her reasons. "During the war, there were many families in Texas loyal to the Union." He'd also noticed she seemed to relax when he talked, so he started his story in a low voice. "Most didn't say much about it, just went about their business. But one farmer, whose place was not far from town, let his feelings be known when Texas left the Union. One night, late into the war when most everyone had lost a son or father to the fighting, a band of men descended on his place. As folks tell the story, the farmer and his sons had just sat down to supper and met the mob without a single gun in hand.''

Wes paused, picking his way down an overgrown road no one traveled. ''The band demanded the farmer and his sons come outside. Then in front of the women and children, they hanged the men from the barn rafters. As they rode off, they set fire to the barn.

''No one did anything about the crime. The farmer's youngest son to die was thirteen. Folks didn't talk about it much at the time, some probably from fear, some from guilt. It was just something that happened in war, and there was nothing to be done.''

Allie leaned her cheek against Wes's back. While she'd been living alone in her cave all those years, the world must have gone mad. She wished she could go back to her hideaway. People made no sense.

Wes turned toward the sunset. Along the outline of gold, she could see the remains of an old, burned barn beside an abandoned farmhouse.

''The farmer's wife took her youngest children and her widowed daughters-in-law and left here. No one wants to buy the place. Not after what happened. But we can stay the night there.''

He headed toward the house. The grassland had almost reclaimed the road, and ivy lapped over the fences. ''The locals are half afraid of this place. They say it's haunted. But if it is, I don't figure the ghost will bother us.'' He turned to wink at her. ''After all, they were Northern sympathizers.''

Allie didn't join in his mirth. She felt like she was trespassing on a burial ground and the spirits would not be pleased. She could almost hear them whispering in the evening breeze, telling her to leave, pushing her from their home, warning her.

Wes helped her down from the saddle and headed into

the house with their supplies over one shoulder.

"Wait," Allie called after him. "I'll not stay in their home."

He turned around and walked back to the edge of a crumbling porch. "It's safe enough. I'll light a fire and chase any critters out."

"No." Allie stood her ground. "I'll not go in."

"Me, neither." Jason slid from his horse. "If Allie ain't going in, I'm not going in."

Wes glanced skyward. How was it possible for his near mute wife to pick up an echo? After four years in the Army, leading men, and two years of pushing cattle to market, it took Allie to make Wes realize that a leader wasn't a leader unless he had a follower.

"All right, where would you like to sleep tonight?" She was developing a habit of being particular about where she slept.

Allie didn't answer, she just turned toward the skeleton of the barn. In one corner, near a charred wall several feet high, a willow had grown. Maybe it had been a sapling when the tragedy happened. Maybe it had sprung from the fertile soil of the ashes, but it stood tall and proud now. The charred wall protected it from the north wind, and the morning sun warmed it. The long, thin branches were almost touching the ground.

She spread her blanket beneath the low limbs of the willow.

Wes stepped off the porch beside Jason. "Looks like we're sleeping beneath the tree. Want to help me with the horses before we settle in for the night?"

"Sure." Jason patted the bay as though they were old and dear friends. "Has this horse got a name?"

"Not that I know of." Wes grinned as he removed the saddle and left it beneath the tree. "My dad used to say a horse shouldn't have a name until it belongs to one man for good. Since it looks like he's your horse, I figure you should name him."

Jason followed Wes's actions, needing only a little

help lifting the saddle down. "He ain't my horse, mister."

"He is now." Wes started toward a stream behind the house. "You'll earn him by helping me take care of Allie. And I can tell by the way he responds to your lead that the two of you are made for one another."

Jason walked several feet before he answered. "I'll name him when I earn him," the boy said with a single nod.

A half hour later, Wes returned. He had staked the horses and taken the time to shave by the water. Jason had managed to find a hatful of nuts and took them back to Allie.

Wes pushed the thin branches away and stepped into nature's tiny room beneath the tree. Handing Allie the canteen, he fished in his bag for the last apple and jerky. He gave the apple to Jason, broke the jerky in thirds, and sat down cross-legged to begin cracking nuts.

"Not much supper tonight, folks. I thought we'd be eating with your grandmother. But we've enough."

Jason was so tired Wes had to force him to stay awake long enough to eat the apple. "What is it they say? It's not the food, it's the company that counts."

He laughed to himself as Allie stretched and laid her head on his knee. "I must be a great conversationalist. I'm putting everyone to sleep."

"Ghosts are in the house," Allie whispered. "We shouldn't bother them." She closed her eyes. "Or the ghost at Goliad where you go to search for gold."

"I'm not afraid of ghosts." Wes patted her shoulder, enjoying the fact she'd finally lost her fear of him. All day, she'd been close and not once had she pulled away. Once, he'd laced his fingers through hers. He'd thought such an action would feel foolish, but, surprisingly, it felt good. He liked the feel of her holding to him as they rode.

Before he finished half the nuts, Jason and Allie were both dreaming. Wes sat in the darkness. There was no need to light a fire; any wind was blocked by the barn wall. Jason would be warm curled in his blanket, and Wes would eventually slide down beside Allie to keep her from being cold.

Wes had too much on his mind to sleep. He needed time to think. He'd planned to look for the treasure alone. One lone man would cause no talk riding into the abandoned mission. He figured he could study the map and be in and out in a day or two at the most. But now there were Allie and Jason. A man could live off the land, eat when he had to, ride hard, and sleep only when exhausted. But a woman and boy were something else entirely.

Wes took a long drink of the water in the canteen, wishing it were whiskey. He didn't regret what he'd done this morning. Allie couldn't have stayed with Victoria. It didn't matter that everyone in the world could see they were kin, Victoria would believe her sister. For some reason, Katherine didn't want Allie to be alive. Maybe she was just protecting her sister from what she thought were fortune hunters. Who knows how many others over the years had claimed to be Victoria's grandchild?

The chipped china came to mind. Wes wondered how much of a fortune could be left. Perhaps Victoria was growing poor in her old age, or maybe Katherine saw no need to spend money on what her sister could no longer see.

Wes brushed his hand lightly over Allie's hair. She could go with him; he'd take his chances with her tailing along. Anything was better than the thought of her being yelled at by Katherine.

Wes leaned back against his saddle. For a little while he'd forget about the map and head back to his place outside Denton. He could round up enough strays to feed them through the winter, and his dugout might not be a headquarters, but it was plenty big for three people. Maybe he could catch and break a few wild horses for the Army for extra money. By the end of winter, he could hire on for a cattle drive and make enough to start a herd next fall.

Rubbing his forehead, Wes pushed away the dream. Who was he kidding? Allie wasn't interested in staying with him. The only reason she was with him was that being near him was safer at the moment. The minute she got the chance, she'd take off to parts unknown. He could feel it. And he'd never been a man who just got by. He'd made a name for himself in the war by always gambling big with life. He couldn't settle down and scratch out a living. The treasure was a hand he had to play. The last card he'd been dealt. If it cost him his life, he'd go out with a dream and not some plan to scrape by. Allie wasn't his, and neither was Jason.

Wes slept little. Thoughts kept stampeding through his mind. He wanted to make it big. He needed to prove he could to everyone. Not for the money or power, but for the satisfaction. His younger brothers had found their niches in life. Adam was a doctor; Daniel, a preacher. Wes had to prove he could be more than a soldier.

Toward dawn, when the earth was so still nothing moved, Wes decided Allie was somehow a part of his destiny. She might not stay with him, she might never care for him, but she was a part of him, woven so deeply into the fabric of his life that she'd never be far from his thoughts even if she left. He cared for her.

He watched first light crawling across the horizon, hesitating in the early fog. At first, the riders coming from town seemed like part of the passing shadows, but as they neared, he heard the horses' hooves and picked out the four horsemen slicing the distance between town and the willow.

Wes shifted slightly, pulling his rifle from where it had been propped against his saddle. His movement awoke Allie. She sat up, sensing danger.

He raised his weapon to his shoulder and waited. There was a good chance the men would pass. Even if they stopped, the light wasn't good enough to see beneath the willow. Wes didn't bother to motion for Allie to remain silent. He knew she would.

The men rode directly toward the house as though on a mission. They looked hard and too heavily armed to be farmers. When they reached the porch, one jumped from his saddle and kicked the front door open, his gun drawn.

"It's dark!" he yelled. "But no one's in there. Squirrels ran in every direction."

A wiry man twisted in his saddle. "We'll keep going. They couldn't be far. A fellow said he saw the three pass through town just before dark last night. If we were after one man, he might have covered more ground, but the woman and the boy will slow him down. He can't be far ahead of us."

Wes fought the urge to fire. These men were looking for him and, from the hurry they were in, they hadn't come to help. The wiry man reminded Wes of a tree that had been twisted early on and hadn't grown straight. He patted his handgun as if it were a pet at his side.

The man off his mount walked to the edge of the porch. "There's a farm about three miles down that takes in travelers. They may have stayed there for the night."

The leader grunted. "Or a hundred other places along the streams and rivers. But don't worry, we'll find them if we have to comb every mile of this land."

Wes's fingers tightened slightly on the trigger. These men were after him, there was no doubt. But why? For the map? For Allie? Or, who knows, Angela Montago was so mad at him, she might have hired them to see that he never bothered her again. Wes could even think of a few men from the war who hated him enough to track him.

As the men rode away, Wes frowned. That was his problem—he'd made too many enemies and not enough friends. When a man has several reasons to choose from why a band of no-goods might be chasing him, maybe it's time to mend his ways.

Wes was a good enough judge of people to know that the four riders were not trained trackers. They would have seen signs, even in the poor light, that would have pointed directly to the willow. And there was something not quite professional about them. They were not hired guns.

Allie watched Wes closely. He'd been prepared to kill the men if they'd come too near, but she wasn't sure why.

He'd saved her again, that was all that mattered. She owed him now. And honor demanded she pay him back. All she had were the pelts in the cave. Somehow, she'd get to them and give him half her wealth. It was the only fair thing to do.

But they'd ridden over country she'd never seen. Not even all the moving around she'd done when she'd been passed from tribe to tribe helped her now. Allie wasn't sure where to start to head for home. If she were alone, she might not be able to find her way back to Fort Worth. From there, she knew the direction. But here, this land was different. She wasn't sure.

"Good morning." He pushed her hair back from her face.

How easily she'd gotten used to his nearness. "Good morning," she answered, feeling the words on her tongue so early in the morning. "Who were those men?"

"I'm not sure, but I'm guessing they were looking for us and that they were probably men we don't want to meet."

Jason slowly turned toward them. His wide eyes told Allie he hadn't been asleep for a while and had seen the riders.

"I know who that was." Jason raised slowly. "That was the meanest man I ever met. I saw him kill a dog with his hands once just because he made a bet that he could."

"Who?" Wes asked.

The boy looked down as if afraid even to say the name. "Michael Catlin," Jason whispered. "I'm sorry about speaking bad of your kin, Allie."

Allie felt Wes stiffen beside her. Somehow this trouble was her doing. Catlin was looking for her, she knew it. And he'd kill anyone in his path to get to her. She'd found her family. And they not only didn't want her . . . they wanted her dead.

"What will we do?" she asked, already knowing what she would have to do. She must get away from Wes and Jason as fast as she could so that they would be safe. Catlin had no reason to chase them. He wanted her.

"We'll go back to town," Wes answered calmly. "It's time to send a few telegrams. I could have you on the next stage to Adam's place if you like."

"No." Allie wanted to run, but not back to Nichole and Adam. That might put them in danger. "I stay with you, or I go on my own."

Wes stood and pulled her from the branches into the morning sun so that he could read her expression. "Then stay with me, Allie. Promise. I can see the look in your eyes. There will be no running. If I found you when you ran, they might find you. Promise you'll stay with me until it's safe."

Allie didn't turn away this time when he stared into her eyes. She knew what he was saying. He was telling her that he'd stand and fight for her. No one had ever done that. Somehow, this strange man had everything backward in the world. Somehow, he thought she was worth fighting for. Maybe even dying for.

"I'll stay." She knew it would be a promise hard to keep.

SIXTEEN

AN HOUR LATER, WES WROTE A TELEGRAM TO THE only man he could ask for help—Wolf Hayward. They'd fought on different sides in the war, but they were both bound by Adam and Nichole. Wolf was Nichole's big brother. Wes was Adam's, and, somehow, that one thread had started their friendship.

"Last I heard, Wolf lived near Austin. If he's close, he'll come." Wes glanced at Allie, who didn't look pleased.

"A man named Wolf?"

Wes laughed. "Wait till you see him, he looks more like a bear. He's the hairiest man I've ever seen. And big, my height, but double the width. But he's an honorary brother in the McLain clan."

Handing the telegram to the clerk, Wes motioned to Jason, who was doing his best to stand still and be invisible. "How about we go over to the cafe for breakfast while I wait for an answer?"

Allie followed along, her thoughts simmering in worry. Wes wouldn't have asked for help unless he thought this trouble she'd caused was great.

She didn't say anything while they ate, only listened as Jason asked one question after another about horses. She could hear people all around her talking. But she couldn't think of anything that would change one way or the other if she said a word.

Wes showed Jason a compass he'd carried all through the war. He tried to explain how it worked, but Jason was more interested in food than direction.

While Wes finished his coffee and Jason his fourth buttered biscuit, the room emptied. Most folks hurried out to start their days. Allie wondered what it would be like to live in a town and be around so many people all at once. They were like one huge tribe. But many didn't seem to know one another, for they didn't even nod as they passed.

When they finished all the food, Wes leaned back in his chair and Jason hurried out to check on the horses. Wes watched the other people for a while, then turned his attention back to her.

Allie shifted in her seat. She was getting used to being alone with him, but she still wasn't sure what he expected of her. Though his wife, he asked no duties of her. It seemed, in his world, the marriage would last only until she found a family.

"I'm not much of a talker, even in the best of times," he began. "But I figure we've got a few things to say to one another, and they need to be said while Jason's not around."

She glanced at her hands and waited. Maybe the time had come for him to tell her he could no longer be responsible for her. After all, she was of no use to him, and she cost him money when she knew his supply was low. Maybe he would say some word, and the marriage would be over, just as his brother had said words to make it begin.

"Will you talk to me, Allie?"

The question surprised her. Most of their conversation to date had been him talking and her listening.

He drank his coffee and waited.

"I don't know what to say," she finally admitted, feeling his gaze warm her. The phrases of her first language were coming back to her, but how could she just talk?

Wes looked up at the ceiling and took a long breath. "After the night in the barn, and the way you kissed me, I've been thinking of lots to talk about, but the words don't seem to come out in rational order. I know there needs to be something said between us if you felt anything like I did. I've tried to give you time, thinking you'd tell me something about how you feel."

He looked directly at her as though he'd judge her answer carefully. "Why'd you kiss me like that?"

"Like what?"

"Like you were planning to crawl in and homestead my heart," Wes answered, "when we both know you're just waiting for a chance to leave me and all of civilization."

"Is kissing you wrong?" Allie had no idea what he was saying. She'd only kissed him the way he'd kissed her, and she'd never told him she wouldn't leave him until this morning, when he'd asked her to promise to stay until the danger was past.

"No, the kiss wasn't wrong. It was about the most right thing that ever happened to me." Wes leaned closer. "I just wondered why."

Allie knew talking came too hard for her to lie. "I . . ."

All the languages began to blend together in her mind. It seemed all her life people had told her not to talk. Now this strange man wanted her to tell him how she felt, something she could never remember anyone asking her.

She forced herself. "The summer I turned ten, I was traded from one tribe to another. The chief of the tribe had a widowed mother, so I was given to her. The old woman's husband had been a great warrior, and her son would follow his path. But the old woman was dried up and angry most of the time. She wanted me as property, not as company. She told me if I talked, she'd cut out my tongue." Allie swallowed hard, remembering those

early days. "I don't believe she would have, but for
years I didn't say a word in any language. She made
sure I worked hard and only ate after she judged there
to be plenty. I lived with her five winters. The dawn
when the raid came, I ran. I didn't even look back when
I heard her death cry."

Blinking back tears, she whispered, "Until you, the
old woman was the kindest person I'd ever known."

Wes leaned across the table and touched her hand.
"I'm not kind, Allie. Most men I know would say I'm
hard and cold. Before I thought of myself as grown, I
fought in a war and proved myself a good soldier. Over
the years, I didn't think about much besides staying
alive.

"Once in a while, I'd need to be near a woman, and
there were always those willing. But with you it's different. When I'm around you, I'm not just near a
woman, I'm near you."

Allie tried to listen closely, but his meaning was un-
clear. Was he talking of the war, of women, or of her?

"I'm not making any sense," Wes tossed his napkin
on the table. "We'd better get over to the telegraph office. There should be a reply by now."

Allie reached out her hand and touched his, stopping
him from rising. "I have a question," she whispered.
"Why did you take me from the cage?"

Wes raised an eyebrow as if he thought the answer
obvious. "I couldn't stand the thought of them treating
you like an animal. You were like some kind of wild
creature with your hair flying all around you and dirt
caking your face." He smiled. "But when I looked in
your eyes, I knew you were enchanted."

He seemed uncomfortable, but continued, "There you
were, trapped in a hell, and you stared at me like you
were worried about my pain. No one's ever done that
before."

"And why did you take me from Victoria's house?"

"That Katherine lady would have picked you apart.

You deserve to be with people who take the time to see inside you . . . who want you.''

Allie watched him closely. ''And do you want me?''

The question was too honest not to be answered.

''Yes,'' he finally said.

One word didn't answer her question. She had to have more. ''How do you want me?'' she pushed. ''As property? As company?''

''I want you safe,'' he answered. After a moment, he added, ''I want you with me because, for some crazy reason, it feels right to have you close. You make me believe in a better world than either of us has ever seen.''

''I can take care of myself in my world. I lived for many winters alone. I won't be anyone's property again. You'll have to cage me to hold me that way. And I'd fight. Eventually, I'd escape, so don't think you can hold me just because you want to. It's not your choice.''

Wes looked frustrated. He'd finally gotten her to talk to him, and she suggested something he'd never do. Maybe they should go back to silence. ''I wouldn't lock you up, Allie. My life is a mess right now. Someone should probably lock me up. I sometimes question why you'd stay of your own free will. I'm chasing a dream that may never come true. I should be traveling fast and light, but all I can think about is you. I thought when I found your family everything would work out fine. Now I'll have to think of something else. Until then, don't threaten to run. When you go, it will be to someplace you feel is right.''

Allie thought of telling him that she had a place to go, and if he'd just help her find the way, she'd be fine on her own. But she didn't speak. Since the night in the barn, she was in no hurry to leave. She couldn't seem to put it into words any better than he could, but she'd felt something when he'd kissed her. It was as if an invisible part of her reached out and laced into an invisible part of him, binding them, making them both stronger.

"Will you ever kiss me again?" she asked, wishing she could feel that way again.

"Would you like me to?"

"I think so," she answered.

He leaned near and lightly touched her cheek with a kiss.

"No," she pouted, "like you did in the barn."

Wes laughed. "I'm afraid I can't do that in public. Folks are watching us enough just because we're strangers in town."

"I can." She stood suddenly and closed the distance between them. Before he could move, she tilted his head back and kissed him full on the mouth as he'd taught her to do in the barn.

Wes gently broke the kiss, his laughter tickling her lips. "We can't . . ."

"Why not? Are we doing something wrong?"

"No." He held her several inches away. "We most certainly are not doing something wrong. I'd say you're doing it just right."

"Then, again, please." She strained against his hold.

"It's just that people usually don't show affection so openly . . . not that it's wrong. We'll be the talk . . . not that I care about what anyone thinks in this town. But proper folks . . . even husbands and wives"—he pulled her gently to him— "Oh, hell, Allie. Who cares if we're in public?"

She felt his warm, wonderful lips touch hers. His hand released her arm and spread lightly across her back just above the waist. It had been far too long since he'd last tasted her and she felt his hunger for the kiss equal her own.

A few minutes later, when she raised her head, everyone in the restaurant was looking at her. She leaned close to Wes and whispered, "Oh, I understand. The people no longer talk. They all watch us."

"I'm guessing by the time we leave, they'll have plenty to say." He laughed as his nose brushed against her hair. "You know, if we don't want folks to notice us, maybe we should act more like everyone else in the place.''

"Agreed." Allie glanced around and saw no one else kissing, so she moved back to her chair. "I will not kiss you again."

"Until we're alone?"

Allie nodded. "Until we're alone. This I promise you."

A loud cough sounded from behind them. "I see you can act like newlyweds, Mr. and Mrs. McLain."

Sheriff Hardy limped into view. He looked tired and road-weary, but he was smiling as though his journey was now at an end.

"Morning, Hardy." Wes's voice was calm, but Allie didn't miss the way he'd shifted his hand to within an inch of his gun.

Hardy lowered himself into the chair Jason had abandoned without waiting to be asked. "I've had quite a hunt trailing you two. By the time we figured out you were gone from the ranch, you had an hour start on me. In the old days, before I took the lead in my leg, I could have caught you by nightfall. Nowadays, I move a little slower."

"Get to the point, Sheriff Hardy," Wes interrupted. "If you've come to ask us to go back, forget it. Allie doesn't need relatives who don't welcome her. She can stay with me."

Hardy pulled out two cigars and offered Wes one.

Wes refused even though Allie saw the way his eyes followed the cigar back to Hardy's pocket.

"I know she can," the sheriff admitted. "After you left, I went to town and telegraphed your sister-in-law, telling her you'd kidnapped Allie from her own grandmother's house. She answered that as far as she knew in Texas a man can't kidnap his own wife. Not if she goes willingly."

Hardy leaned back in his chair and lit his cigar. "I didn't believe it until I walked in this place and saw the way this little lady kissed you." His smile was somehow sad. "You're a lucky man, Wes McLain."

"So, why are you still here?" Wes grumbled. "You must have figured out by now that she's not being held against her will."

The sheriff laughed again. "I know you're not going to believe this, but I'm here to protect this little lady from the storm a-coming. You see, Victoria still doesn't believe Allie's her granddaughter, but Victoria's son, Michael, isn't taking any chances on having to split the family wealth. He'll come looking for her. And when he does, I'll have my gun loaded and ready."

To the sheriff's surprise, Wes nodded. "He already has. We saw him and three other men at dawn. Luckily, they didn't see us. They rode past, heading south, but Jason told us who he was. Tell him he has no worry from Allie. She doesn't want anything from the Catlins."

Maxwell Hardy shook his head. "You'll never convince Michael of that. I'm the only one he might listen to, and he hates me."

"Mind my asking why?"

"He owes me his life," Hardy admitted. "So until he shows up and I talk to him, I'm traveling with you."

"I already have a crowd traveling with me."

Hardy took a long draw on his cigar. "Well, then, you won't notice one more."

Wes stormed out of the cafe and headed to the barn with Allie and the sheriff in his wake. "I'm leading a damn parade!" he mumbled. He fought the urge to yell to the town, "Does anyone else want to come along on this secret treasure hunt?" Maybe he could get a band, or a medicine show. Maybe they could form a wagon train to Goliad. Hell, they were starting to follow him like he'd been appointed head cow on a long drive.

Wes stopped in the middle of the street. "I'm not going back to Victoria's place, Sheriff. I can take care of Allie without any help." Max might tag along, but

Wes wanted it plain the old fellow would be giving no directions.

Max shrugged. "I didn't figure you were a man to backtrack." He glanced down the length of Wes. "And I didn't live this long without being able to size a man up. If it were just you and Michael, my money would be on you. But it's not just you and him. Michael always takes along a few friends to increase the odds. He'll follow you wherever you go."

"Well, aren't you even going to ask where I'm headed?"

The old man shook his head. "It don't matter. I'll find out when I get there. All I know is, wherever you're going, I'm tagging along."

Wes turned around and stomped onto the porch of the telegraph office. He felt like a fool. For some reason, Hardy was trying to protect Allie. The same thing Wes was trying to do. But instead of thanking the man, Wes was angry. After all, protecting Allie was his job.

As Wes entered the telegraph office, he thought about where to turn next. He could outrun Hardy with horses, but the sheriff would probably have every lawman in the state looking for him. And he had to admit, even in the dawn light, Michael did look like he could be meaner than a rattler, and four against one wasn't very balanced. Plus, he had Jason to think about. He could shield Allie, but the boy might be caught in the crossfire if there was shooting. Hardy was older than used dirt, but he knew his way around trouble.

Wes accepted the return telegram. As he read a message from Wolf's landlady, his hope faded. Wolf had already left for Fort Worth. She didn't say more, but Wes sensed something was wrong. Nichole wasn't due for another month. Whatever it was would have to wait a few days. Wes had a bucketful of problems to handle here. Nichole had Adam to doctor her and Wolf to look after her. She didn't need him. He was worthless where babies were concerned anyway.

"You can ride along as shotgun." Wes folded the

telegram, wishing he could fold away the problem as easily. "For Allie and Jason's sake. But stay out of my business."

"Of course." Hardy nodded respectfully. "And what business might that be, Mr. McLain?"

"None of your business!"

Hardy laughed and winked at Allie. "Interesting job your husband has, Mrs. McLain."

"And stop calling her that." Wes's mood clouded over. "Her name's Allie."

Maxwell's head made tiny little shakes. "Of course. Your *wife* is named Allie."

"That's right." Wes's temper promised thunderstorms. Hardy wasn't a man who knew how to keep his nose out of other people's lives. Wes couldn't help but wonder how he'd lived to be so old.

The weather echoed his disposition, for as they walked back outside, it began to rain. Wes pulled the hood of Allie's blue cape over her hair and tucked her under his arm and they ran for the barn where they'd left the horses.

When they reached the shelter, Maxwell's buggy stood beside the mounts.

"Allie will be drier riding in the buggy," the old man offered.

Wes agreed but hated not having her with him.

Hardy reached in the boot of his buggy and handed Jason a leather jacket that almost reached to the boy's knees. "Better wear this, boy," the old man coaxed. "And if I may offer, Gideon packed us blankets and rations in the boot to last a week."

Wes thought of turning him down. But in truth, the rations might come in handy. "Thank Gideon for me when you see him."

"I will," Hardy answered. "I'll see him when I take back Michael's body. I've kept him alive and out of jail for Victoria's sake. But I'll not let him kill Allie, and he's never been a man to listen to reason."

Wes lifted Allie into the buggy. "Do you know how to use a gun?"

She nodded. She'd seen them used, that should count. It didn't look all that difficult.

Wes slipped a Colt from his saddlebag and laid it in her lap. "Keep this handy. I'm not sure what kind of storm we're riding into."

She watched him closely as he covered the gun and her hands with a thick lap quilt.

"I may ride up ahead in this storm. It'll be hard for you to keep sight of me. But don't worry. I won't be far away. If you think there might be trouble fire a shot. I'll be by your side as fast as I can."

Without a word or caring who was watching, she leaned over and brushed his lips with hers.

Wes pulled back, looking surprised. Then, suddenly, he cupped the back of her head and kissed her soundly.

When he finally pulled away, her eyes were shining with pleasure.

"We'll talk more later," he whispered and vanished from her side.

SEVENTEEN

THE WEATHER DIDN'T COOPERATE. RAIN POURED down in their faces. The wind whipped around, slapping them from every direction. After a few hours, Wes ordered Jason into the buggy with Allie, but he was little better protected there. Riding a horse was hard, but driving a buggy became impossible by noon. They pulled into a stagecoach station to wait out the storm.

A friendly old-timer named Owen ran the place and knew the sheriff from as far back as the Republic days. He welcomed them inside and offered them what lodging he had. Maxwell and the boy took two bunks in a long room lined with beds on the second floor. A single hook hung beside each cot for clothes, reminding Wes of a barracks. The owner insisted Wes and Allie take the only private room upstairs. It held only a bed, but he said it was the best he had.

Wes brought Allie's things in, then excused himself to see to the horses. By the time he returned, Maxwell and the innkeeper were sharing a bottle by the fire. Jason had curled up to sleep on a bench in the kitchen area.

Climbing the stairs, Wes noticed it seemed like evening in the large log greatroom that served as a seating area, dining room and kitchen. The stairs ran along one wall and were open on one side, giving Wes a view of the entire room. The second floor didn't extend over the main area, leaving the ceiling high in that part of the house.

Owen's voice drifted through the open area as he talked of the days of President Houston when Texas stood alone as a nation.

A stable hand told Wes a stage was due in a few hours before dark. He said it usually only stopped for a change of horses and a quick bite for the passengers. But the weather might delay it or hold it here for the night.

Wes walked down the hallway on the second floor. He didn't want more people showing up. There were enough folks around as it was. The more people around, the more he had to watch or worry about.

Opening the door while deep in thought, Wes was totally unprepared for the sight that greeted him. Allie had just stood from her bath and was reaching for the towel. The rainy, pearl-light from the windows made her wet skin glow. If ever he'd thought her eyes were enchanted, now her whole body seemed so.

He stood staring at her, unable to look away even if the thought had crossed his mind. She was the most beautiful woman he'd ever seen. Her breasts were high and round, her waist small. He'd always thought of her as thin and short, but everything about her, without the oversized clothes, was in perfect proportion.

"Is something wrong?" She pulled the towel around her and faced him, totally unaware of the effect she had on him.

Wes couldn't speak. He wasn't even sure he could breathe. All he could do was watch her as she walked around the bed.

She fingered her undergarments. "They're still damp," she said. "Do I have to get dressed yet?"

"No," Wes managed to force out, thinking he'd like it very much if she stayed just the way she was forever. "Why don't you rest until dinner's ready?" He tried to make sense of the way he was reacting. "By then, your clothes will be dry." Wes figured his would be also, for he could almost feel the steam coming off his damp shirt.

Allie let the towel slip as she crawled beneath the covers.

Wes backed out of the room, allowing his gaze the luxury of watching her for as long as possible. He stood in the hallway wondering if he had the strength to walk away. She'd finally started to trust him. If he moved too fast, he'd destroy that trust and maybe never get it back.

If he moved too fast? The words slammed into the corners of his mind. Until now, he'd never planned to move any way at all, fast or slow. He'd simply wanted to keep her safe. Then she'd kissed him and somehow started a hunger within him that might shatter every plan he'd ever had in his life.

And now he'd seen her, all of her. An invisible clock had been set in his body, ticking down the hours. He didn't know when, or how, but at some point, he knew he'd make love to her. When he closed his eyes, he could feel her body against his. When he drew in air, her scent filled his thoughts. The taste of her kiss lingered on his tongue.

Wes walked down the stairs and out the front door as if the day were clear.

Just before he closed the door, he heard Owen mumble, "That fellow'll be struck by lightning if he goes out."

Hardy laughed, "He already has been."

Allie closed her eyes. The layers of blankets warmed her body. The gentle tapping of rain on the window lulled her to sleep. As always, she was back in her cave, moving through the pattern of passages to get to her place. The air felt damp and cool against her face, the ground smooth from where a river ran through the entrances years ago.

When she entered her place, fresh air from a crevice far above welcomed her and a thin ray of light lit the little room she called hers. Everything was still there as if waiting. Her pots, her robes, her pelts. Everything she needed to survive.

In her dream, she spread out on her bed and pulled the thick buffalo robe over her. The nightmares would not come with her to her cave. She would sleep.

Hours later a sound whispered in her cave, then in the darkness of the room, pulling her from her dream.

"Allie? Allie, are you asleep?"

She rolled over. "Jason?"

"Yes," he answered. "It's long past dark, and I can't find a candle upstairs."

"What is it?" She blinked, trying to make out the outline of the boy at the door. "Where's Wes?"

"He left here a few hours ago with the stable hand. The stage didn't make it in, and Owen was worried. Wes said he'd ride out and look for it."

She heard Jason shifting in the darkness and knew something was wrong. She reached for her undergarments and dressed, knowing the boy would not have awakened her unless he felt he had to.

"After they left, Owen and the sheriff decided to have another bottle and relive the battle of San Jacinto. I think Owen passed out at the table. I can't get him to wake up."

Jason paused as though hating to continue. "The sheriff was going to bed, but he only made it up four of the steps before he tumbled. I wasn't close enough to help him. He didn't seem too drunk to make the stairs when he started climbing. But with his bad leg, he fell. I . . ."

She pulled her dress over her head. She slipped her boots on and moved out the door, buttoning the bodice as she hurried down the hallway and the stairs.

Just as Jason had said, the sheriff lay at the bottom, twisted and unconscious.

"I didn't know what to do." Panic made the boy's voice high. "I tried to help him up, but his leg is busted bad. He tried to stand, then must have passed out."

Allie knelt, her fingers running along the length of the

old man as she'd seen medicine men do. She wanted to say she didn't know anything, but that wasn't what Jason needed to hear. The boy was almost as pale as the old man. He needed someone to help, not complain.

"Help me get him to the table." She tried to think of something. Maxwell's crippled leg must be broken, for blood stained the knee of his trousers. A bump the size of an egg had formed on his forehead and scrapes crisscrossed his cheek.

Jason seemed to calm with having something to do. He moved beneath one arm of the sheriff and tried to pull his part of the load as they half carried, half dragged the wounded man across to the table.

Straining, they lifted the sheriff onto the end of the long table and rolled him onto his back.

"Get blankets and a pillow," Allie ordered. "Then build up the fire, and see if you can find a few more lanterns."

Allie unbuckled his gunbelt and draped it over one of the kitchen chairs. Pulling her knife from her boot, she slit the material covering his leg. As the bloody fabric peeled away, Allie saw a jagged rip in the flesh and a bone, snapped like a twig.

She stood back and tried to breathe without the thick smell of blood filling her lungs. She'd gutted animals, she'd even seen babies born, but now blood seemed to be everywhere. Warm, red blood. Her fingers were covered in it, and her dress stained.

"Holy . . ." Jason whistled behind her. "That looks terrible!"

Allie swallowed hard. "No worse than an animal's insides." She forced herself to look at the break. "All we have to do is straighten out the bone and sew up the gash." That sounded like a plan. Simple, just straighten a bone and close the opening. How hard could that be?

Jason moved an inch closer. "And stop the bleeding and put all the bloody parts back in order. And hope the sheriff don't die before we get through. Who knows, maybe as bad as this is, it's the bump on his head that will kill him.''

They both glanced at the old man's face. The bump did look bad, but there was nothing Allie could do about it.

Hardy looked ready for the funeral fire now. He was either too drunk or too hurt to feel any pain, which could be good. Allie didn't care which—she just wanted her doctoring not to kill him. But if she didn't do something, he would surely die from the rate blood poured out of him. So she had to try.

She remembered seeing the way Adam had sewn up Wes when he'd been shot in the back. She could do that part, she told herself. As for the other, she wasn't sure. It wouldn't do much good to sew him up if the bone just poked another hole in his flesh as soon as he moved.

Jason took short quick breaths and turned whiter the longer he stared. ''How much more blood you reckon he's got in him?''

''Enough.'' She prayed she spoke the truth.

''Get water and something to use for bandages,'' Allie ordered, hoping to keep Jason from being her next patient. She moved around the room looking for something to use for sewing. The room only had an old desk and a round-toppped trunk. In the trunk they found women's clothes and a small sewing kit. After Jason brought the water, he set about ripping a petticoat into strips while Allie tried to clean the gash.

But blood kept dripping out, slowing the process. In one swipe of a rag, Allie felt something hard in the soft, open flesh. At first, she thought it was part of the bone, but then the light caught its shine.

She glanced up to show Jason, but he'd disappeared into the kitchen area.

Allie pulled a bullet from the tissue and tossed it in the pan of water without taking time to examine it. When he woke up, if he woke up, he'd no longer have lead in his leg.

''I'm ready,'' Jason called triumphantly as he ran toward her. "I pulled this board off the back wall. I think we have to stretch the leg on it." The board was about four feet long and six inches wide. "I seen a doc do that once with a friend's arm. He said he had to hold the bone straight until it grew back."

Allie nodded. She knew for the bone to heal straight it must be tied to something. She'd seen a medicine man tie a broken leg to a man's straight one, claiming they would both grow the same. For a full cycle of the moon, the man crawled around dragging his tied legs behind him. But when the ropes were removed, he stood straight on two legs once more. If that worked, the board might work.

They placed the wood beneath Hardy's leg and pulled as hard as they could.

"Harder!" Allie kept saying as she tried to keep Maxwell still while Jason pulled.

The sheriff moaned in pain, but the leg straightened. Allie and Jason tied it in place, leaving the gash untouched. Blood dripped out on the ties as they worked.

"You think we pulled it too hard?" Jason whispered. "What if this leg is longer when we untie it from the board?"

"We'll worry about that later," Allie answered, thinking the boy needed an extra pocket to carry all his worries in.

Allie held the flesh together with her fingers and began to sew the skin closed, but blood kept bubbling in her way.

"Wait!" Jason ran to the bottle still next to the sleeping innkeeper. "I saw a doc do this once in the bar. Every time there is doctoring to be done at the bar, I like to help if I can. Hope I learned something that will help."

He began dripping the whiskey over the wound, washing away blood as Allie stitched. The whiskey sizzled on the raw flesh. She could see where to make the X's to hold the skin together.

When the gash was closed, she wrapped the wound

tightly and bound the leg, from hip to foot, to the board. The sheriff moaned. Jason dribbled watered-down whiskey into the sheriff's mouth.

"Is he going to live?" Jason sounded near tears for the first time. His hands shook. "He was always nice to me, never yelled or nothing. I don't want to watch him die. I've watched enough people die."

"I don't know if he'll make it." Allie picked up soiled rags. "I never doctored anyone before, but if he does, he'll have you to thank."

"Me?" Jason answered. "I think we both did a fine job. If he lives, of course."

"Of course," Allie liked the feel of the phrase. Words were coming easier to her tongue. "We'll watch him closely and rewrap the wound every time it gets soaked in blood."

They sat on either side of the table and stared at the sheriff for an hour. Slowly, his breathing grew long, and he slept.

Jason finally could sit still no longer. "I made a stew while they was drinking, just in case those folks from the stage come in. I made cornbread, too." He ran to fetch her a bowl. "I can cook pretty near anything. There were some days, back at the hotel, that I was in the kitchen from before dawn until after the bar closed. I was only supposed to clean up, but the cook taught me to do things so he wouldn't have to hurry."

Allie watched him moving about the kitchen. He was proud that he'd helped, and that he could cook. The pride made him taller, she thought.

They ate in the center of the long table with the sheriff lying at one end and Owen resting his head at the other.

"The stew is very good," she complimented. "Will you teach me?"

Jason swelled with pride. "Sure. I'd be glad to. Does that mean I can stay with you and Wes?"

"If you like," she answered. "And you can leave when you're ready. It will be up to you."

The door rattled, and both of them froze. It rattled

again. Allie reached for her knife; Jason tried to pull the sheriff's heavy Colt from its holster hanging on the back of a chair.

Wes blew in with the rain as the door swung open. His hat was pulled low and saddlebags hung over one shoulder. "Found no sign of a stage . . ." he began. His tired gaze scanned the room and came to rest on Allie. "What happened?"

She could see the worry in his eyes.

Suddenly, all the panic of the past hour shook her. Dropping the knife on the table in her haste, she ran toward him in one swift movement.

The saddlebag slid to the floor. He swept her up in his arms. He held her tightly against him and moved into the room.

"It's all right," he whispered, brushing her hair back from her face. If she was alive, nothing could be too wrong in the world.

Allie didn't say a word, but Jason filled Wes in on all the details.

Jason finished by saying, "And he's still alive, so we must have done something right."

With Allie leaning against him, Wes examined the old sheriff. "I'd say you did more than something, son. I've seen a hundred field dressings in my day, but I've seen none better. It's a good splint. Who knows, the leg may heal straight."

He kissed Allie on the forehead and winked at Jason. "I'd say Hardy was lucky to have you two around. From the looks of Owen, Hardy would have been in big trouble if you hadn't been here. He would have bled to death before his friend sobered up."

While Wes brought a cot down, Jason dipped him a bowl of stew. By the time Wes carried the sheriff to a comfortable bed by the fire, his meal waited for him: stew, a wide slice of cornbread, and cold buttermilk.

The boy never stopped talking while Wes ate. When he'd finished his second bowl, Wes knew every detail of what had happened.

Allie hurried about the room, first cleaning up the blood, then checking on the sheriff.

When she made her third trip up the stairs with a bucket of rainwater from the porch, Wes asked what she was doing.

Allie looked down at her dress. "I thought I'd take a bath and wash the blood off me, then my clothes."

Her drab brown dress was stained in several spots. The blood seemed to be drying the same shade of brown as her dress.

"Mind if I come on up?" Wes asked as casually as he could. "After a day fighting this storm, I'm ready to call it a night."

"No." She turned around and headed up the stairs once more. "I don't mind."

EIGHTEEN

WES CHECKED ON THE SLEEPING SHERIFF AND TOLD Jason to call him if Hardy woke up. Then he slowly moved up the stairs. The thought of seeing Allie in her bath warmed his blood. He'd spent hours in the cold rain telling himself that she meant nothing to him. What he did for her he would have done for any human. She didn't care for him any more than he did for her.

But after hours of talking to himself, only one picture came to mind . . . the vision of Allie reaching for her towel with her body glistening with moisture.

As he opened the door, he braced for her beauty, telling himself that he could look at her and even enjoy the sight of her without making any promises or attacking her like an animal. He'd just watch her and then kiss her goodnight. Maybe he'd hold her as they slept. Nothing more. Nothing.

When he stepped into their small room, the low glow of one candle greeted him. Allie knelt over the tub, scrubbing her dress. She wore her underthings, but the thin clothing did little to hide what he knew was beneath.

Forcing himself to move slowly, he crossed to the far side of the bed and removed his mud-covered clothes. Unlike Allie with her cleanliness, he planned to let his clothes dry and shake them out in the morning. It was a habit he'd learned in the Army. One that would have sent his mother into a sermon on cleanliness.

Allie looked up at him standing by the bed in his long-handles and undershirt. "No," she said firmly, as if answering a question only she heard. "You are not getting in bed like that."

He raised an eyebrow, wondering if his mother hadn't yet come back to haunt him. "I'm not?" He thought about reminding her how tired he was, or informing her that he had every right to climb in her bed. But her statement shocked more than angered.

"No," she answered. Her lifted chin reminded him of her grandmother. "There's water enough to wash you first. Take off the rest of your clothes."

He froze. The idea of lying next to her totally nude with their bodies pressed together had crossed his mind a few thousand times today. But the thought of standing stark naked in front of her was something altogether different. The first was sensual, erotic. The second somewhere between unseemly and downright dirty.

"Turn around," he found himself saying in a voice gruff as ground anger. He'd not have her watching him bathe, even though that was exactly what he'd planned to do to her.

Allie did as he asked. Slowly, watching her all the time, he removed his clothes and walked over to the tub and stepped in. He grabbed the first bucket of water and poured it over his head. As the cold rain dripped down his body, he picked up the soap and began to wash.

She kept her back to him, moving around the edges of the room until she reached his pile of muddy clothes. Then, without a word, she picked them up and was gone.

Wes laughed and finished scrubbing. In truth, even a cold-water bath felt wonderful. When he dried off, he realized he had nothing, not even his longhandle underwear, to put on. So he slipped between the covers and waited. The warm blankets felt soft and grand against his tired muscles. The day had been endless, and now flickers of the single candle seemed to be waving him to sleep.

The rain still tapped on the roof, and the familiar sounds of horses in the corral reminded Wes of the home of his childhood.

Sleep had almost won over when Wes heard the door open and close softly. He didn't bother to open his eyes as Allie lifted her side of the covers and slid beneath the quilts.

"Are you asleep?" she whispered.

"No." He didn't move. Just the sound of her voice made him very much awake.

She waited several breaths before asking, "Is now the right time to kiss?"

He thought for a moment. It seemed like a decade ago that they'd kissed in the cafe. Could it really have been only this morning?

"So, you're interested in kissing?"

"If you're not too tired." She moved closer. "No one would be watching us."

Wes extended his arms, and she rolled against his side with covers bunched between them. He waited as she wiggled into place, moving her hair above his arm, finding just the right spot for her head on his shoulder.

He leaned slightly toward her and brushed her wild hair from her face. Even in the shadows, he could see her beauty. Featherlight, he touched his lips to hers.

"Again," she whispered.

He laughed against her hair, loving the way it smelled like rainwater tonight. When his lips lowered again, the kiss was deeper, drawing her response.

He pulled away. "Again?"

Her face was calm, as though she were ordering dinner and not making his heart pound double-time.

"Yes. I would like another."

He didn't move. "First, pull the covers away from between us."

Rocking slightly, she tugged the covers and rolled back against his bare skin. The thin material she wore did nothing to bar the warmth of her body from his.

Wes felt like he was being tortured in paradise. "Closer," he asked against her hair. "Move closer, Allie. You feel so good."

She followed his order, pressing against him.

He rewarded her with another kiss. If his mind could have worked at the moment, he would have wondered at this strange creature who thought a kiss was so wonderful. But he couldn't think, all he could do was feel. He was drowning in a pool of pleasure and making no effort to swim to the surface.

The kiss deepened as he parted her lips and tasted her. His hand moved slowly along her back, stroking her gently, treasuring her. As the strokes grew stronger, she molded like liquid fire against him.

The feel of her enchanted him. Her nearness made him believe there was more than hardness and struggle in life. With just a kiss, she took him to where no other woman ever had . . . to a place of peace.

Finally, when he broke the kiss, she rolled onto her back and let out a long sigh. "Thank you," she whispered, as though he'd given her a gift.

Wes raised to one elbow and watched her. He felt like a youth in his first encounter with love. He had no idea what to do. What she'd let him do. He was looking at a banquet of pleasures with a teaspoon in his hand. If he moved too fast, if he took too much for granted, she'd run. He could feel it.

"Talk to me, Allie." He gently placed his hand on her abdomen. Her slow breathing didn't quicken with his touch. Her calmness brought him great pleasure.

She didn't answer.

"Talk to me. I need to know what you're feeling." Wes almost laughed aloud. He'd never said such words to a woman. Most of the time he'd only been interested in *how* they felt, not *what* they felt. But Allie was different. She was like fine china. The wrong move might shatter her.

"I like you to kiss me," she said with her eyes closed.

"I didn't think I'd like it so much, but I do."

"And?" He spread his fingers across her stomach. The perfection of her so near was intoxicating.

"You don't frighten me as other men have." She opened her eyes. "You've never harmed me. With you, I no longer wait for a blow to strike."

Wes didn't want to know. He never wanted to know. He knew he'd hate hearing it. But he had to ask. She had to tell him. "Allie, how have you been hurt?"

The soft glow of peace faded from her eyes. He felt her breathing quicken beneath his hand. He could see terror jolt through her . . . pain too great to put into words.

"Allie, tell me," he said. "It was more than beatings, wasn't it?"

She clamped her mouth tightly closed, but couldn't seal away the hurt in her eyes. Her whole body had gone cold, as if what she'd endured had killed something deep inside her.

He touched her hair, stroking it lightly. "It's all right," he whispered, wishing he hadn't asked. "You don't have to say anything."

But panic still flickered in her eyes. In one swift movement, she slid out of the bed and ran from the room.

Wes wasn't sure if she was running from the nightmare she'd seen or from him. He lay on his back and swore to the ceiling. Without a word, she'd told him all she needed to. She'd suffered what polite ladies call "a fate worse than death."

He'd once heard his mother say that, if a man ever forced himself on her, she'd kill herself rather than live with the shame. But Wes saw no shame in Allie's stare, only fear. How many times had she been attacked and used until now the mere thought brought panic?

His mind filled with visions he didn't want to see. He'd seen all the horror he could handle in war; he didn't want to view more. But the visions of Allie kept coming. Wes felt a ball of hate knot in his stomach. He wished he'd killed the preacher and the cripple who drove the wagon with the cage. And every man who'd looked at her and thought her less than a woman. How many days had they made her life a hell?

Slowly, he calmed. Allie had survived. No matter what happened, she'd survived. And there had been enough of her spirit left to reach out and take a chance with him.

"Allie," he said, knowing he was alone. "Thank God you survived."

She sat in the corner by the fireplace where the brick connected with the wall. The sheriff rested quietly, his bleeding lessened with each bandaging. Owen, the station manager, had stumbled off to his room in the back. Jason slept soundly on a kitchen pew. The room was almost as quiet as her cave.

Tucking her knees beneath her chin, Allie watched the way the firelight danced on the walls of the room. She didn't want to think about her life before Wes. The nightmares would come back. He had no idea how hard she'd fought to forget what he asked her to remember. She could never tell him of the horror in the nights when her door was unlocked, and she'd fight until she couldn't fight anymore. She couldn't even tell him of how the wagon driver used to hold her and let men grab at her breasts as if they could pull the tender flesh off in their rough hands. She could tell Wes nothing. She knew she never would. The name she'd been called drifted across her mind . . . *throwaway woman.* Wes was the only one who thought she had some value. If she told him, he'd think less of her.

There would be no sleep tonight, she promised. The sheriff's moaning would keep her awake and Jason, even asleep, somehow guarded her from evil. She would stay awake and not let the nightmares bother her. Then, with dawn, she'd start trying to forget all over again.

Allie didn't look up when she heard Wes come downstairs. The shadow of a man draped in a quilt moved across the dancing firelight along the far wall. She could hear him lifting his saddlebags and guessed he was getting fresh clothes.

Staring at the floor, Allie thought of her home in the cave. This house was larger and warmer, but a place like this would never be home.

A blanket slipped gently around her shoulders. She looked up into Wes's warm brown eyes now dancing with firelight.

"I thought you might be cold." He'd put on his extra pair of trousers and a dry undershirt.

"I'm fine." She rested her chin back on her knee.

He knelt in front of her and smiled as he pulled the blanket tight over her shoulders, cocooning her in its warmth. "I was thinking." He picked his words slowly. "You may very well be the bravest woman I know."

Without commenting on what he was doing, he lifted her, blanket and all, into his arms. "I had a colonel once who said the hardest part of being brave is staying alive. Any fool can get himself killed. But a brave man, a true warrior, is the one who can stay alive, no matter what."

He started up the stairs with her in his arms. "What happened to you isn't as important as the fact that you survived it. I figure that makes you about the bravest person I know. No matter what life's thrown at you, you live on like a strong tree that stands against all weather."

He reached the door to their room. "So, if you don't mind, I'd like the bravest person I know to sleep beside me." He lowered her on the bed. "To keep *my* nightmares away."

She watched him move around the bed and slip beneath the covers. "You have nightmares?" she asked.

Wes smiled, knowing he'd guessed right. "Horrible nightmares." He stretched his arm toward her. "Mostly of the war. In daylight, they seem far away, but with the dark, they drift into my sleep."

Allie cuddled into his embrace. "Me, too," she whispered. "Sometimes I try not to sleep so I can keep them away."

Kissing her forehead, Wes slid his free hand to her waist and closed his eyes. "Maybe I'll keep yours away the way you keep away mine."

Studying his face in the candle's light she watched as he relaxed. In truth, she hardly noticed the scar anymore. There was so much more to this man. The thin white mark on his cheek seemed only a character line. His hair was longer than his brothers'. As his breathing slowed, she decided she liked his mouth the most. She liked the way he kissed her as if he were touching something treasured.

He'd called her brave. Proof that he was crazy, she thought. All she'd ever done in her life was try to run and hide. But he was right about one thing: she wasn't afraid of him anymore. And if she could trust one person, maybe someday she could trust another.

All the men of any nation she'd ever known had been hard. At the worse, they'd been cruel. At best, indifferent to her. No matter how much she'd tried, she could remember nothing about her father except that he yelled and seemed angry. He'd set the pattern she'd grown to expect.

No man had ever called her brave or treated her so kindly. Allie studied Wes carefully. She must stand brave in front of him. It was wrong of her to allow him to see her fear as she had earlier. He was a good man and, little by little, he'd help her lose her fear of people. But tonight, she'd start with this one man.

"Wes?" she whispered, testing to see if he was asleep.

He didn't answer.

Allie moved her lips to his, tasting while he slept.

She raised to one elbow and lightly traced his jawline with her fingers. When he didn't react, she felt his thick walnut-colored hair. He was of the earth, this man, with his brown hair and eyes.

Slowly, she lowered her hand to his throat where she could feel his pulse. He slept soundly, telling her how tired he was or, maybe, how much he trusted her. She knew he'd been a warrior, and he wouldn't have fully relaxed if he thought he was in any danger.

Allie rolled on her back and took a deep breath. Now she could sleep, and she knew the nightmares wouldn't come. Somehow, they'd fight them together as they slept.

Before she closed her eyes, there was one more thing she had to do. She had to know that the feel of all men was not the same.

Her fingers circled his wrist, resting at her waist. With determination she pulled his hand up until his fingers spread across her breast.

Allie held her breath, waiting for the pain.

But it didn't come. His hand relaxed over her flesh, curving around her mound gently.

She took a deep breath and felt the rise and fall of his hand over her. Her breast seem to swell to fill his palm. Through the thin cotton, she could feel the warmth of his fingers. To her surprise, his touch felt good, brushing away memories of pain.

Spreading her smaller hand over his, she pressed. But his touch brought her no pain, and no terror blocked her screams.

Quickly, she moved his hand to her other breast. No pain again. Clearly, the past harm had come from the man and not from the act of being touched. For Wes's hand brought her only the warm feel of his fingers touching her sensitive flesh.

She returned his hand to her waist. Somehow, her testing had removed an ounce of terror that she knew would no longer haunt her dreams.

"Thank you," she whispered.

"You're welcome," he answered.

NINETEEN

WES POURED HIMSELF A THIRD CUP OF COFFEE AND pulled a chair by the window so he could watch the sun rise. From the kitchen, he heard Owen swearing that he'd never drink again.

Looking out on the gray morning, Wes set his mind to what had to be done. The dream of the Goliad gold was just that, a dream. He had to turn it loose. Allie was in danger, and the best way he could protect her was from his home base. The ranch he'd bought the first year he came to Texas hadn't been much of a home. He'd mostly used it as a stopping-off place between trail drives. But it had a bluff backing up to the dugout, making it accessible from only one side. She'd be safest there.

He also had to consider that the sheriff needed a place to recover and Owen was worse than nothing as a nurse. Wes didn't know of any relatives the sheriff might have, so he'd have to recover at the ranch. Adam was close enough to ride over and check in on the old man now and again.

And then there was Jason. He needed a place to grow. Being on the run from trouble was no place for a boy.

Wes took a long drink, allowing the coffee to warm him. He knew the gold wouldn't wait. Vincent had told him there were other men looking for it. This had been his one chance. He was within a day's ride from it, but he was outgunned, fighting an uphill battle. He couldn't leave them unprotected, even for a few days to follow his dream. Allie meant more to him than the gold.

Sheriff Hardy moaned and tried to rise.

Wes moved to his side. "Easy now, old man. You'll break a few more bones if you fall out of bed." Sweat dotted the sheriff's face, warning Wes the fever had begun. He only hoped that Hardy was strong enough to fight a fever and the pain.

The sheriff grumbled. "Get this contraption off my leg!"

Wes placed a firm hand on Hardy's shoulder. "I can't. You've got to give that leg time to heal. I figure I can take you back to my place for a few months. It's not much, but we'll make it work."

The sheriff leaned back as realization cleared his bloodshot eyes. "No," he finally said. "Take me to Victoria."

"More likely hell than there," Wes answered as he tried to put a towel across Hardy's forehead.

"No, listen," the old man mumbled, his voice growing weak. "That's the only place we know Michael won't go. He hasn't set foot on his mother's land in twenty years. It's the only place in Texas where I'd be safe. I can't let Michael find me when I'm down. It'd be the chance he's been waiting for."

"I thought you said you saved his life?"

"I did, and the fact that he owes me a debt has been festering in him ever since. He's been waiting for me to get old and drop my guard."

Hardy grabbed Wes's arm with surprising strength. "If not for me, take us to Victoria for Allie's sake. You can't protect her and the boy every moment. Michael's getting closer, I can feel it."

Wes knew the old man was right. "Are you sure he won't show up at Victoria's?"

"I'm sure. When he left, in his youth, he swore he'd never return, not even to bury her."

Nodding, Wes gave in. "How long until you're able to leave?"

Hardy relaxed, as if he'd won a fight. "I'm ready now."

Wes knew the longer they stayed here, the greater the chance Michael would find them. If what Maxwell Hardy said was right, it might be worth risking the old man's life to get him to safe ground. "I'll see if Owen will trade your buggy for a wagon. We'll pack it with straw and blankets."

Ten minutes later, he'd made all the plans and had Jason help Owen get everything ready. All that was left to do was go upstairs and tell Allie.

Wes didn't hurry. He knew she wouldn't want to go back to Victoria's. But Hardy was right. It was the safest place for them right now.

When he entered the room, Allie was dressed, looking out the window. She'd cut a strip of cloth from the bandages and used it to tie back her hair. She wore the other dress Nichole had given her. The muddy blue color was even less flattering than the brown had been. But Wes hardly noticed. He remembered what lay beneath.

"Allie," he said, knowing she'd heard him come into the room.

She didn't turn around. "We're leaving, aren't we? Even in the rain."

"Yes." He moved behind her, standing close enough to feel her warmth without touching her.

"Do we go to look for your treasure among the ghosts?" She stared into the gray morning.

"No." He lightly touched her shoulder. When she didn't pull away, he allowed his hand to rest. "We have to take Hardy to a safe place. He thinks Michael will kill him if Michael finds him wounded. Hardy wants to go back to Victoria's place."

"But what about your treasure? You need the gold to buy cattle for your ranch." She leaned slightly, brushing her shoulders against his chest. "I heard you tell your friend that it would be your one chance to start over."

"It can wait," Wes lied. He knew if he stopped now, he'd never make it back. He also knew she didn't want him to bother the ghosts at Goliad. Victoria must frighten her more than any ghosts.

She turned and placed her arms around his neck. "I'm sorry," she whispered. "You must change your plan."

Wes had expected her to balk at the thought of going back to Victoria's, but instead, she understood. She knew what he was giving up because of Hardy and her.

"It's all right. I'll find another way." He pulled her close, wishing he could tell her all of how he felt. He'd always been alone, worrying about himself. Now he had her. It felt good to worry about someone else for a change.

"We'll take the sheriff to my grandmother, but then we must leave for Goliad. We will not stay at the head-quarters."

"No," Wes started.

"Yes," she answered. "If it hadn't been for me, you'd already have been to the gold. I will go with you to look. I will help you fight the ghosts."

"No, forget it."

"I will not," she said the words as though ending the discussion.

For the first time, he saw a stubbornness in the set of her jaw. Maybe because she didn't talk much; maybe because she was so tiny, he'd always thought of her as a little bit childlike. But she'd understood his loss of a dream. There was nothing childlike in the way she faced him, or the way she'd felt last night.

"We'll talk of it later. Right now, we need to get started if we plan to reach Victoria's place by mid-night." He looked into her wonderful blue eyes. There was so much to her, the blue seemed endless. The more he learned and understood her, the more he cared.

Without thinking of how little time they had, he lowered his head and kissed her tenderly. The taste of her lips could easily become addictive.

She accepted his kiss willingly, wanting a moment's warmth before the long ride ahead.

When the kiss ended, Wes hesitated.

His hands rested at her waist, but he didn't pull her closer. "About last night." Slowly his hand moved up the front of her dress. "Why did you put my hand . . . here?" His fingers slid over the material covering her breast.

All she had to do was move and his slight touch would be gone. But she didn't even breath. "I . . ."

His hand gently covered her, warming the skin beneath the cloth.

"I wanted to see if it hurt." She fought to catch her breath as he continued touching, pressing enough for her to feel.

"And does it?"

"No," she answered.

"All you have to do, Allie, is step away," he whispered against her ear. "I'm not holding you, only touching you."

She didn't move.

Wes kissed her cheek lightly as he crossed to the center of her dress and began to loosen the buttons.

"Step away," he said against her ear, "and I won't follow."

The buttons tumbled open easily to his touch. He knew there was no time, but he couldn't stop. The memory from the night was too strong.

"All you have to do is back up, and what's happening now will be over between us without another word being said. I'll never touch you again."

She closed her eyes and tried to stand still as he pulled the material away.

"But I want you to feel my touch when I'm awake. I want you to know that I'm here, whenever you want."

His fingers gently lifted her lace strap and pushed it from her shoulder. Then, very slowly, he placed his hand at the base of her throat and lowered his fingers over her flesh.

Allie leaned her head back and let the feel of his hand caress her. She steeled herself for the pain as he explored lower, cupping her breast in his grip. But none came. Only the warmth of his touch.

His free hand gently braced her back as his mouth covered hers. His kiss was hungry, hurried, his touch tender, hesitant. Sensations exploded inside her, shaking her body with the force.

He broke the kiss and stepped back suddenly. "Are you all right?" His brow wrinkled in worry.

Allie staggered forward from the sudden loss of his nearness. "I think so." She placed her hand on his chest, steadying herself. "I never felt anything like that before. My whole body had a fire running through it."

Wes relaxed. "I thought I'd hurt you."

"No," she answered, thinking she'd like to ask him to do it again but unsure she should. She wished there were someone, anyone but Wes, to ask if what he'd just done was right. She knew what the men had done before was wrong. It hurt her, and they made sure no one else saw them. But when Wes touched her, there was no pain, only the warmth. And he'd offered to repeat the action any time as though he were giving her a gift.

"Is it right, for a man to touch a woman so?" She pulled her dress together.

"It's right for a husband to touch a wife as I touched you," Wes answered.

"Then you will touch me so again, tonight?" She passed him and headed for the door. "Is this also done only when we are alone?"

"Yes."

She reached for the door. "Until we are alone tonight." She vanished before he could answer.

Wes braced against the window frame, reminding himself he was her husband in name only. Only to protect her. Only until she found a home. Only til she was out of harm's way.

But if he touched her again tonight, he'd be her husband in more than name.

He told himself he didn't want a wife. He didn't need a wife . . . he could barely feed himself. But from the looks of things, the only one who would stop him was himself. Wes wasn't sure he was strong enough to fight that battle alone.

He was still trying to decide what to do ten hours later as he neared Victoria Catlin's ranch. He'd noticed riders following them a few hours back, but they hadn't drawn closer. If Allie or Jason could have driven the wagon, Wes would have ridden back to take a look. But Allie had her hands full trying to keep the sheriff settled. The old man was well into his second bottle of whiskey by nightfall. The team was too inexperienced for Jason to handle, but the boy was quick to jump out and help guide when the road was muddy.

By the time they were well onto Catlin land, the men following had disappeared. Wes thought maybe they'd just been going in the same direction, but, with his luck, that was doubtful.

When they sighted the ranch headquarters, it was near midnight. No light shone from the fortress, and Wes wondered if they hadn't made a mistake returning. How safe could they be at a headquarters that didn't post a guard at night?

They reached the gate with still no sign of life from inside the wall.

Wes handed Jason the reins and climbed down. The horses were too tired to walk, much less run, so the boy could handle them.

Walking up to the small door on the side of the huge gate, Wes pounded. Once. Twice. No one came.

With a shove he forced open the door that had been locked but not barred. Inside the compound, the night was black. Shadows closed upon shadows, making the blackness complete.

"Hello!" he yelled. "Gideon! Hello!"

A light flickered on from the second floor, then another in the servants' quarters. Footsteps echoed. A door opened somewhere in the blackness.

"Gideon, it's Wes McLain. I brought Sheriff Hardy. He's wounded." Wes waited for an answer.

In the inky blackness, he thought he heard someone tapping down the stairs with a cane.

"Mr. McLain?" A whispered voice drifted around him.

Wes reached for his gun then paused. The voice was only a few feet away.

"Miss Victoria?"

The soft sound of aging laughter drifted to him. "You can't see me? But I can hear your breathing as loud as a drum."

"Where are you?" Wes asked in the general direction of the voice. "It's black as midnight out here."

"It's always black midnight to me." A thin hand touched his sleeve. "Will you take me to Maxwell? I heard you say he was wounded."

Wes helped her through the door. As they walked to the wagon, he tried to explain what had happened.

Victoria held up her hand. "I wish to touch his chest first."

Allie took the woman's withered hand and placed it over Maxwell's heart. "He's still alive." Allie knew the blind woman was testing to make sure.

Victoria smiled as she felt a heartbeat then moved her hands to his face. "He's burning up with fever and long past drunk, from the smell of him. Gideon!"

The stout man appeared at the door, still trying to dress himself. "I'm here, Miss Victoria," he mumbled.

"Of course you are. I heard you coming from the time your feet hit the floor by your bed. Now, unlock the gate. Send a man to town for that quack who calls himself a doctor, and order him to bring plenty of medicine. And tell Katherine to get the study ready to use as a sickroom. Maxwell will be easier to take care of on the first floor."

Gideon looked flustered. "All at once?"

"All at once and right now! I've no time to waste

being questioned or repeating myself. This is Maxwell Hardy we have here.''

Wes almost laughed out loud. Blind and old, she was still quite a woman.

"And you, Mr. McLain, pull the wagon carefully to the main door.'' She grabbed Maxwell's hand. "And don't you worry, Sheriff, I'm not turning loose of you until I see you cared for.''

The place turned into an ant bed of activity. Gideon was shouting orders and pushing everyone who got near him to hurry them along. Torches and lanterns were everywhere, lighting the courtyard and the steps bright as day. Only the wagon moved slowly to the door with Victoria Catlin walking beside it.

Wes lifted Maxwell from the wagon with Jason holding his leg straight out. The sheriff moaned in pain, but he was drowned out by Victoria's rapid fire of endless orders.

They were halfway up the steps when Katherine appeared before them, blocking the doorway like an aging Amazon warrior.

"These are the people who—''

Victoria's cane struck her, none too accidentally, mid-thigh. "Hush, Katherine and get out of the way. I know who these people are, but all that concerns me right now is that Maxwell is hurt. Now you can help or remove yourself from the area. I don't care which.''

Katherine took one look at the sheriff's blood-covered leg and ran for the stairs.

Victoria walked into her house without using the cane. "Put him in the first room, Mr. McLain. And be careful when you pass through the door.''

As Allie followed, Victoria grabbed her arm with strong, bone-thin fingers. "Did you bandage the sheriff and set the leg?''

"Yes,'' Allie answered. "With Jason's help. We did the best we could.''

"Good, then you'll be my eyes.'' She pulled Allie along the hall. "We're going to take the bandages off and check the wound. I don't want someone fainting on me while I do my doctoring. If you've seen it once, the wound will be nothing new to you.''

"You've doctored people?" Jason asked from just behind Victoria.

"I have. I doctored all my husbands through gunfights, steer-gouging, and every other ailment you can think of.''

"Your husbands?" Jason asked. "They're all dead, ain't they?''

Victoria held her chin a fraction higher. "That's beside the point. They all had cleaned wounds when they passed on into the hereafter.''

TWENTY

By dawn, Victoria had learned everyone's name and the sounds they made when they moved, so that she was never surprised with where they were in the room. She kept Allie by her side, making Allie tell what she saw and often asking to feel the stitches or Maxwell's forehead.

The servants stood just outside the door, waiting to be called. And call them Victoria did. She constantly wanted clean water, or more bandages, or wood added to the fire. Once she even demanded a full meal of steak and eggs, then ordered Wes and Jason to eat.

Wes found himself of little help in the makeshift hospital. Instead, he walked the perimeter of the headquarters. Checking for perfect vantage points along the wall. Wes quickly fell back into his military thinking. For the length of the war, all he'd thought about was staying alive. Several times, his preparation had saved not only his life, but the lives of his men.

The headquarters had been built by a military mind, there was no doubt. Thick walls formed a square, with only two openings large enough for a horse and rider to pass. The front gate was barred with an oak log. The other opening could be easily seen and defended from any spot inside the compound.

Wes understood why Sheriff Hardy insisted on this

place. A few men could hold off an army.

Gideon silently relinquished his command of security to Wes, seemingly glad to have the younger man's advice. Keeping an eye on two old women was one thing, protecting a fort from attack with only a handful of servants was another. It didn't take long for Wes to realize Gideon saw himself more as doorman than defender. His chain of command had been from Victoria to the kitchen help, no further.

By midmorning men started arriving, slowly filling the courtyard like migrant birds returning after a hard winter. Old men. Aging fighters who'd fought for the Republic and maybe served a few tours as Rangers during Indian trouble. None looked young enough to have fought for Texas in the War Between the States.

"Who are they, Gideon?" Wes asked as the two men watched thirty visitors milling around below, setting up camp, apparently planning to stay a while.

"Victoria's army. They must have gotten word when we sent for the doctor," Gideon answered calmly, as if his words made sense. "For years, Victoria's ranch has been a place men knew they could come and, no matter how old or stove up, still be treated like a full man. Back in the '30s and '40s Texas was packed with Indian fighters and fortune hunters, outlaws and worn-out lawmen looking for that last time to stand tall."

Gideon looked over the gathering. "As time passed, they either lost what family they had or never married. What's a man to do who's no longer strong in a land where only the strong survive?"

Wes studied the men more closely. A few wore tattered parts of uniforms with pride. Most still carried single-shot rifles and handguns made generations before the Colt. But they stood proud. A waiting army a day away from the grave.

Gideon continued, "A few were Catlin's men from his Army days, others Victoria met over the years. One by one they showed up at the gate, and she insisted on treating them like returning heroes. A few were so down on their luck, they walked through the gate without a horse. Victoria would have a great dinner for them and, in her way, beg them to stay on to protect the ranch. She'd offer a house on the land and a full hand's pay in exchange for their watchful vigilance over the place.''

Wes raised an eyebrow. "You mean this is the Catlin ranch's security?"

Gideon nodded. "I call them the Old Guard. They may be crippled and all used up, but one thing you got to know. To the man, they'd die for Victoria . . . or kill for her."

Wes pushed back from the railing. "Take me to meet these heroes."

As he walked down the stairs, he thought of what happened to a man who had no family when he aged. These men weren't farmers. Their skills had kept them alive long enough to leave them starving when their fists no longer struck hard and their aims wavered. No one else would have hired them. There weren't enough homes to take in orphans, much less the aging loners and warriors. Old women were valued for all they could do to help, but who would value an old buffalo hunter or frontier fighter?

Wes met them one at a time. Listening to their stories, remembering their names. He could see it in their eyes, in the strained hardness of their handshakes. These men were an army. They didn't need a commander. They only needed direction. Each would man his post until the end of his watch.

Wes stepped up on the edge of the fountain and raised his hands. "Thank you for coming so quickly to my aid."

"We didn't come for you!" yelled a barreled-shaped man with gun belts crossing his chest. "We come to protect Miss Victoria."

Several others nodded.

Wes took a deep breath. This wasn't going to be easy. "I've outlined a plan of defense."

"Don't need no plan!" A bald warrior who looked

like he ate men for breakfast grunted. "We know what to do, sonny."

"Yeah," another complained. "We don't need no pup of a Yank telling us nothin'."

"But I was a captain in—" Wes began.

"And I was a colonel when you was still having your mama hold you out the window to drip."

The crowd laughed. These men were loners who balked at suggestions. Who knows, Wes thought, they might shoot at a direct order. He didn't feel like being used in target practice.

Anger boiled in Wes. He needed their help, but his pride wouldn't let him beg, and he'd be a fool to bully. None of them looked like they had a heart anyway. He'd been wasting his time. "Look!" he yelled. "Trouble's coming."

If he'd expected to alarm them, he was greatly disappointed.

"Trouble's always coming!" hollered a one-eyed man who called himself Dillon.

Wes glanced at the man to argue, but found himself trying to decide which side of Dillon's face was uglier— the side with an evil eye staring him down, or the one with a sunken socket.

"Trouble's my middle name," Slone, the one whose bullets hung in an X across his chest, answered. "I'm already here."

"I've been itching for a fight so bad I done scratched to the bone," another shouted. "If there's gonna be fighting, ain't nobody better kill them all before I get my shot."

Several agreed that, if they were attacked, each man only got to kill one until every man had had a turn. Each suddenly seemed to feel the need to describe a killing he'd participated in.

"Young fellow, you go on in with the women," ordered the one who called himself a colonel. "We'll take this watch."

Wes fought the urge to slug a man old enough to be

his grandfather. In the army, the bars on Wes's shoulders had always won him respect. But now, he didn't have the time to figure out how to unite them. They began moving away, talking in small groups, paying no more attention to him.

Wes felt a small hand slip into his. He looked down into Allie's tired blue eyes. He'd left her asleep in a chair. Sleep still drifted across her face, along with worry.

"What's wrong?" He guided her onto the step.

"The sheriff is asking for you." She didn't turn loose of his hand. When she moved beside him, her body brushed his.

Wes nodded in response to her request, but for a moment he just wanted to be near. And from the way she leaned against him, he guessed she wanted the same thing. All night, he'd watched her work beside Victoria. The only time he'd touched her had been when he'd covered her up after she'd fallen asleep.

Every time he'd entered the room, his gaze had been drawn to her, as if he had to locate her before the world was in balance.

"I missed you," he whispered next to her ear.

"I've been right here," she answered.

His free hand cupped her chin, and he turned her face to the sun. "Not near enough."

Just as he lowered his lips to hers, he heard it. Silence. Wes froze, an inch away from her mouth. Slowly, he turned his head.

Every man in the place silently stared at Allie.

He felt her fear. Her grip on his fingers tightened. She moved closer, as if she could vanish against him.

"What is it?" he snapped, angry that they'd frightened her. In truth, he'd forgotten the "Old Guard" the minute she'd touched his hand.

But none of them answered. Several removed hats. A few walked closer without taking their gaze off Allie. One even scrubbed his eyes with the back of a dirty hand as if trying to improve his sight.

"They see it," Gideon whispered from behind Wes. "They all do. They see Victoria reflected in her face."

Wes leaned down. "It's all right," he said to Allie. "You've nothing to be afraid of."

She straightened. "I'm not afraid." Her grip didn't lessen on his hand, but the touch of stubbornness was back.

Wes faced the army. "Gentlemen," he almost choked on the word, "I'd like you to meet Allie, my wife. We need your help protecting her and the others here within these walls."

The man who'd said he'd been a colonel marched toward Wes. "Luther Ashford Attenbury, reporting for assignment." His words were for Wes, but his gaze never left Allie's face.

He drew a saber from his waist and saluted Allie in true cavalry style.

The one-eyed man was next. He tipped his slouch hat and mumbled, "Dillon, ma'am. My folks were too poor to give me two names. Just Dillon. I'm at your service. All you have to do is call."

One by one, the others followed, most using titles that had prefaced their names years ago. A marshal, a sergeant, a scout, a captain.

There was no need for Allie to comment. They were not meeting her, only pledging allegiance to her with their introductions.

Wes helped her down from the fountain ledge and walked toward the house. He knew he'd have no trouble with passing out assignments when he returned. Their love for Victoria spilled over to Allie.

He walked past Katherine as he entered the hallway. "You two will not get away with passing her off as my sister's granddaughter." Her words were layered in hate.

"I'm not trying to get away with anything. Allie doesn't want the Catlin money. You and Michael can have it all when the old woman dies, provided she doesn't outlive you both," he shouted over his shoulder as he hurried to reach Hardy. "Just stay out of my way."

Katherine didn't have time for rebuttal. She stopped at the doorway as though she'd been banned from the sickroom. Her brittle frame stood rigid a moment, looking as though she might storm the place, then she vanished.

Victoria raised her head at the sound of Wes's footsteps. "Mr. McLain. Maxwell wishes to talk to you."

Without the use of a cane, Victoria moved away from the bed that had been made on a couch.

Wes knelt on one knee. "Maxwell?"

The old man smiled. "Thanks for bringing me." His voice barely passed his lips. "Allie will be safe here. There's no way into the compound unless someone unbolts a door from the inside. With a few guns you could hold off an attack."

Wes agreed.

"You met the Old Guard?"

"I met them."

"Good, make sure one of them is at every entrance every hour, night and day. Let no other take a watch. Trust none but the Old Guard. There are several young hands I saw around when we came last time that I don't know."

"I already figured that out. I'll keep them busy with the horses." Wes had thought he'd have to use the male servants for a turn at watch. But once he saw Victoria's army, he'd changed his mind.

"Michael won't come, but he might send someone. There are enough men out of work who'll do anything for a price, even kill a woman. Keep Allie by your side whenever she isn't in this room."

Maxwell patted his side. "I got Allie to put my pistol right here. If anyone should get this close, he'll never leave the room." Even injured, the sheriff hadn't lost sight of his mission. "With the doors open I have a clear view of the hallway and stairs."

"I'll station the guards, then I'm going to get a few

hours' sleep.'' Nights without rest started to catch up to Wes. ''It could be a long night ahead.''

Hardy touched his arm. ''Tell Jason to find Crandall Cutler. He likes kids more than most and loves to talk about horses. He'll keep the boy busy and safe.''

''Thanks.'' Wes glanced at Jason sitting in the windowsill.

The boy nodded and hurried out, thankful to have been freed.

Thirty minutes later, Wes asked Victoria if she had a place he could bed down for a while. The old woman hadn't said a word about the possibility of Allie truly being her granddaughter, but he'd learned there was little the blind woman missed.

''The second room off the stairs has been made ready for you and Allie.'' Victoria sat beside Maxwell while he slept, showing no sign of needing to rest herself. ''The door next to mine.''

Wes climbed the stairs, too tired to think about anything but closing his eyes. He didn't bother striking a light when he noticed the windows were closed and shuttered. He pulled off his gun belt and boots. Now, while Victoria's army was fresh, would be a good time to sleep. He figured if an advance came, it would probably be in the night hours. Michael seemed the type.

Stretching out on the quilt, Wes folded an arm over his eyes to block the thin rays of sun shining through the shutters. All he needed to do was let out a breath and he'd be sound asleep.

''Wes?'' Allie whispered from the doorway. ''The sheriff told me to stay close to you. Can I stay in here?''

He stretched out his arm in welcome. ''Come along, Blue Eyes.''

He'd expected her to slip into bed as she always did, quietly. He'd noticed a small step stool had been put on her side to make climbing onto the high bed easier. But she jumped forward in a mighty leap, tumbling against him as she bounced.

Opening his eyes, he laughed. "You're a hard woman to get in bed."

"I've been waiting to be alone with you. You should have told me you were coming up to our room. I would have followed."

He leaned back against the pillows. "I didn't figure you'd be too tired, the way you were curled up in that overstuffed chair for several hours early this morning."

"I'm not sleepy." She sat cross-legged beside him and wiggled until she felt comfortable.

Wes opened his eyes once more, thinking he was getting to the point of being too tired to hear. If she wasn't sleepy, why was she here?

Allie sat facing him, calmly unbuttoning her blouse. "I've been waiting for you to touch me again. You said you would."

She had the nerve to look like she requested a favor. Her huge eyes stared at him, as if she were bracing herself to be disappointed. "You will, won't you? Touch me like you did before we left the station? You said we could do it when we were alone."

Wes's blood pumped from dead-tired slow to full gallop in one heartbeat. All he could do was stare as the top of her dress fell away. He told himself he had to stay alert to protect her, and in order to do that, he needed a little sleep. But he could see the outline of her entire body as she slipped from her dress. The undergarments were wrinkled from having been pressed against her and now, even without the dress, held their place.

"Would you like me to take off more?" she asked as though trying to encourage him to keep his promise. "I don't mind you watching me undress now that I know that's the way it is between husband and wife."

He couldn't believe what she said. He must already be dreaming. He found it impossible to fathom that all night, while he'd been pacing, she'd been thinking of asking him to touch her again.

Raising his hand, he lowered first one of her straps,

then the other. The camisole draped over her breasts lightly, threatening to fall at any moment. The sight was intoxicating. He wet his lips and took great pleasure in just watching her breathe.

She waited.

"Why are you doing this?" he whispered as his fingers brushed over the soft flesh at her throat.

"I have to learn not to be afraid."

He moved his hand lower. She drew in a breath. Her chin lifted slightly with determination.

Her action strained the material, outlining the peak of each breast beneath the lace. *This is too good to be a dream*, Wes thought. Studying her closely, he tried to understand.

He saw it then, in the set of her eyes and the carriage of her body. She was testing the limits. Like a man taking one more step into a lion's cage each day. Being near him was her way of conquering her fears.

Wes rose to his elbow and brushed her mouth with his thumb, pulling slightly so that her lips parted. He wanted her not to be afraid, but he needed her to want him. She meant more to him than any woman ever had in his life, but he wasn't sure what he meant to her. Sure, she turned to him when she needed him. But did she want him?

There was no doubt he wanted her. Lord, how he wanted her. She'd been like a flash flood that washed over him all at once when he wasn't even expecting it. A few days ago, he would have been happy to help her and let her go on her way. But now, looking at her like this stirred something deep inside him. She didn't even know the games played between men and women. She didn't have to.

The thin layer of cotton and lace slipped beneath the left side of her breast, and Wes no longer breathed, much less thought.

He leaned forward and kissed her peak lightly, then shoved the material away to her waist with only the tips of his fingers.

Her chest rose and fell rapidly, but she didn't pull away. His light touch made every nerve alive. Barely brushing her flesh, he allowed his fingers to drift from her waist to her throat. She closed her eyes, wanting the full press of his hand against her, but waiting. If he wanted to lightly touch her first, she could wait for the warmth.

Lying back against his pillow, Wes watched her. Again, he lightly brushed her skin from waist to chin, only this time, he slowed to circle the borders of each breast.

Allie let out a cry.

"Did I hurt you?" His voice was low and thick with a hunger.

"No," she whispered, out of breath. "It didn't hurt. Again, please."

Yes, he could take his time in the touching, she thought, for he made her feel treasured. She sat very still and allowed him to continue.

His fingers circled her breasts once more then moved upward, brushing her mouth open with his touch.

She closed her eyes, feeling his thumb press against her bottom lip and his fingers caress her face. Then his hand moved downward, brushing her throat. As his fingers closed gently over her breast, Allie straightened slightly.

"You're beautiful, Allie," he whispered as he circled lightly over the tip of one breast.

"Come to me, Allie." He placed his hands behind his head, letting her know this would be her advance, not his.

For a long while, she didn't move. Then, very slowly, she leaned over him, kissing him fully. As before, the taste of him blended with the smells that always surrounded him, giving her a sense of safety and warmth.

Wes fought the urge to reach for her as she played with his lips until she coaxed just the kiss she wanted from him. Dear Lord, the way she kissed him was perfection. But he allowed her to end the kiss.

Hesitantly, she raised above him until the tip of her breast touched his lips. She shook with uncertainty, but she offered freely.

His hands moved along her rib cage, holding her tenderly just above him. The feel of her flesh in his hands blended with the taste of her breast moving with each breath against his tongue to explode his mind in senses.

He sampled her fully, enjoying the way she paused timidly but didn't turn away. Her heart quickened as he circled her flesh with his mouth while he stroked her sides with his hands.

A sigh escaped her. She leaned away long enough to offer him the other breast. As his mouth savored new flesh, his hand crossed over her damp breast and the warmth of his palm pushed slightly into her softness.

Fire shot through her, jolting her with a pleasure she never dreamed existed.

She pulled away suddenly, drawing back from indulgence into too much joy. Crossing her arms over her chest, she sat in the center of the bed.

"What's wrong?" Wes rubbed his face as though he too were being dropped too quickly into reality. He rose beside her.

"Nothing." She looked down. "I just never felt anything like that before. I never knew anyone, anywhere could feel like you make me feel just now." She closed her eyes, trying to force her thoughts into words. "I'm burning up inside. You give me such great pleasure and ask nothing in return. It is not a fair bargain."

Wes laughed and brushed her hair over her shoulder. "You don't understand. It is you who bring me great pleasure." His arm slipped around her shoulder. He pulled her with him to the pillows. "I thought you knew." He couldn't believe she thought he was somehow giving her joy when he felt nothing.

He didn't wait to be asked this time. He rolled on his side and kissed her. As his tongue parted her lips, his hand moved over her breast, warming her with his touch. When she was breathless, he broke the kiss. "It's you who, by allowing me to touch and taste such beauty, pleases me." He had to make her understand. "You let me feel paradise in my hand. I'll be happy to touch you whenever you like, I swear."

As she relaxed in his arms, his kisses grew deeper, his touch bolder. She could feel his heart pounding against her chest. His actions went from being smooth and practiced to being suddenly jerky.

He stopped, burying his face in the pillow.

"Again," she ordered, holding him to his word. She had not had her fill of this pleasure. "Touch me, please."

Swearing beneath his breath, he rolled onto his back and forced himself not to look at her.

Allie leaned against him. The top of her camisole had disappeared amidst the covers. "Is it over? You will do no more? I thought you enjoyed it. More, please."

Wes didn't look at her. "There is more, Allie, far more. Other places I can touch you. Other places I'd like to touch you."

"But I like this."

"Yes, but there is more to what we're doing." Wes took in air as if knowledge would somehow come with it. He was a fighter, never a lover. How was he supposed to explain the facts of life to a woman walking around with the most perfectly built body he'd ever seen, much less touched? How could he tell her that her polite begging for more was driving him insane?

"How? Where would you touch?"

Without a word, he moved his hand from her chest down. As his fingers slipped over the thin cotton of her underwear and pressed between her legs, she understood.

Allie shoved herself from the bed as if the covers were afire. "No!" She picked up her dress and held it over her, ashamed of him seeing her for the first time. "No!"

Wes felt like an idiot. There must have been some other way to tell her. Maybe he could have just kept kissing her and touching her until it happened. No, that didn't make sense. At some point, she'd become frightened and he'd be so far lost in the paradise of her body he might accidentally scare her before he could stop.

"Allie. It's a part of loving. As much a part as the kissing and touching. It's what man and wife do."

"No!" she screamed. "Never! You will never touch me there!" Tears fell unchecked. "I know the pain. Never!"

She looked at him with hate and fear and terror back in her eyes. As if she might bolt and run. As if she might pull her knife and try to kill him at any moment. As if she wished him dead.

"Allie." He fought his own battles. They'd come so far, and now they were back to where they started. "Allie. Have I ever hurt you?"

"No," she answered.

"Do you trust me? Do you sleep beside me and know that I will bring you no harm?"

"Yes."

"Then trust me now. I'll do nothing until you are ready. Until you want it. Until it's the right time." He made himself relax on the bed, even though every part of his body wanted to grab her and pull her to him and make her understand.

"Now, get back in bed," he ordered in a far gruffer tone than he meant. "There is nothing to be afraid of."

She didn't move for a long while. Then slowly, she placed her dress back in place over the chair and slipped into the bed. She spread out beside him no longer soft and ready for his embrace, but stiff and cold as stone.

"It will never be the right time," she finally said. "You will never touch me there."

"Go to sleep." Wes locked his hands behind his head and stared at the ceiling. *Never* suddenly took on a sound lonelier than any he'd ever heard.

TWENTY-ONE

Wes PACED THE TEN-FOOT WIDOW'S WALK ON THE roof above the second floor. He could see for miles across the rolling land and anyone out there could probably see him.

"Go ahead and shoot me," he mumbled toward the open range. "I'm too much a fool to live."

Ten minutes ago he'd walked away from a beautiful woman sleeping almost nude next to him. At the rate things were going, he'd probably never sleep again. There must be a kind of madness that comes with never resting. But he couldn't lie in bed with Allie and not touch her. And if he touched her, he'd want more. And if he took more, she'd hate him. And if she hated him, she wouldn't have to kill him, he'd kill himself. After, of course, Victoria's aging army took turns shooting him.

Wes got dizzy thinking about it.

He looked out onto land withering in winter. "Shoot me now and save air!" he yelled. "Go ahead! Take your time and aim. Make sure you hit my heart, because God knows I don't have a brain. A bullet to the skull would just rattle around in a vacant shell." What kind of man explains the art of loving by putting his hand between a woman's legs?

He should have said . . . oh, hell, what difference did

it make what he should have said? At least she hadn't wasted words. She'd told him exactly what was *not* going to happen in their relationship.

He was madder than hell and so proud of her at the same time. A few weeks ago, she would have done anything he said, no matter how much it hurt her. But she'd found the pride this morning to tell him what she wanted and didn't want. The tiny little half-pint of a woman was growing stronger by the minute. But instead of thanking him for her newfound courage, she was threatening him. The woman had no gratitude in her soul.

He paced, telling himself he was never meant for love. She needed someone different. Someone sensitive. Someone patient. Not a soldier. A loner. A man who's grumpy on his good days. Even when he'd paid women, he couldn't remember thinking he'd been all that great a lover. And now he'd tried to teach Allie. If it weren't so ridiculous, it might be humorous.

Wes told himself that he was the kind of man who did best with a woman of the night. A woman he didn't feel the need to remember her name. He wasn't made to have to think about anything but the business at hand. He didn't want to feel in his heart.

He couldn't teach her of the art between a woman and a man. He'd never taken the time to learn. Somehow, he missed that lesson in school, or life, or wherever a man is supposed to learn how to make love to a woman. It was obvious he'd missed them, he didn't even know where the lessons were taught.

Wes stopped and widened his stance, as if facing a firing squad. All he could do was protect her. He was good at that. If he did more, he'd be the harm that came her way.

The trapdoor behind him rattled. Victoria Catlin stepped out onto the flat walkway.

"Miss Victoria?" Wes couldn't believe what he saw. Not only blind, but frail and crippled with age, she walked into the sun like it was not only her right but her duty to do so.

"Stop looking at me like I'm a fool," she snapped.

Wes laughed. "How do you know how I'm looking at you? You're blind."

"Of course I am. I don't need reminding, young man. But even blind, I can guess how a man looks at me. Always have been able to. When I was young, I could read what men were thinking as clear as if they were shouting from the rooftops." She took a step and reached for his arm.

He offered his support.

"Which in your case is no great feat since you're up here doing exactly that."

Wes couldn't help but like the old woman. Victoria was full of vinegar and meaner than a two-headed rattler, but she had a point. "Should you be up here?"

"I've been coming up here for fifty years. I like the feel of the sun on my face by day and the nearness to heaven by night."

"So you came up for some sun?"

"Of course not." She slapped his arm. "I came up to talk to you. I have a few questions."

"If it's about Allie, she doesn't need your money. As soon as it's safe, we'll be out of your hair. We only came back because of Hardy."

"Stop trying to answer before I give the questions. That's always been a habit of men that has pestered me from time to time."

"Yes, ma'am."

"Maxwell told me how you found Allie tied in a cage and what, he guessed, she'd been through before you came along."

"She can handle it." Wes felt somehow disloyal to Allie talking about her. "It's none of your concern."

"Of course she can handle it," Victoria said. "But the question is, can you?"

For a moment, he thought she was looking directly at him as she repeated, "Can you handle all that's happened to the girl?"

Wes fought the urge to turn and run. He didn't want

to talk about Allie with anyone, much less some withered-up old woman who wouldn't claim her for a grandchild.

"I don't have to handle anything. I promised to see her safely home. That's all. Since this isn't her home, I'll search until I find another."

"And if her home is by your side?"

"She doesn't want that."

"Doesn't she?" Victoria's hand tightened on his arm. "Are you sure?"

Wes could only guess at how much the old woman heard from her bedroom next to theirs. She seemed to hear everything that was said in the house. He hardened his jaw, forcing the truth out. "She doesn't want me. I'm sure about that."

"If you believe that, Wes McLain, then you are a fool and someone does need to shoot you right now and put you out of your misery."

"I don't know how . . ." He couldn't say the words. How does a man admit he never bothered to learn how to love?

"Of course you don't. No man does. Believe me, I've had enough men to prove the theory."

Her voice softened. "All you have to do is open your arms. She'll show you the way. I had to teach every one of my husbands everything. A woman feels deep down in her gut what's right. She'll let you know when it's time."

Wes couldn't tell her that it wasn't that way between Allie and him. They weren't meant to be lovers. He wasn't even sure how it happened. Allie wasn't the kind of wife he needed and he sure wasn't the kind of husband for her.

Victoria pulled at his arm. "Get me off this roof, young man. What kind of fool takes a blind woman up to the roof?"

"At least we agree on one thing: I'm a fool."

"Don't let it bother you. Half the population has the

same problem." She carefully lowered herself down the ladder steps.

Without another word, she walked down the hallway and disappeared into her room.

Wes watched her go. She measured her steps so that she didn't have to touch a wall to know where she needed to turn.

He didn't see Victoria again until nightfall, when she took her turn at Maxwell's side. Jason gladly gave up the watch. Wes had told the boy he could sleep with the army tonight. Hardy had been right, the man called Cutler was full of horse stories. Jason thought it a great honor, but Wes knew that if Michael came, his two targets would be Hardy and Allie, and Jason would be safest away from them. Plus, the men would take care of him if any trouble did come riding in.

Wes had walked the grounds so many times he felt he could do it blind as easily as Victoria did. He'd checked and rechecked each of the doors opening out. The main gate was bolted with a log it took two men to lift. The two side doors framing the main gate had double guards to keep each other awake. The corral doors and barn were the least fortified, so Wes put not only guards, but most of the sleeping army along that wall.

There was also a small door off the kitchen and another by the well. Both were old solid doors with thick bolts. Anyone breaking them down would make enough noise to wake up everyone in the headquarters.

At sunset, Wes sat across from Allie and ate a few bites of supper. He couldn't think of anything to say, and she never wasted conversation. Someone had placed a stack of clothes on their bed. She now wore a soft blue dress that fit her as though it had been made for her. It was simple, with old-fashioned lines but made of fine-quality material and workmanship. The dress molded to her body perfectly, showing off the balance as Nichole's clothes could never do.

Wes shoved his plate away. "I like the dress." He'd finally thought of something to say.

Allie didn't answer.

"I like the way you've done your hair, too." She'd let one of the housekeepers tie the sides back, leaving it down, but no longer in her face.

She stared at her plate.

"Allie, are you ever going to talk to me again?" He tried to keep the anger from his voice.

She looked up at him. The dress made her eyes even bluer.

"I thought you were mad at me." She studied him carefully. "Are you?"

"Hell . . . I mean, no. I'm not mad at you." He leaned toward her, hoping no one else listened. "When this is over, we need to talk. I feel like someone poked a stick in me and stirred up all my insides."

She stood without a word and moved next to his chair. "I know how you feel." Her hand stroked his hair as though she'd been longing to touch him for hours.

He didn't react as her touch grew bolder.

She was doing it again, he thought. Proving she wasn't afraid of him, testing, pushing the limit. Her fingers combed through his hair once more and he circled her waist with his arm, pulling her onto his lap.

"Say it, Allie," he insisted. "Say you want me near. That I didn't make you so afraid of me you never want to set eyes on me again."

"I want you near," she answered a little breathlessly.

He didn't kiss her, although the need to do so washed over him like flood water. He only stared at her, hoping she could read his feelings as easily as he could read hers.

She leaned against his chest and allowed him to hold her.

A moment later, he heard footsteps and lifted her up. When he stood her on her feet, his hand spread out across her back to steady her.

"I like the dress," he commented as though their conversation had just started.

Gideon hurried to the table as Allie whispered, "I'm glad."

Their talk was at an end. Wes pulled himself back to the problems at hand. He knew he would not see her again or have a chance to talk with her until the night was over. But somehow in the few words they'd said, they'd made a peace.

Gideon drew him back to reality.

Just after midnight, Wes made the rounds again. He took his time, even stopping to visit with the one-eyed man called Dillon at the door near the kitchen, though the man was still short on being friendly and long on being irritating.

At least in the dark he looked better, Wes thought as he returned to the house. It would have to be a moonless night at the bottom of a well before that man would ever find a woman to couple with.

Wes swore. With two eyes, he was doing little better.

Walking the ten feet to the kitchen door, he stepped inside, deciding he needed more coffee to stay awake. He was halfway through his second cup when Dillon clambered in.

"I'm here," he grumbled. "What's so all-fired important?"

Wes stood, smelling trouble. "Why'd you leave your post?"

"Miss Katherine said Miss Victoria sent for me. Said you had a dangerous job only I might be able to do. Katherine brought two replacements. Slone and one of the stable hands."

Wes grabbed his rifle and ran for the door, almost knocking Dillon out of the way.

"Wait just a—!" Dillon shouted as he grabbed Wes's collar.

"I didn't send for you!" Wes jerked free.

Realization dawned in the old man's one eye. "Hell's fury!" Dillon breathed the war cry in like liquid rage. He swelled up, shoved Wes hard, and ran from the room. The old soldier had only been gone from his post for a minute, maybe two, but it might have been a minute too long.

Wes was a step behind him when they stumbled over the body of the huge bald man. The gun belts across his chest had done him no good. He'd been stabbed in the back.

The moon through the open side door reflected off the dead man's blood.

Gunshots rang from the barn area.

Dillon rose and took a step toward the noise.

"No!" Wes shouted. "There hasn't been time for more than a few to cross through the door. Let the others take care of anyone near the barn. You get to the front gate and warn the men to stay put. If several are within the compound, they'll have to open the gate to let more in. The main entrance would be the fastest way to enter."

Dillon nodded.

Shots volleyed again from the barn.

Wes closed the open door, bolted it once more, and ran for the house. He wasn't sure how many rats were inside, but one thing he knew. At least one of them would be headed straight for the study and Maxwell Hardy.

Allie jumped from her chair at the sound of gunfire. She was halfway across the room before she realized she wasn't in the middle of a raid. Everything looked exactly as it had since she'd arrived. Maxwell was resting with Victoria by his side. All was still around her.

But Victoria's head turned toward Allie. "You heard it, didn't you, child?" she whispered.

"Gunfire."

"Gunfire." She motioned for Allie to move closer. "Maxwell told me you'd been in raids. Well, if this is what I think it is, I'm facing a raid on my place and no one, *no one* invades my home and lives."

She stood slowly and paced her way to the corner of the room without touching any furnishings. "Once during an Indian uprising, I found the perfect place to hide. In plain sight." She pointed up, toward the top of an eight-foot bookshelf framed into both sides of the wall. "It's an easy climb. Go, child, we've no time."

"But . . ." Allie couldn't leave Victoria and Maxwell alone.

"You're the one they've come to kill." Victoria pushed her toward the shelves. "We'll be safe enough. Now go and don't come down until it's safe."

Allie placed her hands and feet on the polished wood and climbed as easily as if it had been a ladder. Once she reached the top, she spread out across the dusty wood, melting into the ceiling shadows.

She felt like an observer, no longer part of the room. Victoria seemed very small from this height.

The old woman returned to her chair and lightly brushed her hand along Maxwell's arm. Several rounds of gunfire exploded from the direction of the barn.

"Maxwell," she said simply, "we take to arms."

The old sheriff opened his eyes and winked at her as though she could see. "I'm ready, Victoria." He patted her hand. "Is the girl safe?"

"She's safe."

Neither one of them showed any surprise when the door shattered open with a loud, cracking sound. An instant later, Maxwell's gun fired, as did the intruder's.

Allie watched the sheriff jerk backward onto the couch, his side splattered in blood. The intruder stumbled forward a few steps before falling dead. Only one drop of crimson marked a wound on his forehead.

The old sheriff whispered Victoria's name before letting the gun slip from his hand onto the covers at his side.

Victoria grabbed his hand. "Don't you dare die on me, Maxwell." She stood slowly without releasing her grip on his hand. "Katherine," she called toward the door. "You can come out now."

To Allie's amazement, Katherine stepped past the shattered door. Just behind her stood a man dressed in black. He wore his hat low and walked with a swagger of one who thought himself above such surroundings. He was the man Allie had seen mornings ago. Michael. He advanced, using his aunt as a shield.

"Who is that with you?" Victoria asked. "I hear another crawling behind you like a snake."

"Don't you recognize your own son?" Katherine snapped. "Has it been so many years you'd forget the sound of his footsteps?"

Victoria's face softened for a moment. "Michael, I thought you'd never come home."

"I didn't, Mother. I came to take what's mine before you give it away. You've dominated everything and everyone in your life for years. But you never could dominate me. Not even with your slave-dog, Hardy, to keep tracking me down. I took my freedom years ago, and now I've come back to take what belongs to me."

Allie watched. He raised his weapon.

"Good-bye, Mother!" He said the last word with pure hate in his tone.

Victoria stood like a ruling queen before him. She didn't look surprised or even hurt by his words. She silently accepted a fate she'd known would come with the same courage with which she'd faced all problems in her life.

Just as Michael drew his mother into his gun sight, a shot rang out from the hallway, hitting him full in the chest. Blood splattered over the fine lace tablecloths and handmade cushions as he fell.

"You've killed him!" Katherine screamed as she dropped with Michael to the floor. She tried to break his fall, but her body was too frail.

Victoria didn't move as Wes stormed the room, his gun still aimed at Michael as though the man in black might yet rally to fight.

"Are you all right, Victoria?" Wes yelled.

She nodded slightly.

"And Allie? And the sheriff?" Wes advanced, laying his weapon down when he saw Hardy's wound.

Before Victoria could answer, Katherine screamed a full war cry. "Who cares about them? They're nothing! Michael's been shot. Victoria, McLain's killed your last son."

The old blind woman blinked back tears, not allowing them to fall. "I know. It had to be done, and I couldn't have pulled the trigger. He was rotten from childhood. By the time he could talk I knew something was twisted in his soul. He hated me for everything I ever did to help him. Just as he hated Maxwell."

"Well, a man like McLain is not getting away with killing one of *my* kin." Katherine rose with Michael's gun in her hand. "A life for a life, that's what the Good Book says."

Wes jumped for his Colt as twin blasts shattered the room. For a moment he froze, surprised he felt no pain. Then Katherine crumbled, her body falling protectively over Michael's. Her blood blended with his on the multicolored rug.

Victoria calmly laid Maxwell's gun back at his side and walked slowly to her sister. Her steps were not as sure as they had been. She felt her way, stretching her hands low in front of her, searching for her sister.

The tip of Victoria's boot touched the bundled fabric of Katherine's dress. She knelt, pulling Katherine into her arms, holding the wounded woman to her chest.

"Why?" Victoria whispered. "Why'd you unlock the gate, Katherine?"

"It wasn't—"

"Of course it was. Don't lie to me now. I stood just above the kitchen door listening to the swish of your skirts. Nothing sounds like your skirts moving about the place. I should have yelled to warn Wes and the guard, but I couldn't believe you'd truly open us up for attack."

Neither of the old women seemed aware of the action going on around them. Their world was only one another. They didn't notice Wes calling for Allie and then helping her down from the shelves.

Katherine gripped her side in pain as her face twisted

with hatred. "All right. I opened the door. I let Michael in. I couldn't let you give everything away to a little tramp of a girl who lived wild like a savage. Michael has always had a man in Austin watching for her to surface. He thought he took care of her when she was given to a preacher who swore he'd take her north and keep her caged. But McLain didn't mind his own business, then Hardy interfered when the preacher failed."

Victoria moved her hands gently over her sister's cheek. "Michael wanted the ranch that badly?"

"Bad enough to kill anyone who got in his way. Including you, dear sister." Katherine almost spit the words.

"But why you?" Victoria asked. "Did you hate me so much?"

Shots continued outside. Wes ordered Allie to do what she could for the sheriff and Katherine, then vanished through the window with both Colts drawn.

Katherine's voice weakened. "Yes," she choked out the words, "you've always had everything. The love of many men, children, wealth. I've had nothing. Nothing."

Victoria cradled her sister. "But you had my love."

"I didn't want your love." Her words were only a faint whisper now. "I wanted your life."

Victoria rocked her little sister to sleep with the same lullaby she'd used when they were children. She'd lost her Michael years ago. She'd only been hanging on to memories and hope. But she'd lost her sister tonight.

Allie watched her, not knowing how to help. Victoria was in a world of darkness now without a guide.

Though gunfire still sounded outside, in the study all was quiet.

TWENTY-TWO

THE GUNFIGHT FINALLY STOPPED. TORCHES AND lanterns were lit in the courtyard. All told, seven men had passed through the door. And seven men, including Michael, lay dead . . . along with three of Victoria's army.

Wes checked Hardy's wounds and hurried back toward Allie. He'd sent Gideon and Jason on ahead to see if the sheriff was still alive, but Wes held little hope.

"McLain!" yelled the guard manning the main gate as Wes reached the center of the courtyard. "More riders coming in fast. Do we fire?"

By now, the moon was up, giving any man a clear shot from the level of the gate. Snakes, like Michael's men, would be holding to the shadows.

"No!" Wes climbed the ladder to the lookout post. "Stand ready, but let them come closer."

He looked into the night. Three riders sliced the distance between them and the headquarters. Wes could tell by the way they handled their mounts they were experienced horsemen who'd spent most of their lives in the saddle. As they neared, he shouldered his rifle, holding his call to fire until they were nearer.

Their hats were low, their dusters flying in the night like huge capes. If men could truly ride the wind, these three appeared to be doing just that. A bag bounced on the side of one rider's saddle—a medical bag.

Suddenly Wes lowered his weapon and jumped from his post. "Hold your fire!" he shouted. "Open the gates!"

For a moment, the guards stood staring.

"Open the gates!" Wes ordered again. "Let my brothers in!"

Dust flew as the men rode through the gates and pulled their powerful animals to a stop.

Daniel jumped down first. "We heard shots!" He spotted Wes and rushed toward him. "Is everyone all right?"

Wes slapped his little brother on the shoulders. "Showed up a little late, preacher. The fighting's all over."

Adam swung from his saddle, unstrapping his medical bag as he moved. "We came as soon as we could. The sheriff in Brady didn't know where you'd gone, but the doc said he'd been out here and seen you and Allie."

The huge hairy man who made up the trio remained in his saddle. "My housekeeper telegraphed that you might need us. You're not an easy man to track down, Wes McLain." His voice was loud and deep, like a rumbling river. "'Course, I had to go to Fort Worth first. You Yanks can't bring a McLain into this world without me. I'm getting to be a regular midwife . . . even if this one did jump out of Nichole so fast Adam barely had time to catch it."

"Welcome, Wolf," Wes laughed as he motioned his brothers up the stairs. "And what do we share? A nephew, or a niece?"

"A niece. But don't worry, I'll teach her to ride and shoot just like I did my Nick." Wolf shook his head, as though to say he had his work cut out for him as an uncle.

"Adam, you'll need your bag." Wes motioned with his head toward the house. "We have one man down. As soon as he's taken care of, I want every detail of the new McLain, except the birthing, of course."

Wolf grabbed the reins of Daniel's and Adam's mounts. "I'll see to the horses. I'll get there in time for the bandaging or the burying. I'd just as soon miss the doctoring."

The three McLain brothers walked through the double doors, shoulder to shoulder. Wes wasted little time with introductions as Adam went to work on the sheriff. Daniel helped Wes clear out the bodies of Michael and his gunman. Victoria insisted her sister be taken upstairs to her own room so that she could be properly dressed.

Wes saw to all that had to be done, then dozed in the chair as Adam continued to work on Hardy. He couldn't explain the peace he felt at having Adam, Daniel, and Wolf with him. He now had someone to cover his back if there was more trouble.

He slept while Allie helped Adam. Wolf and Daniel bedded down outside with the men, and Jason watched, fascinated by every stitch Adam made. The boy finally had a real doctor he could put questions to—and he appeared to have been storing them up for years.

At dawn, Victoria walked behind Michael's casket to the family graveyard. She listened without emotion as Daniel said the last words and prayed. She didn't move from her place until she heard the thud of the box hit bottom. Then, she raised her hand to Gideon's arm and they walked back to the house not saying a word.

An hour later, she made the same journey behind Katherine's casket. This time, tears flowed from her eyes. Victoria didn't wipe them away or try to hide her sorrow.

By midmorning, the marshal had come from town to collect the bodies of Michael's men. He didn't bother asking too many questions. Most, he said, he recognized as troublemakers from as far back as he'd pinned on a badge. As far as he was concerned Wes and Victoria's Old Guard had done the state a favor.

He also brought news of a stranger asking questions about a woman who fit Allie's description. The marshal hadn't been too loose with information, because the stranger claimed Allie was being held against her will. The lawman wasn't certain about Wes, but half the town remembered seeing Allie in the restaurant. He had twenty witnesses who would swear the little lady didn't appear to be in bondage when she kissed her husband in front of half the town. Also, he knew Victoria would tolerate no such thing at her ranch.

At exactly noon, three more dead were delivered to the cemetery. Fallen warriors. Wolf, Allie, and the McLains stood beside Victoria as her men were given a full military funeral. Republic of Texas flags draped the coffins and a full-gun salute resounded in the countryside.

When they returned to the house, Victoria and Jason took their meals beside a still-breathing Maxwell. The McLains congregated in the kitchen.

Wolf related every detail of the birth of his niece, ending with how Nichole ordered them all out to help Wes so she could get some rest. She swore if they didn't ride to his aid within the day, that she would do so herself.

The men laughed, marveling at how easily a woman ran their lives. Adam even told a story of May, Daniel's wife. The healing from her death had begun, and the memories were no longer so painful to voice. The way the McLains treasured their women hung thick in the room.

When Allie entered, the men fell silent, self-conscious of a woman seeing such vulnerability. They all watched her as she filled her bowl and joined them at the table.

After several minutes of silence, Daniel could hold his tongue no longer. "Is this the same girl who held a knife on us all the morning I married her to you, Wes? Or did you trade wives somewhere long the trail?"

Wes smiled. "Allie, you've met everyone but Nichole's brother, Wolf."

"Howdy, ma'am," the bear of a man said as he slid along the bench to within a few feet of her. "I'm real sorry to hear about you having to marry Weston. He's meaner than a polecat in quicksand. You want me to kill him for you and make you a happy widow?''

Allie's eyes widened in panic.

Wes smiled. "Stop it, Wolf. You're scaring her. She thinks you're serious."

Allie relaxed and continued her meal.

"Well, maybe I am," Wolf bellowed. "One look at this lady tells me she's far too fine a woman for the likes of you, Yank. And she's little, too. You should have married a few hundred pounds of woman who could box your ears good and hard now and again." He grinned and danced his bushy eyebrows. "You want me to skin him for you like we do down in Tennessee?"

Allie's eyes widened and she dropped her spoon.

"That's enough, Wolf," Wes warned. "She doesn't get the joke."

"What joke?" Wolf teased. "There's getting to be a pile of McLains in this world. I could thin the herd a bit."

In one swift movement, Allie grabbed her knife from her boot and swung along the table to stick the blade to Wolf's throat.

All laughing stopped.

Wolf held his hands up. "I was only—"

"Do not touch Wes," Allie stated without humor. She let the knife remain a moment longer then pulled away and slipped it back in her boot. "I will kill him myself if he gets bothersome."

Wolf's laughter rumbled from deep within him, and all the men relaxed. "Mighty nice to meet you, ma'am," he bellowed when he could gain enough control.

He slapped Wes hard on the back. "That's one fine woman, Wes. To think I was worried about her being so small up against the likes of you. Now, I'm thinking maybe I should worry about you."

Wes watched Allie closely. He'd done it again. He'd judged her short. She'd understood the teasing and played along in just the way Wolf would understand. If she'd cried or panicked, Wolf would have never stopped pestering. She was changing before Wes's eyes.

Jason hurried into the room as the men laughed. "Doc, the sheriff's asking for water."

Adam stood. "I've got a feeling Hardy's out of danger. I'll check the bandages."

He went back to Hardy. Daniel and Wolf excused themselves for the night. All at once, Wes was alone with Allie.

He sat drinking the last of his coffee and watched her move about the kitchen. It seemed like it had been a month since they'd been alone in the bedroom. There was still much to be said between them, decisions to be made, plans.

He could feel her nervousness as she moved about. She was busy doing nothing, but she didn't leave the room.

Without a word, he stood and walked to the fireplace where she poked at the embers. He took the iron from her hand and replaced it, then pulled her into his arms.

For a moment she didn't react, then she softened against him. Slowly, she raised her hands and circled his neck.

He lifted her up, molding her to him as he buried his face in her hair. He wanted to hold her tight, to breathe her inside him. But he knew he could have only a part of her and Wes wasn't sure that would be enough.

TWENTY-THREE

WES SAT ALONE ON THE WIDOW'S WALK, WATCHING the sun come up. He'd slept in the study until almost dawn, knowing he couldn't go up to the bedroom he shared with Allie. Another day was coming, and he had some decisions to make before everyone woke up.

Maxwell held his own despite continued loss of blood from his chest wound. Now that the trouble was over, Adam and Daniel were in a hurry to start home. But the doctor in Adam wouldn't allow him to leave until he knew Maxwell was out of danger.

"But what of me?" Wes mumbled to the rising sun. "Where am I headed?"

He unfolded the map and spread it across his leg. The Goliad gold. Maybe it was only a legend. He might be chasing something that never existed.

But what were his alternatives? He could take Allie back to his ranch and scratch out a living until next spring. If she'd go. She'd only promised to stay with him until the danger was over.

Maybe she could remain here while he looked for the treasure, or she could ride back toward Fort Worth with his brothers.

Wes took a swig of an almost full whiskey bottle, making a face as he lowered his liquid breakfast. The liquor wasn't going to do it this time. It couldn't make the emptiness go away.

Never, she'd said. Never was a long time.

He tried to tell himself it didn't matter. He could just be around her and protect her—that was all he'd signed on for in the first place. If she were hurt or dying, then her not being able to make love to him wouldn't make him turn away. He'd still stay by her side.

But she wasn't hurt or dying. She was healthy and more than able to feel the passion in his kisses and to react to his touch. She just didn't want him as a woman should want a man. As he wanted her.

He propped his foot on the railing. What was he going to do with Allie? Or maybe the question was, what was he going to do about the feelings churning inside himself? For, according to Allie, he was going to do nothing with her.

The trapdoor rattled. Wes turned with dread, figuring he was in for another lecture from Miss Victoria. The old woman had been almost silent since the shootings, but he didn't think it would last.

Wolf squeezed his bulk through the opening. "You reckon this little walk will hold us both?" He glanced at the ten-foot length and three-foot width, as if doubting.

He took one look at Wes and laughed. "Who cares. We'll have quite a ride down if it doesn't. Right?"

"Right." Wes offered him a drink.

Wolf raised one bushy eyebrow. "I think I'll wait until I've at least had my breakfast. But thanks for the offer."

Wes turned back to the sunrise. He liked and respected Wolf, but Wes wasn't in a mood to talk. Something told him that wouldn't matter much to Wolf.

The huge man bumped into the railing as he sat down. "I've been elected to come up here and talk to you. Hell if I know why. Grumpy seems like your natural state to me, and if it's female problems, I'm not the man to give advice. I haven't kissed a woman in so long, I forgot how to pucker.''

Wes took a drink. "Tell my nosy brothers nothing's wrong with me, would you?''

Pulling out his pipe, Wolf nodded. "Sure.'' He stuffed the bulb with tobacco. "Well, that was easy. And to think your brothers were worried about you. But I told them there weren't nothing strange in a man moping around all night, refusing to eat, and not sleeping in a real bed when he had the chance.''

Wes cut his eyes at the man. "Getting rather chatty in your old age, Wolf.''

He lit his pipe. "Comes with not having to listen for the next bullet flying toward my head. You know, it don't make any sense, but in a strange way, I miss the war. Not the killing and hardship, of course, but the way you feel all alive all the time.''

Wes understood. When there's a chance a man might die any minute he doesn't spend too much time worrying about how many head of cattle he's lost. Also, during the hard times of war, a man spends his free time dreaming of once there's peace. But what does a man dream of when there's peace? Wes hadn't figured it out yet.

"What I wouldn't give for an adventure about now. Something to make my blood pump.'' Wolf stared out into the loneliness of the land.

Wes handed him the map as he made up his mind. He couldn't follow Allie around for the rest of his life waiting for her to heal. If she didn't want him, she didn't want him. It was as simple as that. Wolf was right, he needed something to get his mind off her. "Want to go treasure hunting?''

Wolf looked at the map, interested but not excited.

"Thirty years ago when Texas fought for independence from Mexico, men congregated at an old mission about two days south of here called Goliad. As the Alamo fell, they were headed in that direction to help. A few days out, they were attacked and captured. Santa Anna's men held them in the mission chapel then marched them out on Palm Sunday morning of 1836 to be killed.''

Wolf forgot his pipe and leaned closer to Wes. Interested.

"Legend has it, hundreds of men buried all their valuables in a tunnel running below the mission. But the few who escaped were never able to go back and claim the treasure.''

Wolf shook his head in doubt. "Thirty years is a long time to have a map around. Someone's been there before you.''

Wes smiled. "Only thing I forgot to tell you, the treasure's cursed. Men have died over just the map. They say the ghosts of Goliad protect it.''

Wolf raised and lowered his eyebrows several times. "Sounds interesting, but I'm not fool enough to believe in ghosts. If I were, a company or more are bound to be following me around trying to haunt me.''

"If I knew Allie was safe, I'd be on the trail by tomorrow morning.'' Wes folded the map. "Time's running out, and I'd love a shot at finding the treasure.''

"I am safe,'' a voice drifted from the trapdoor opening. A moment later, Allie was in sight. "Both your brothers have offered to have Jason and me stay with them. Jason is excited about going with Adam. He says he will learn all about doctoring then take care of horses, not people.''

She stepped over Wolf's legs and sat down next to Wes. "Victoria also offered to let me stay for a while if I liked, though she said nothing about believing I'm her granddaughter. Not that it matters. I'm not staying.''

Wes kept his voice calm. "You're going with Adam?''

"No.'' She looked him directly in the eyes. "I'm going with you. You said I could stay with you until I found a home.''

Wes took a long draw on his breakfast. "Goliad's no place for a woman. I'll take you back to my ranch.''

"The treasure will not wait forever. We should go.

We could leave at first light tomorrow morning. I can keep up with you.''

Wes glanced at Wolf for support.

"Don't look at me. I took my little sister with me to war. What do I know?'' Wolf stood and headed down the steps. "I'll be ready when you decide to ride out. I don't know about going treasure hunting, but I'll travel with you until the road splits.''

He vanished, leaving Wes and Allie alone.

She faced the sunrise. Silence drifted between them, reminding Wes of how very little she talked to him. At first her voice had seemed stilted, hesitant, as if she were getting accustomed to every word. But over time, he'd grown used to her ways. So much so that other women's conversations seemed hurried and high pitched.

Finally, when her words came, they were soft, carried on the wind. "I have a place to go to deep in the hill country. A cave with robes and pots, everything I need to be safe. I remember your friend, Vincent, saying his grandfather ran from Goliad to the Guadalupe River. That is the river that runs close to my cave. All I would have to do is follow it upstream once we look for your gold.''

Wes listened, wondering why she'd never told him of this place. Had she been afraid he'd follow her? Had what happened between them made her want to be alone?

"After I ran during a raid, I made my home there for five winters. After years of never seeing anyone, I got careless and wandered too far from safety. I'll not make that mistake again. I wish to return.''

"So you don't want this pretense of a marriage anymore?''

Allie looked down at the ring on her finger. "In this life, I will have no other husband.''

"And I will have no other wife,'' he answered. "You're the only woman who's ever gotten under my skin. I've told myself it was just a need to protect you, but it's more, Allie.''

He stood suddenly, worried he'd say something he'd regret. "I'll take you back to your home, if that's what you want. Then I'll look for the treasure."

"No." Allie faced him. "We go to Goliad first."

"But—"

"We go to Goliad first, and each night we have left, you will hold me so that I can remember what it is like to sleep beside a husband."

"And then we say good-bye." Wes tried to keep his voice as void of emotion as hers.

"Agreed." She moved away, her head high. "If I help you find the treasure, I will have paid you back for some of the kindness you gave me. It is a fair bargain. Then I'll follow the river, and you can head north to your home."

Wes watched the sun pull away from the earth on its journey. "It wasn't kindness," he whispered as she closed the trapdoor. He knew anything between them was hopeless. She'd set the rules. A part of him couldn't help but be proud. A strength had blossomed inside her that surprised him.

The day filled with plans and preparations. Several men in Victoria's army rode out, checking to make sure none of Michael's men remained. Adam spent the day doctoring the sheriff and treating the signs of aging among the remaining troops. Wes and Daniel rode to town to see if anyone remembered the man who'd been asking questions, but the description the townfolks gave could have been half the men they knew.

Wes crossed Allie's path several times as the day passed. Her manner was cold. He thought of reaching for her, if only just to touch, but she didn't want a man. Allie only wanted a protector, a pretender who would hold her at night without any depth to his passion, without any warmth in his soul. She wanted the very thing he'd asked for in Angela Montago, a marriage without love, without passion.

At least she knew what she wanted, or, better yet, what she didn't want. Wes had no idea. A month ago, he wanted to be rich. Then he'd seen Allie and he'd only wanted her safe. And last night, he wanted her beneath him.

By twilight everyone had returned to the headquarters, and Victoria's staff cooked a feast. The warm autumn night allowed tables to be set up in the courtyard, but nothing improved Wes's mood.

Forcing himself to look away from Allie, he watched Victoria's staff. They made sure the old woman's world of darkness held no surprises. Her meals were prepared so that nothing had to be cut. Her place setting was exactly the same as for the meal before. She didn't seem handicapped by her blindness within the walls of her home.

As soon as Victoria finished, she excused herself to return to Maxwell Hardy's side. Adam might be a great doctor, but the sheriff's improvements could mostly be credited to the blind woman's constant supervision.

As Victoria moved away, Wes leaned across the table toward Adam. "Is the old man going to live?"

"I don't know. The bullet wouldn't have killed him by itself, but with the broken leg, he was already short on blood." Adam shrugged. "If he dies, he dies in the place he wants to be."

Wes agreed. "The old fellow's crazy about Victoria. He's spent his life worshipping her."

"You should see her fuss over him. She checks and double-checks everything I do for him."

"Wonder why they never married?" Wes kept his comment low.

"Maybe all her life she needed him as a protector. A knight in shining armor to call. If they'd married, it might have diminished his role."

"Maybe." Wes nodded, wondering if that's all he'd ever be to Allie. Someone to help her out when she was in trouble, but not someone to spend any more time with than necessary.

Suddenly the feast seemed too crowded. Wes excused himself and went upstairs to his room. He had an hour before his shift with the sheriff started. Miss Victoria might cover the days, but they all took turns keeping watch over Maxwell at night.

Frustration had been brewing in him all day. Every time he looked at Allie, he remembered the way she felt all soft in his arms and the way she'd said "never" when he'd touched her. He had to put some distance between her and his heart before he exploded.

Their room was still in the evening shadows, but signs of Allie were everywhere. Her clothes stacked neatly on the dresser, hair ribbons rolled beside her brush, a nightgown spread out across the bed. She'd settled into the room as easily as she'd settled into his thoughts.

He'd just finished shoving a clean shirt in his bag when she opened the door.

She looked quite the lady tonight with her hair pulled up on the sides and tied with a real ribbon. She wore the blue dress that matched her eyes and a hand-crocheted shawl about her shoulders.

"We leave tomorrow?" She glanced at his saddlebags.

"*I* leave tomorrow," Wes corrected. "There's no need in your coming to pay me back for some service you think I did you. You'll be safer here for a few days." He watched her closely as she folded her shawl over the chair back and placed the key she always kept in her pocket on the dresser. "You don't owe me anything, Allie. I'm not taking you along."

"I will go with you and help you." She faced him, shaking her head as though refusing to believe his words. "We will sleep beneath the robes together until it is time for me to return to the cave."

Wes stared at the corner where the servants had already prepared her bath. He didn't want to look at her beautiful eyes filled with tears, but the sight of the tub brought memories vivid in his mind.

He turned to the windows, but the vision of her wouldn't leave his thoughts. What he did was for her own good. For his own good. He would only be putting her in danger if she went along. She could stay here, safe for a few days, and then he'd take her to her cave.

"No." He fought to keep his voice calm. "We will not sleep in the same bed together or beneath a blanket or robes. Not ever again."

She moved closer and brushed his back with her hand.

Wes stiffened as though she'd scraped skin away with her touch.

"But I thought you—"

"You thought wrong!" he snapped. "Maybe I don't want to pretend to be man and wife anymore."

Allie touched him again, feeling his withdrawal even though he didn't move. "I thought—"

Wes twirled, grabbing her by the waist and lifting her onto the footstool so she was at eye level. "You thought I liked this?" He kissed her hard, holding her head back. One hand plowed into her hair while the other pulled her body against him like a vice.

Breaking the kiss as suddenly as he'd started, he shouted, "Well, I don't!" He had to make her believe he didn't want her. It was the only way he could keep her safe . . . from danger and from him.

He backed a few feet away, leaving her balancing on the stool. "I don't like kissing you." He wiped his mouth. "Or touching you, or sleeping with you pressed against me. So we can stop that pretense right now."

He saw her chin quiver slightly and almost abandoned his attack. But he had to settle this here and now. She wasn't going with him. If she wouldn't stay here, he'd see her safe somewhere else. He would not take her into danger just because she wanted to sleep beneath his robes and pretend what they had was all there was between a man and a woman.

"Leave me alone!" He couldn't face her and say the words that had to be said. He turned to the windows. "Don't tempt me one minute and sentence me to hell the next. I wasn't the one who hurt you, and I'll be damned if I'll pay the price."

He told himself he was doing what had to be done.

A clean break. He couldn't play games. He couldn't kiss her and touch her and not make love to her. And he couldn't take what she didn't freely give.

Wes wasn't sure what she'd do, but he never expected a full attack. He turned just in time to see her jump at him with both fists flying like a wild animal cornered.

They tumbled to the floor like children, Allie swinging and Wes trying to defend himself.

Downstairs, the brothers sat finishing off the last of the coffee.

"Ah, marital discourse." Wolf smiled as he toasted the ceiling. "Reminds me of home."

"Sounds like she's beating some sense into him." Adam laughed. "Nichole almost killed me, making me see the light."

Daniel looked worried. "Allie's small. You don't think Wes will hurt her accidentally?" He might be a big man, but Daniel wore his heart on his sleeve.

Both older men laughed aloud. "More likely, she'll hurt him," Wolf answered. "Right about now, he's probably wishing we'd come up and save him."

A loud thud resounded from above.

Daniel stared up. "Are you sure?"

Wolf patted the younger man's shoulder. "Up north, love may come in like a soft breeze on the wind, but in this rough country full of hard men, love has to smack a man solid between the eyes to get his attention."

TWENTY-FOUR

WES TOOK THE BLOWS, TRYING TO CATCH HER FLY-
ing fists and guard his eyes at the same time. He rolled
with her, bumping into the chair and sending it flying
backward into the wardrobe. Kicking the footstool out
of the way, he rolled again, slamming into the corner of
the bed and making the headboard pound several times
against the wall.

He tried to stand, but she threw him off balance, sending them both tumbling once more. She continued to
swing from every direction, hailing fists upon him.

Frustrated beyond patience, Wes rolled atop her and
pinned her suddenly to the floor.

"Enough!" he shouted as she twisted beneath him.

Her hair was wild around her, her eyes filled with
fight. She was not afraid, but angry. There was a zest
for life in her blue depths he'd never seen before—not
just survival, but the courage to fight for what she
wanted in this world.

"Enough," he said more calmly as he pressed his
body against her. He loved the way her eyes sparked
with fire when she was mad. He'd never seen her look
more beautiful.

She still fought, trying to jerk free so she could land
another blow. There were no words in her; her actions
spoke her feelings.

"Enough," he whispered as he lowered his mouth over hers, unable to resist drawing closer to the fire. Her body twisted beneath him, allowing him the pleasure of feeling every part of her.

For a moment she fought, trying to move away, then she stilled and suddenly returned his kiss with the same zeal she'd used to fight.

She'd won the argument without a word, but he was too busy to notice.

Wes released her wrists and filled his hands with her hair as the kiss deepened. Her body softened beneath him, as she became aware of how he moved above her.

Allie sighed as the wall of his chest pressed her against the wooden floor. His tongue parted her lips in hurried demand. He tasted deeply as he molded against her, making every part of her alive.

He shifted, lessening his weight over her and allowing room for his hands to stroke her. The need to touch her pounded through him, driving all thought away as the fresh smell of her filled his senses.

When he felt her breasts covered in layers of material, his kiss grew wilder, and the longing to capture her flesh in his hand outweighed even breathing.

Frantically, he pulled the buttons free and shoved her dress open enough for his fingers to enter her blouse. The soft mound filled his hand in welcome. Her breathing came in gasps as he pressed his palm slightly. Her heart pounded beneath the intoxicating velvet of her flesh.

Then, she surrendered all struggle. She was his, moving to his every wish. Her fire had turned to passion and his anger to desire. He could lie to her no more, the need to hold her was too great.

He turned her away from him, enjoying how she cried out softly for more as he broke the kiss. But she molded as his hands twisted her until her back rested against him.

He pulled her close. His fingers moved beneath the material of her blouse and coveried her breast once more. "Lay your head on my arm," he whispered as his hands slid low over her dress and pulled her to him, allowing her to feel him fully.

She melted against him, taking in his nearness like a long needed drink of water.

"Pull your hair away from your throat, Allie."

Following his orders, she moved her hands above her so that he had full rein to gently stroke her, drawing her closer against him with each passing. She was a creature made for loving and hadn't learned the subtleties of holding back the pleasures she felt. She wanted his touch and had no idea how she made him feel when she responded so willingly.

Shoving her blouse from her shoulder, he kissed the long line of her throat. The flesh was warm and inviting, tasting slightly salty on his tongue.

She curled like a kitten against him. He pushed the material lower, revealing her back. Thin scars crossed over her flesh beneath his fingers as he stroked her gently, washing away painful memories with his caress.

"This is what you want when you say you want me to lie beneath your robes?" Wes whispered against her ear. "This is what you need, don't you, Allie? You want me to hold you like this."

"Yes," she answered breathlessly as he tightened his grip on one breast then moved low over the front of her dress to pull her hips against him once more.

"You need my touch, Allie, don't you? You need to feel your blood rushing. You need to feel the fire."

"Yes." She saw no reason to lie. "More, please."

He rolled her to face him. With one quick tug, the front of her blouse opened wide.

Allie stretched, loving the warm, wonderful way he made her feel. She knew once she was alone, she'd never have the fire spread through her again. He was her one blaze of pure pleasure. He made her feel beautiful and treasured. His hands were rough, yet his touch gentle.

When he pulled away suddenly, she opened her eyes

in surprise. He was doing exactly what she wanted him to. There was no need to stop.

Wes sat up and wiped his lips slowly. His gaze moved over her like a caress but the words he mumbled were a curse. He raised one knee and locked his arm around it with both hands white-knuckled in fists.

Confused, she rose, kneeling in front of him. She wanted him to continue and had no idea what could have made him stop the pleasure. "Thank you." She wouldn't beg, even though her body ached for him to hold her longer.

Wes winked then looked away suddenly. "You want more of the same?"

"Yes, please." She didn't cover herself. He could look at what he'd already caressed. "If you are not too tired, I would like more before we have to go back downstairs."

Wes sat staring at the windows for a while, then he slowly tugged his shirttail free.

She leaned forward, pressing her lips to his, but he gently pushed her away. Watching as he unbuttoned his shirt, she felt the coldness of the room against her bare flesh. But she didn't move. The fire would come again when he touched her.

Staying perfectly still, she studied him closely, knowing that he was aware of every rise and fall of her breasts. He would pleasure her again. She would not have to fight this time.

He closed his eyes and took in a deep breath before looking straight at her. For a long moment, he stared, then reached toward her. "Give me your hand, Allie."

Hesitantly, she lay her fingers in his. He turned her hand palm up and brought it to his lips. Allie fought for control as he kissed first her fingers, then lowered his lips to her palm. His open mouth drew her very soul as her hand throbbed from the pressure of his kiss.

Allie shivered with pleasure. She felt as if she'd captured the fire of his nearness in her fist.

He lowered her hand slowly, smiling at her reaction. "Now, the other."

She quickly offered him her palm. He repeated the action, making the nerves in her fingers come alive to the slightest touch.

Only, this time when he'd finished, he didn't turn loose of her. Instead, he spread her fingers out over his heart. The hair of his chest tickled across her hand as he moved her fingers over his skin, feeling the deep rhythm of his heart beneath her hand. There was no softness in the feel of him, only a wall of warmth.

"Allie. Open your eyes. See me as you touch me. See only me."

She looked up as he guided her hand over his chest, teaching her to touch. She could see the fire in his eyes grow with her action.

He kissed her then so tenderly it brought tears to her eyes. When she pulled away, he whispered as his hand fell away from hers, "Touch me, Allie. Keep your hand over my heart."

Timidly, she felt of him once more, and his kiss continued. Slowly, the feel of him became less frightening. She liked the way his muscles tightened slightly as she caressed them. She liked the pounding beneath her fingers.

He allowed her time, to feel, to explore. And again and again he rewarded her with warm kisses.

Finally Wes leaned against the bed, stretching his long legs in front of him and holding her against his side.

"You're one strange lady, Allie McLain. One minute you're kicking me out of our room, and the next you're fighting because I won't 'lie beneath the robes with you.'"

"McLain," she whispered. "Is that my last name?"

Wes kissed her forehead. "That's it. Whether Victoria claims you or not, your last name is McLain."

"And I will ride out with you tomorrow?"

Wes looked down into her blue eyes. All the reasons why she shouldn't come with him came to mind, but his mouth mutinied and he heard himself saying, "We leave at dawn."

An hour later, he'd just finished explaining his plans to Sheriff Hardy when Gideon rushed into the room with Colonel Attenbury and Jason on his heels.

"We got problems." Gideon shouted, feeling the need to announce Attenbury.

The old colonel shoved past the doorman and crossed straight to Wes. "He's right." Attenbury's body might be aging, but his eyes stared crystal clear. "I can feel it, son, and I've been around long enough to trust those feelings."

Wes stood, noticing Hardy pulling himself up with interest and patting the covers for his guns. "What kind of problems?" There was no doubt the sheriff had been expecting something to happen. Maybe he was like the old colonel, he could feel it in his blood.

Jason moved behind Hardy so he wouldn't miss anything being said. A boy's excitement blended with a man's worry in his face.

"One of the men thought he saw a lone rider at sunset coming up the south side. He said he watched the rider approaching for ten minutes, then the guard blinked, and both horse and man disappeared.

"That alone is simply noteworthy. The light can play tricks on a man at sunset. But Cutler reports a horse in the corral that wasn't there last night. Now, other men I might think to be mistaken, but not Cutler. I took a look at the animal. He'd been rode hard today. Not a man claimed him as mount."

Wes glanced at Hardy, but the man offered no comment. "Are you saying, Colonel Attenbury, that we have an extra man in our midst?"

"Not among my men, but somewhere in the compound," Attenbury answered.

"Any other news to report?" Wes watched the colonel carefully, sensing there was more.

"When I made my rounds at ten, the gate just behind

the kitchen and the one by the well had been unlocked. It was as if someone had walked just ahead of me. Every man on guard swore they'd seen no one."

"Gideon, have your people search the house. Attenbury, take five men and comb the barn and quarters. Order double guards tonight and lanterns placed around the courtyard. I want no one being able to walk across the yard without being seen. We'll meet by the fountain in thirty minutes. If there's an extra man in this place, we'll find him."

As both men left, Wes glanced at Jason. The boy stood bravely, awaiting assignment like the others, but his eyes were wide and his face pale with fright.

"Jason." Wes leaned close. He had to make the boy feel important even though all Wes wanted to do was ensure Jason's safety. "I need you to do something quickly. Go upstairs and warn the women. Ask them to join the sheriff here. Between the two of you, the women will be safe."

Jason nodded with pride and ran to fulfill his assignment.

Wes returned to his chair beside Hardy's makeshift bed. "It makes no sense," Wes mumbled. "Surely, one man's not planning to attack this place."

"Could be he came in to kill a single person." Worry lines rippled across the old man's forehead. "I don't know about you, but I've got a few enemies. Maybe he plans to slit my throat, then get a fresh mount and ride out."

Wes shook his head. "No, if it's personal, looks like he'd wait until we all split up tomorrow. Why attack when the headquarters is full?"

The old sheriff leaned back against his pillows, holding his side as though it were an effort to breathe. "Years ago," he whispered, "back in the days of the first three hundred who came with Austin, I got to where I could talk with the Karankawas who made their camp around the settlement. They saw the settlers as about as important and pesky as mosquitoes. Austin's colony thought the Indians were unfriendly, but mostly, the Karankawas just didn't bother trying to communicate.''

Though Wes was starting to wonder if this story had a point, he didn't interrupt.

"One night, I was in the camp and one of the braves gave a report almost identical to Attenbury's. Seems men had heard a rider coming, but no one broke the trees around the camp. Then they noticed a horse with markings unlike any of them had ever seen.''

"And?'' Wes encouraged.

"I've heard many names other tribes use, but the best translation is 'smoke warrior.' The Karankawas have an old legend that ghosts walk among our midst, unnoticed for the most part. No one can see them most of the time, they float like vapors at sunrise. But once in a while, they get strong enough to take on form solid enough to ride a horse. When that happens, they only have one mission.''

Wes leaned forward. "What?''

"To take another soul with them when they cross over to the next life.'' Hardy's face left no doubt he was deadly serious. "Some folks don't want to cross over to the hereafter alone.''

"But who?'' Wes shook his head. "That makes no sense.''

Sheriff Hardy swallowed hard and opened his mouth to argue, but before he could form a word, a scream shattered the stale night air.

Wes was on his feet running before the sound died in his ears. "Watch the entrance!'' he yelled over his shoulder as he took the stairs three at a time.

Another scream came from above.

"Allie!'' he shouted as he rammed their bedroom door at full speed.

TWENTY-FIVE

Wes broke into the quarters with Adam only a step behind. The room was exactly as it had been an hour ago when he'd left. Only, Allie was missing.

"I'll check on Victoria!" Adam backed out the door and tried the next room. "She had one of the girls show her upstairs ten minutes ago."

Empty!

"Maybe they went back to the kitchen for some reason?" Adam checked the old woman's room carefully, as though he thought she might be hiding somewhere amidst the lace and drapes.

"Then who screamed if they went downstairs?" Wes inspected the windows. They were locked from the inside. No one could have gotten in or gone out and relocked them from inside.

Daniel thundered into the room like a freight train having trouble stopping. "I came up the back stairs from the kitchen. No one passed me. Who screamed?"

Adam shook his head.

Wes stepped to the landing. "Hardy!" he yelled down the stairs.

"Yeah!" the old sheriff answered, out of breath.

"Seen anyone come down?"

"Not a soul! Is Victoria all right?"

Wes raised his gaze to the ceiling. There was only

one place they could have gone. "They may be on the widow's walk."

"And, from the screams, they're not alone," Adam whispered as if whoever had the women might hear them through the ceiling.

Wes glanced toward the end of the hallway where a tiny staircase led up to the trapdoor.

Jason lay curled in the shadows at the bottom of the steps. His body rocked back and forth in pain.

The brothers reached him in seconds.

"What happened, son?" Wes asked.

Adam examined the boy, slowly testing for broken bones.

"Where are Allie and Victoria?" Wes pushed for an answer. "Are they all right?"

The boy jerked when Adam brushed his hair away from a badly bruised forehead.

"Jason?" Adam turned his face to the light. "Jason? Can you hear me?"

Trying to turn away from the men he mumbled, "I can hear you. I'm sorry. I'm so sorry." He looked at Wes. "You told me to watch the women. I tried, but when we were climbing the steps, the man hit me hard in the face. He knocked me down the stairs. The trapdoor closed before I could follow."

"You tried, son." Wes comforted the boy. "What did this man look like?"

"He was real tall, and thin, with a gun in one hand and a long stick in the other. He wore a great coat that folded around him like a bat's wings. He kept shoving the women along with his stick. I heard him whisper that he'd kill Victoria first if any of them made a sound."

Holding his head, Jason rocked slightly. "I didn't cry. Not even when he kicked me. Allie tried to protect Victoria when the man didn't think they were moving fast enough and swung the stick wildly. She didn't say a word when the blows hit her, but Victoria screamed."

Dread shook Wes to the core. There was only one

man who reminded him of a bat. Only one man who would risk anything to kill Allie.

Wes bolted halfway up the stairs before Daniel and Adam's grip pulled him down.

"Let go!" Wes jerked at their holds. "I have to get to Allie. He'll kill her this time for sure!"

"There's no way to open the door without the man on the widow's walk seeing you." Adam stated the obvious. "It would be suicide."

"I don't care!" Wes fought at their arms. "Allie's up there."

"And once it's open, whoever has Allie will have a clear shot at you." Daniel's grip was iron around his brother's arm, but his face showed his understanding.

"You're no help to Allie dead!" Adam shouted.

His words penetrated Wes's mind. He had to fight not only his brothers but himself to keep from invading the walk.

Wes moved back down the narrow stairway barely the width of his shoulders. Storming the roof would be ridiculous, he realized, but he had to do something. If the preacher named Louis had Allie, he'd been willing to risk a great deal, even his life, to kidnap her. After all, he'd been willing to kill Wes for taking her from the cage. There was no telling what the man might do if cornered.

Gideon hurried up the stairs and darted into the first bedroom. "Miss Victoria's missing!" he yelled. "Outside, the guards said they could see shadows on the walk."

"How many?" Wes knew the answer.

"Three. One tall man, two short women." Gideon glanced in Wes and Allie's room. "They're both gone? Miss Victoria must be on the walk!"

"They didn't go willingly. I think I know our intruder." Wes began to pace, reasoning out his strategy. There had to be something he could do.

"The walk was built into the roofline. It would be

impossible to get off a clear shot at night and little better in daylight from a lower angle.''

Daniel and Adam were not military men. They'd spent the war doctoring and preaching. For the first time since the three brothers were together, Wes's expertise was needed most. He had to think of something.

Adam persuaded Jason into allowing him to examine his forehead. Daniel stood guard at the foot of the stairs as though fearing Wes might yet bolt for the trapdoor.

Attenbury slowly climbed the stairs from the ground floor. "I heard shots," the old colonel mumbled.

"Your invisible rider's on the roof with Victoria and Allie," Wes explained. "I was so busy guarding the grounds, I left the house wide open. Somehow, he got past us all to them."

"What does he want?" Attenbury asked. He was too old to be surprised by anything in life, but anger glistened in his watery eyes.

Wes shook his head. "It's what he has that worries me."

"We can pick him off come morning. I've got men who can shoot the left eye out of a rattler at a hundred feet. I'll put them out on the range to wait for sunup."

Wes paced, glad to have someone to voice his thoughts to. "We don't have until morning. The women will be dead by then. Our stranger came to kill. If he sees any sign of men on that side of the wall, he'll probably shoot."

Jason pushed Adam's hand away as the doctor tried to bandage the boy's head. "I could go out the second-floor window on the other side of the house and cross over to the walk. I've got good balance and I've used a gun once."

Wes patted the boy's shoulder. "Good idea, son, but we can't risk it. You might fall because of your injury, and from that height it would be three stories. Or, if you made it, whoever has them might shoot you as you drop down."

"I could try it," Daniel volunteered.

"The roof's not safe," Gideon added. "Tiles fall off, sometimes for no reason. It wouldn't hold the weight of a boy, much less a man."

Swearing beneath his breath, Wes realized there was no way to get to them. He also knew the only reason the two women hadn't been murdered in their rooms was because Louis liked to play with his prey before the kill. But, soon he'd get tired of his games and strike. Wes had to find a way to help the women before then.

But how? He'd promised to protect Allie. Now she was only a few feet away, and he could do nothing. Nothing.

Allie felt Victoria's fingers clamp down on her arm, but the old woman didn't cower in fear. She stood on the narrow walk with her head held high. Her bravery made Allie stand taller.

"Don't either of you move!" the intruder yelled. "I got to think a minute."

"Who are you? What do you want?" Victoria demanded as though she hadn't just been forced at gunpoint to climb stairs to a roof that offered a fall that would surely kill her.

"Why don't you ask the *creature* who I am?" The man's voice was filled with hate. "You might have cleaned her up, but I know she's a wild savage with no soul. She's the devil's child for sure."

Victoria's fingers tightened, but Allie didn't say a word.

"I should have killed her as I was paid to do, but I thought to make a little money." The stranger's voice boomed like that of a preacher with a full house. "But she's evil, the devil's daughter. She drove me to do things to her." He laughed suddenly, a wicked laugh. "Oh, she fought and cried, but in only a matter of days she'd led me down the path of sin again. She's like a fever that poisons a man's blood."

Allie couldn't speak. Fear pulsed so violently through her that no language would come. Somehow the preacher had found her. Somehow, he'd gotten past all the men protecting her.

A part of her wanted to curl down and become the animal he called her. Another part wouldn't allow his words to break her.

Victoria, however, seemed to face him on even ground in the darkness with no fear rattling in her voice. "What do you plan to do?" she demanded. "If it's kill us, you'll never get off this ranch alive. My men will slaughter you and string you up in the courtyard."

The preacher laughed. "I don't want to live. I'm ready to go to my home in heaven . . . or I will be as soon as I send this trash to hell. And as for you, old woman, you'll only be making the journey to heaven a few days before planned. The Lord won't mind my hurrying the process."

The aging woman pushed Allie behind her. "I'll not stand by and let you harm the child." She laughed as if almost enjoying the game. "And I'm not as easy to kill as you might think."

The preacher made his first mistake. He touched Victoria. He might have been six-feet tall and thirty years her junior, but when he touched her, he put himself on even ground. She knew where he was.

Victoria shoved Allie backward as she ran forward like a raging angel.

He wasn't prepared for an attack, not from an old woman. She raked her fingernails across his face before he had time to raise his arms.

Louis screamed. Giving pain might be his pleasure, but he bore no joy when receiving it. His blood looked black in the moonlight as it dripped in his eye and across his face from her scratches.

Louis raised his staff as he shoved Victoria against the railing. The whooshing sound of her breath leaving her lungs combined with the hollow crack of ribs.

Allie watched as he drew in a mighty breath. This blow would be struck to kill. Victoria fought to regain her balance as she turned her head, listening, testing for exactly where he stood behind her. She was alone now and lost.

As the mighty blow lowered toward the old woman, Allie attacked. The knife from her boot filled her palm. Without pulling back to increase the power of the strike, Allie shoved the blade forward into Louis's chest.

The sharp blade sliced into him between his ribs.

For a moment, he stood before her filled with rage, paused to yet render a blow.

Fear and panic drove Allie. Her knuckles whitened around the handle of the knife as she tried to pull her weapon out of his chest. But it wouldn't budge! Somehow the blade had lodged between his ribs.

In the length of a heartbeat, Allie saw him start to crumble, his staff falling to his side. Victoria stood before him, listening, trying to understand what was happening.

Allie had to release her knife. She had to pull Victoria from his path or he'd take her with him in the fall.

She had to give up her weapon!

Like a mighty tree that whispers through the air as it first begins to fall, Louis tumbled. His blood sprayed like a warm shower on Allie as she released her knife and pushed Victoria out of harm's way. As Louis staggered over the railing, the women fell to the floor of the walk.

Allie lay over the old woman, protecting her. At first there was silence, then Allie heard the thud of his body against the hard earth below.

Afraid to move, afraid to believe it was over, Allie clung to her grandmother. But there were only the sounds of the night, and peace.

She rolled away from Victoria. "It is over," she whispered.

The old woman didn't move.

Allie brushed the blood from Victoria's face. Her eyes were closed. Her body limp.

"Victoria?" she whispered. "Victoria!" she screamed.

Light suddenly filled the walk as the trapdoor flew

open. Wes shoved his gun into his holster and knelt at her side.

"Allie, are you all right?" His voice was thick with worry as his fingers brushed over her.

Allie made words form into sound. "Help Victoria! She's hurt."

Wes forced his attention from Allie to the old woman. Gently, he lifted her and carried her to the trapdoor opening, calling orders down to his brothers as he moved. He lowered her to the waiting arms of Daniel.

"I've got her." Daniel's voice reassured Wes. "Adam is already downstairs making ready. We'll take care of Miss Victoria. You get Allie."

When Wes glanced back to help her, he found Allie was leaning over the railing. He moved to her side and gently slid his hands along her sides, reassuring himself that she suffered no harm.

"Are you all right?" He watched the Old Guard below gathering around the preacher's body. "Louis is dead. He'll never hurt you again."

Allie circled her arms around Wes's waist and cried softly. "I want to go home," she whispered. "I want to go back to my cave."

Wes had no idea what to say. He hugged her to him, realizing how close he'd come to losing her, and he knew without any doubt that he loved her.

"I'll take you tomorrow." He kissed the top of her head. "If that's what you want."

"That's what I want," she answered.

TWENTY-SIX

TEARS STILL SHONE IN ALLIE'S EYES AS THEY WALKED into the main room downstairs several minutes later. She felt as though she'd stepped from calm through a tornado to find the other side of the world peaceful once more. No one asked her questions or demanded to know why she'd killed a man. All she saw in their eyes was worry.

Daniel met her at the door. He slipped her knife into her hand. "I cleaned it for you, Allie. Thank the Lord you had it with you," he whispered as he left the room.

The sheriff pulled himself to a sitting position on his couch when she entered. He gripped his side and fought down the pain with a quick smile in her direction, then turned back to watch Adam working over Victoria a few feet away.

Wes didn't loosen his grip on Allie's hand. He knelt beside Victoria's chair opposite Adam. "How is she?"

Adam shook his head. "Folks her age weren't meant to take blows like she's suffered. Daniel and Wolf are bringing a bed down from upstairs. I'll know more after I examine her, but the longer she's unconscious, the worse it looks." He placed a cool cloth over her forehead.

Allie studied the old woman carefully. She looked

as fragile as fine china. It was hard to believe how she'd fought on the walk. If she hadn't, they'd both be dead.

Daniel banged in with one end of the bed. Wolf followed with no greater skill on the other end. The two housekeepers and the cook hurried in with linens and a nightgown. They were like bees around a queen, surrounding Victoria after Daniel placed the bed only a few feet from the couch.

While they worked, Adam and Wes stood several feet away.

"I'd planned to take her to her room," Adam whispered, "but Maxwell here yelled he'd crawl up the stairs and shoot *me* in the leg if I didn't bring her to him. I think he meant it, that is, if the climb didn't kill him first. He said he had to see she was alive."

Maxwell Hardy stared with worried eyes at the backs of the women as they lifted Victoria into bed. Wes thought of how helpless he'd felt when he couldn't reach Allie earlier. There was no doubt in Wes's mind that the sheriff meant every word he'd said to Adam. Even wounded and crippled, he'd still give his last ounce of blood for Victoria.

Wolf, Daniel, and Wes crossed to the cold fireplace as Allie helped the women make Victoria comfortable and dressed her in a nightgown.

Wolf excused himself, saying he had to get back to Jason. Adam had ordered Wolf to keep Jason awake and watch for any change in the boy. Suddenly, the house seemed more like a hospital than a ranch headquarters.

Wes wanted to leave, too. He hated sickrooms. But he wouldn't go without Allie. He didn't want to let her out of his sight for a moment.

When Victoria was ready, Adam began his examination. If she'd been a man, he would have stripped off clothing and checked her over totally. But women, especially aging Southern women like Victoria, would never allow such treatment, no matter how badly they were hurt. Adam had to very carefully cover her body as he checked each limb. He'd heard more than one doctor tell stories of women dying rather than returning to a physician who wasn't quite proper with his examination.

The two housekeepers held the sheet up while he wrapped Victoria's ribs. Both servants turned their faces away, respectfully allowing her as much privacy as possible.

Victoria moaned a few times as he examined her. She seemed to be fighting to come back to the world. Her body might be frail, but her spirit was still strong.

"Well?" Sheriff Hardy asked as Adam ordered the women to mix a powder in a basin of water and brew tea laced with painkiller. "How is she?" The old lawman watched him carefully.

"She's got a few broken ribs, maybe some bleeding inside," Adam said, looking up at the man so he'd know Adam was telling the truth. "I can't tell how much. From the way they're swelling, she may have broken two fingers of her right hand and has a bump on the back of her head." He glanced at Allie for an explanation.

Allie was surprised no one had asked her what had happened before now. She cleared her throat and forced out the words. "She scratched Louis, the man who forced us upstairs, hard across the face, giving me time to pull my knife. He knocked her into the railing. Blood dripped from the marks she left on his face, blinding him." Allie fought back tears. "She hurt her head when I pushed her down so the preacher wouldn't fall into her and take her over the railing with him. It's all my fault. He didn't want to hurt her, only me. She was only trying to protect me."

Wes put his arm around Allie's shoulder, but before he could speak, Victoria's voice drifted through the air like a weak vapor.

"You're right, child," she mumbled as she pulled

herself back to consciousness. "It is all your doing that I'm alive."

Everyone turned to Victoria. She closed her eyes, fighting back the pain. "Is that horrible man dead, Maxwell?"

"Yes." Allie moved closer. "I killed him."

Victoria raised her unharmed hand. "Hold your chin up, child," she said as though she could see Allie. "Don't ever be ashamed of doing what has to be done. There's enough regret in not doing what you should have done to last a lifetime."

Turning her head, listening, Victoria seemed to locate the sheriff. "Maxwell, have one of the men shoot him again once he's boxed just to make sure he doesn't try breathing again."

The sheriff laughed, relief making him look ten years younger. "I'll do that."

Adam leaned over Victoria. "How are you feeling?" He placed a hand at her throat.

Victoria pushed him away. "How do you think I'm feeling? Like a horse kicked me in the ribs. The fingers on my right hand feel like they've swelled double, and my brain has taken up playing the tom-tom. Pester me no more with your silly questions, Doc."

"You need rest, Miss Victoria. I've ordered you a warm mixture to soak your hand in before I set the fingers. And there's tea made that should help you sleep." Adam tried to replace the cloth on her forehead.

"I didn't live this long by giving in to a little pain. I'll sleep after I talk to Maxwell." She raised her head. "Maxwell, are you still here?"

"I'm here, Victoria." Despite the pain, he stretched to touch her elbow. "I'm right beside you."

"You did a lousy job of protecting me." She slowly moved her head back and forth. "I thought I was dead for sure up on that walk. And you were nowhere near."

"I'm sorry, Victoria."

She frowned. As she took a deep breath, the pain showed in her face. "You've never let me down before,

Maxwell. You've always been there when I needed you. But you were nowhere in sight.''

"Now, wait a minute!" Wes interrupted. "You've got some nerve, lady. The sheriff's got a busted leg and—"

"I know perfectly well what the sheriff has and doesn't have, young man." Victoria's voice rose slightly in anger. "Maxwell, shoot that husband of my granddaughter if he says another word."

Maxwell lifted his Colt. "All right, Victoria," he answered, as if she'd asked him to pass the sugar at a tea party. "But he's got brothers. I may have to reload."

"And that goes for anyone else in this room. If you value your life, keep quiet. I wish to talk to Maxwell, no one else." She might be lying on her back, wounded, but she was serving notice that she was still on the throne in her own kingdom.

Wes walked to the windows and turned his back to everyone. If the sheriff was dumb enough to volunteer to shoot him for standing up for him, Maxwell Hardy deserved the dressing-down he was getting.

"The thing I've always been able to depend on is you, Maxwell. All my husbands let me down in one way or the other, but you were always there. My knight in shining armor, ready to fight any battle."

"The knight's getting old, Victoria, and the armor's more bandages than steel."

"I've noticed," Victoria snapped. "You were the handsomest man I'd ever seen in those early years. I remember how you used to ride in here when I sent word and swing off your horse at my steps. I always thought, no matter what the trouble, you could battle it for me. You'd fight all my dragons."

A sadness settled over Maxwell. "I liked it when you asked me. There's nothing I wouldn't have done for you, Victoria. Not from the first time I saw you until now."

"I know," she answered. "But I don't need a knight any more. All my dragons are dead."

Maxwell nodded, pushing his thinning hair from his wrinkled face.

"What I need now is much more than I've ever asked of you." Victoria lowered her voice. "Maybe a hundred times more."

"Name it," Maxwell answered. "I'll do my best. Though there's not much fight left in me, as long as I'm breathing, I'll try." He lifted his leg, trying to move it to a more comfortable position. But the splint made that impossible.

"I want you to stay with me," Victoria ordered. "For whatever time we have left on this earth, I'd like to spend it with you. Live here with me, Maxwell."

The sheriff wiped his hand over his eyes. A slow smile crawled across his wrinkled face. "Why, Victoria, I've never known you to live with a man you weren't married to."

"Of course not, it wouldn't be proper. I guess we'll have to marry, also." She smiled, looking suddenly younger. "And after we pass on, I want to lie next to you in the family plot for eternity. That way I'll know you're still looking out for me."

"I'll do that, Victoria."

"Allie." Victoria's voice was calm, as if allowing another to come into her private world. "Tell that brother of your husband we need a wedding ceremony at sunrise. I'll not allow Maxwell to heal enough to change his mind and ride out of my life as he's done a hundred times. Gideon, make all the arrangements. It's not as if you haven't done it before."

"Victoria?" Maxwell seemed unwilling to think about there being anyone else in the room. "You know I've always loved you."

"Of course," she answered resolutely. "As I do you. But until tonight, you never fell to earth." She stretched her hand toward him.

"One thing." Maxwell frowned, showing a touch of uncertainty. "You'll take the name of Hardy, not stay Catlin this time."

Victoria opened her mouth to argue, then closed it. "Yes, dear," she said simply.

Maxwell closed his fingers around her small hand. "Until tomorrow, Mrs. Hardy."

Victoria nodded slowly. "Until tomorrow."

TWENTY-SEVEN

THE BRIDE WORE A NIGHTGOWN, THE GROOM MORE bandages than clothing. But no one seemed to notice. Just after dawn the windows to the courtyard were opened, and all the Old Guard witnessed as Miss Victoria took not her next husband, but her last husband.

Though Wes watched the ceremony, his mind wasn't on what Daniel said. The promise he'd made to take Allie to her cave filled his thoughts. He guessed she wanted him to come along to protect her until she was safely there, then she'd say good-bye.

She'd curled next to him the few hours they slept last night, and he'd held her tightly. There had been no passion, only the sweet feel of her at his side.

He'd been a hard man all his life. The war molded him as such, and he never complained. He always thought men who fell hopelessly in love were fools asking for heartache. But when he looked at Allie . . . Lord, when he looked at Allie.

"Wine?" Gideon offered a tray.

Wes blinked. He'd been so lost in his thoughts, he hadn't noticed the wedding was over. "No, thanks," he managed to mumble. "We need to be going."

When he knelt to say good-bye to the newlyweds, Maxwell wished him well, but Victoria grabbed his hand and towed him close to her side.

"Will Allie be all right?" she whispered.

He would swear the blind old woman looked directly at him.

"I hope so," he answered.

"Hope simply won't do, young man. You're her husband. You should know and see to her well-being."

Wes tried to pull his hand away, but Victoria's grip was iron, rusted like a clamp around his fingers.

"I invited her to stay here, but she says she has to go back to that damn cave she lived in for five years." The aging queen frowned. "I don't like the thought of her being alone there. Promise you'll keep her safe with you or bring her back here to us."

Wes shook his head. "She's as headstrong as you. I doubt I'll ever take her anywhere she doesn't want to go."

Victoria leaned back and released her grip. "Then tell me, young man, how many husbands will she have to bury before she finds one to love her completely?"

Talking to the old woman was like poking at a red ant bed. Eventually, you knew you were going to get stung.

When he didn't answer, Victoria added, "Maxwell said you signed on to this marriage with Allie only 'til she found a home. Well, she has a home here, but she's not staying. Maybe she thinks the marriage ends if she stays. Does it?"

"I've offered to take her back to my ranch." Wes couldn't help but wonder if the old woman spoke the truth.

"Did you tell her it was just until all was safe, or did you promise her forever?" Victoria shook her head. "Sounds to me like you've got some proposing to do before you're really a married man. Maybe a few days alone will loosen your tongue and make that knee of yours bend easier."

"I don't need any advice."

"Then get on with your trip to the cave. I've a wedding to celebrate. But you'd better not come back across

my land without my granddaughter at your side, or I'll
have you stripped, tied, and left as live buzzard meat."

Wes stood, thinking it must be something in the Catlin
women's blood that made them so hard to reason with.
What bothered him more than the fact that he thought
the old woman might carry out her threat, was that she
might be right about Allie believing the marriage to be
over when she found a home.

Wes said his good-byes to the others as quickly as he
could. Daniel and Adam were already in the saddle by
the time he reached the barn. Wolf had left before dawn
to take Louis's body to town. He didn't think a body
should be anywhere near a wedding. He'd left word that
he'd catch up to Adam on the road. It seemed seeing his
niece outweighed going with Wes to look for gold.

"Change your mind about taking Allie back to the
cave?" Adam asked when he saw Wes walk in alone.

Wes shook his head. "I gave my word. She's getting
her things together now."

"She belongs with you," Daniel said. "Much as I
feel sorry for her. Surely you're not planning to leave
her in some cave in the middle of nowhere."

"She doesn't want to be with me. She wants to be
alone." Wes loved his brothers but sometimes resented
them following his life as though it were the weekly
installment of a dime novel. "I'm not sure what I'll do."

Adam settled his horse. "Well, big brother, as soon
as Jason gets here, we'll say good-bye. We ride north.
Keep an angel on your shoulder and your fist drawn until
we're together again to cover your back."

"I'll do that." Wes laughed at the old saying they'd
always used when parting. "Give Nichole and the baby
a hug for me." He turned to Daniel. "And those twins."

Adam and Daniel rode toward the house as Wes
walked in the barn.

One of Victoria's men stood among the shadows.
"Mr. McLain." He stepped forward. "Miss Victoria
asked me to saddle your mounts if you and Miss Allie
are still set on going."

"We're still set," Wes answered.

The ranch hand brought out their horses and a pack mule.

Wes opened his mouth to object to the mule but the man didn't allow him time.

"Miss Victoria insisted. She'll have my hide if I don't follow orders. A pack mule, loaded with supplies and one of her own stock of horses for Allie."

Nodding, Wes surrendered. The old woman would only argue if he declined the offer. Hell, she'd probably have him chased down and tied to the mule. He might as well help load.

Allie also packed. She suddenly had more dresses and ribbons than she'd ever imagined one woman owning. Two bags were already filled. She tried to get everything remaining into a third one. Victoria never threw anything away. She'd explained that she had rooms with trunks of clothes and furniture. Allie could have her pick.

Allie turned down all but a few dresses and nightgowns. Yet every day, more seemed to show up in her room, already cleaned and pressed for her. She found them hard to refuse. Everything, even the leather riding gloves, fit her as if they'd been made for her.

"Allie?" Jason's voice drifted from just outside the open doorway. "You mind if I come in?"

"No." She watched him walk into the room. He also wore new clothes. The bandage on his forehead had been replaced by a bandanna.

"I come to say good-bye. Adam and Daniel are waiting for me." He sat down on the bed, making it plain he'd come to say more than good-bye before he left.

"I will miss you," Allie answered honestly. "We are the same tribe, you and I."

Jason smiled. "I love you, too."

"You will be happy with Adam?" She almost felt as if she should take him with her, but life would be much easier for him with Adam.

"He's got the magic to heal in his hands. That's something I'd like to learn." Jason stood and awkwardly hugged her. "Thank you," he whispered.

There were no more words needed. He left her. Allie stood alone in the room she now thought of as hers. She knew Victoria didn't want her to go. Wes and his brothers were worried about her. But she had to make this journey. She had to be in the one place where she felt totally safe. And she had to be there with Wes.

She slipped the key Nichole had given her into her pocket. There would be no more locks where she was going.

When Allie stepped from the house, Wes almost didn't recognize her. She wore a wine red riding skirt with a jacket and hat to match. Her hair had been curled and tied to one side as Victoria's had been fifty years ago in the portrait. There could be no doubt to anyone seeing Allie that she was a lady. A fine, beautiful lady. The wild creature had disappeared.

If she'd been smiling, Wes thought, she would have been perfect. But Allie never smiled. He wasn't sure she even knew how.

"Are you sure you still want to go?" he asked as she paused on the step above him. "Victoria tells me you've a home here if you want it." He'd done what he set out to do, he'd found her family. She would someday inherit a ranch far bigger than the Montago spread.

"You said you'd take me back to my cave," she whispered. "Do you go back on your word?"

"No. I'll take you, if that's what you want." He handed her the reins to her horse. "Let's ride."

She didn't say a word as they rode south toward the Guadalupe River. By nightfall, they were both too tired to do more than build a fire and eat the leftovers from the lunch the cook had packed.

Wes knew they should talk, but he didn't know where to start. It didn't seem right that he should tell her how he felt without having some inkling of what her feelings were. He wasn't a man who spilled out his longings like some actor on a stage. And Allie never said anything unless she had to.

He leaned against his saddle and stretched his feet toward the fire, watching as she removed her jacket and hat. "There's a cot packed in the supplies, and a tent. I'll put it up if you like."

She shook her head and lifted a blanket from the stack. Without a word, she crossed to his side and lay down beside him.

He pulled her next to him. This might be their last night together, but he didn't kiss her. Wes just wanted to hold her and remember what she felt like against him. She'd said she wanted to go back. He wasn't the kind of man who'd beg or even ask again. He'd offered to take her to his ranch more than once, and she'd said no.

Wes fell asleep thinking of all the things he should say to her, but not knowing where to start.

By midafternoon the next day, they reached the Guadalupe River and stopped along its banks for supper. Allie felt her heart pound within her when she recognized the land. Suddenly, she could follow no longer. She raced ahead of Wes.

He seemed to understand and mimicked her movements as she picked her way through familiar landmarks. The trees had been green with late spring when she'd last seen them. Now, winter made the land seem cold and unwelcoming. But Allie could hardly wait to see her cave.

Darkness enclosed them as they reached the clearing that had once been a campsite years ago when the raid came. Now, a tiny thread of a stream cut into the land where once teepees stood. Grass grew over former campsites and the blood of a slain people had been washed away by years of rain.

"We can leave the horses here." Allie jumped down and studied the clearing in the moonlight. "There's water and grass."

"How much farther to the cave?"

"Just beyond the trees and up the hill a little."

Wes unsaddled the horses but left the mule loaded. He hobbled the mounts and swung one saddle over the pack while he carried the other. "Lead the way. I'll take the mule as far as I can, then unload and bring her back here. You sure you can find this place at night?"

Allie took his hand and led him into the blackness of the trees. She didn't explain that most of the times she'd left the cave had been at night. She knew every tree, every branch. She was no longer in a strange world. She was home.

When she reached the entrance, she stopped and turned loose of his fingers. "I'll pull the brush back and you can unload."

Wes lit a lantern and made several trips depositing their belongings at the opening.

While he took the mule back to the clearing, Allie waited in the darkness. Not all the seasons had changed since she'd seen her home, yet it seemed smaller than she remembered. The air was heavier, and the smell of decaying leaves penetrated the cold night.

When Wes returned with the lantern, he stood just inside the opening, almost brushing the top of the rock. She didn't remember it being so small. She'd always thought of it as big.

"I can sleep here for tonight if you want your privacy," he offered.

"No," Allie almost shouted. "Come back with me. Tonight you will sleep beneath my robes." She almost added, *as I've planned.* But she couldn't tell him she had a plan. Not until she knew she could carry it out.

They collected a few of the supplies and moved deep into the cave.

After several turns, Wes asked, "How'd you ever find your way to this place?" His low voice echoed through the tunnels, creating a lonely sound as if a voice had lost direction.

"It took me many tries to find the chamber. At first,

I brought sticks and lit one after the other, using the charred ones to mark the walls.''

Wes lifted the lantern to see markings along one wall. They looked like the scratchings of a child, reminding Wes of how young Allie must have been when she first began her search. What courage it must have taken for a child to enter this world where most adults would hesitate to go.

"When the lights burned out, my exploring was over. So I brought freshly cut branches and spread the sap to mark my way. Even when it dried, it left the walls smooth at finger-level. Then, even in total blackness, I could feel the once sticky syrup along the rock. Every time I turned down a dead-end tunnel, I brought fresh horse droppings to place in the opening so I'd know not to turn that direction again. By the time I'd learned my way, the droppings had dried.''

Wes laughed. "You were just a kid exploring this place.''

Suddenly, they turned the last corner and were in a cavern twice the size of Victoria's greatroom.

Wes set the lantern down and slowly circled. "This is grand, Allie. Grand.''

She'd only seen the room in firelight and by the thin light that filtered from far above. Now, with the lantern, she could see her home clearly. The jagged walls, the poor array of handmade bowls and baskets. Dirty buffalo robes others had discarded spread on the hard rock to make a carpet, and ashes from dozens of fires were swept into one corner. Compared to all the homes she'd now seen, her cave looked terrible, little more than the den of an animal.

Allie knelt in the center of the room, fighting back tears. She stopped thinking about being safe in her cave. All she could remember now were the cold nights and days without sunshine. And the terrible loneliness of never hearing a human voice.

"I'll build a fire,'' she managed to whisper. She

couldn't bear to allow Wes to know she was unhappy after she'd made him bring her here.

Wes wasn't listening. "This is a great place, Allie. Did you make the bowls? And the baskets? Of course you did."

With the fire started, Allie lifted the lantern and moved to the space where she kept her treasured pelts. "You can have these." She held the lamp high. "I have no need for them. Maybe you can start your herd with the money you get from them. They will repay you."

Wes knelt beside the pelts. They were not the fine winter pelts found farther north, and they looked to have been tanned and cut by a child with a dull knife. Maybe, on a good day, with a blind trader, they'd bring enough money for a dozen head of scrawny longhorns. But they were her gift. Her most valuable possession.

"Allie, I can't take these."

"You must. I decided long ago that they would repay you for all the trouble I've been to you. I decided to give them to you."

"I can't." Wes stood, guessing the pelts were the reason she brought him here. Not because she wanted to stay with him a few days longer. Not because she wanted to sleep one more night with him. But only to pay him for his services.

"You must," Allie insisted when he didn't answer. "You saved my life."

Wes knew she had no idea of the value of the pelts. She thought she was giving him a great prize. If he turned her down, he insulted her. "Allie, you are my wife. All you have already belongs to me."

She raised her head slightly. "That is true."

"And all I have belongs to you," Wes added. "These pelts are of great value, but they are nothing compared to your life."

She could never remember a time when she thought of herself as having any value, much less great value. She moved around the cavern, turning over in her mind what he'd said. The memory of his words warmed her face. Her pelts were her greatest wealth, but he'd said they were nothing compared to her.

Wes followed her out of the cave and back down to the stream, surprising her by how fast he'd learned his way. While she washed, he checked on the horses. When they returned to the cave, he made coffee while she unrolled a huge buffalo hide and began undressing in the center of it.

"Aren't you going to wear a nightgown?" Wes watched her over his coffee cup.

"I never have in the cave before. The fire is warm, and the fur feels soft against my skin."

She lay on the robe nude and spread one of Wes's wool blankets over herself.

Wes continued to drink his coffee, but each swallow became a battle.

For several minutes, he studied her, wondering what she wanted of him. He could barely play her game of not loving her all the way now. If she were nude beside him, he wasn't sure he could obey the rules she'd set.

"Wes," she whispered. "Are you going to sleep beside me tonight?"

"I can't," he mumbled as he stood. "I'm a man, Allie. Much as you'd like to think I'm some kind of guardian angel, I'm just a man. There is a limit."

He grabbed the lantern and was several feet down the tunnel before she wrapped the blanket around her shoulders and caught up with him.

"Wait!" She placed her hand on his arm, as though it somehow chained him to her. "Don't leave me. Please, don't leave me tonight."

"I can't stay." He looked down at her. Rock walls forced them closer than they'd been all day. "Another night of sleeping beside you and not making you mine will drive me mad."

The torture showed in his warm brown eyes, and Allie knew she'd been unfair. Somehow in keeping herself from harm, she'd hurt him. She'd always thought of how she needed him and how he'd protect her. It had never occurred to her that he might need her.

"No harm has ever come to me in this cave," she whispered. "Sleep next to me. Do whatever you wish, but don't leave me alone tonight."

Wes bent closer, but he didn't touch her. "No, Allie. I can't sleep with you just because you feel you owe me. I can't be your husband and not be a man."

"I owe you nothing. That is not why I asked. I gave you the pelts, so we are even. And I do not ask for you to sleep with me, but to mate with me. I want to know the rest of this act you call loving."

"No." He couldn't believe what he was saying. She was offering the very thing he'd longed for every night when she was so close against him. But he couldn't. Not on her terms. Not because she wanted one night.

All his life he'd looked for a love for a night, but she was a love for a lifetime. One night would never do. He loved her too much to leave her here with the possibility of a child. His child.

"You do not want me?" She tried to keep her voice from shaking.

Wes leaned near, pressing her against the wall of the cave. "I want you so bad I can taste the need in my throat. But not this way. Not the way you think. I don't want to take you. I want to make love to you."

He pressed his face into the fresh smell of her hair. "The act of loving can't be taken, only given. Don't offer just because you don't want to be alone, Allie. Offer because you want me."

"Teach me of this loving." She raised her arms to him. "Please."

The blanket floated to the floor of the cave along with all of Wes's defenses.

TWENTY-EIGHT

WES CARRIED ALLIE BACK TO HER ROCK-WALLED room and gently set her down on the soft fur bed. He wasn't sure why she wanted him to make love to her, but he could no longer turn her away.

Standing, he tried not to hurry. He removed his gun belt and laid it on the pile of pelts.

Then he undressed slowly, as though removing his clothes in front of her was the most natural act in the world. Between the lantern and the campfire, light danced off the walls, allowing her to see him fully. Wes wanted her to know every second that it was he and no one else making love to her. He wanted her to be able to see his face and the truth in his eyes.

Her huge blue eyes watched him. Wes could see emotions churning within her. Fear, longing, stubbornness, panic, desire. There was no telling which would win out this night. But whatever happened, he'd be with her.

He lay down several inches away and surveyed her beauty. Fear flickered in her eyes, but she didn't turn away or hide herself from his view. He peeled the blanket away. Slowly, he leaned forward and kissed her. Only their lips touched, nothing more.

When he pulled away, tears shimmered in her eyes.

"Are you frightened?" He fought to keep from pulling her into his arms.

"A little," she answered. "But I know you will not hurt me. I don't want to live with the nightmares anymore. Show me there is more."

"You really have no idea how beautiful you are, Allie. Maybe I can even please you," he offered, feeling as if this were the first time for them both. She'd never made love, and, in truth, neither had he.

He ventured closer, cupping her face as he kissed her once more. She tasted as he knew she would, of liquid pleasure. Her bottom lip trembled slightly as his kiss gently brushed over it.

Easy, he told himself. Make love to her slowly.

His kiss touched the corners of her mouth, teasing it open slightly before he kissed her once more. She responded as he hoped she would.

When he pulled away the second time, a bit of the fear was gone from her eyes. He waited, unsure of what to do next to keep from frightening her. How could he show her the other side of an act she'd only seen as evil? If one moment reminded her of her nightmares, any hope he had of loving her for a lifetime would be lost.

He couldn't bring himself to touch her. The stakes were too high. He hesitated.

She grew impatient and reached for his hand. Placing it over her breast, she asked, "Is the kissing and touching a part of your loving?"

"Definitely."

"Then you will do that part first."

Wes laughed. "If you insist." He moved his hand over her warm skin as his mouth touched hers once more. The kiss deepened to a point he knew she enjoyed. She sighed against his lips and rolled closer, pressing her breast deeper into his palm.

Wes stroked her gently. He kissed her until all the stiffness and hesitancy in her body vanished. Then he leaned away slightly and lifted her hand to his mouth. As before, she enjoyed capturing his kiss within her hand. And when he placed her fingers on his chest, she didn't pull away.

"Touch me," he whispered. "Like you did a few nights ago."

She followed his lead, feathering her fingers across his chest and through his hair as he rewarded her with light kisses. As she moved, their bodies came into contact again and again, a tap, a brush, an accidental pressing. She seemed unaware of the impact her touch had on him. It was as though she accepted his nearness as part of the kiss and the touching she did.

Watching the fire build in her eyes was like watching passion's birth. A touch at a time, she became aware of him. An accidental brush of her body against his was repeated. A slight embrace became bolder on the next passing.

Slowly, his kisses deepened. His hand covered hers and moved over his body, encouraging her to touch where she hadn't dared. At first, she pulled away. He tried again and again, pulling her hand over his flesh, making her know every part of him with his gentle persuasion.

After the first few jolts of panic, she relaxed. His kisses drew her back to the paradise, the warmth. Finally, when he lifted his hand from hers, she didn't pull away, but continued to touch him.

His kisses moved to her throat, and then her breasts, making bolts of pleasure shoot through her and warmth grow within the very core of her. When she was deep into the middle of paradise, he moved close against her ear, his words more a kiss than speech.

"Say you want me, Allie." He kissed her cheek. "Look at me and say you want to make love to me."

"I want . . ."

His hand lowered over her abdomen as she began, intentionally venturing into territory she'd said was forbidden.

"I want . . ."

His hand was firm across her stomach, moving downward, making her forget words.

His fingers pressed over the place between her legs, where she said he'd never touch again.

"Say it, Allie." His voice was low with need. "Say you want me."

Suddenly there was no air in her lungs, no air in the room. Allie wanted to fight and run. She wanted to get away from all the world, all the hurt and all the pain. But his body leaned warm and protectively against her side. His hand rested low, holding her in place, holding her to him.

His soft kisses rained against her cheek. "Say it, Allie. Look at me and say the words."

She looked at him then as her blood pumped through her veins in panic. Thoughts of fighting filled her senses. She'd fight. She'd kill if she had to. No one would hurt her again.

Only she saw no devil. She saw only Wes with his warm brown eyes filled with worry and doubt. His strong body held her still, but she knew he understood her pain. He was not the enemy but there beside her to help her fight the nightmares.

There was no overwhelming desire, no passion-driven look about him. There was only concern. And she knew he wasn't doing this for himself, but for her.

She took a deep breath, feeling the weight of his hand over her. "I want you," she forced the words. "I need you to make love to me."

Wes kissed her and whispered against her mouth, "Say it again, darling."

"I want you," she answered as she felt his hand began to explore. "I need you to love me."

When she stiffened suddenly, his voice filled her world.

"Look at me, Allie," he ordered gently. "Don't close your eyes." His hand grew bolder, but his stare never left her face.

She held her breath, expecting pain, but none came.

His eyes told her all she needed to know. He'd never hurt her.

Suddenly, a fire exploded within her, and she began to move with his touch.

He slid a few inches away so that he could watch her. Only his hand rested on her now. She could have pulled from his hold easily if she'd wanted, but she didn't want to leave the pleasure.

His fingers were bold as they moved, making her cry out for more. She'd expected him to kiss her, but his mouth closed over the tip of her breast and the pleasure she thought could grow no greater increased.

When his mouth returned to her lips, she pulled him close, needing his kiss as she had never needed anything in her life. She wanted to be kissed fully, and he gave her what she wanted. A kiss so full of desire it took her breath away.

When she relaxed back on the bed, he smiled down at her, his hand still touching her. "You're ready now, Allie. There will be no pain."

She'd expected him to move above her, but he pulled her atop him. She went willingly, unafraid.

He kissed her tenderly as his hands slid along her hips and lowered her body over him. A warmth spread through her as he moved within, filling her completely with his passion.

Any noise she would have made was muffled in the depths of his kiss as the joining of their bodies became complete.

His hands on her hips, he taught her the dance of loving, one step at a time. Emotions overwhelmed her as his kisses continued. Her breasts molded against the wall of his chest, and a part of him touched deep inside her, stirring a fire . . . a fire that built until she moved without his encouragement.

As pleasure suddenly shot through her like a cannon, Allie felt him tighten every muscle. He wrapped his arms around her and held her to him as his body shook from the passion.

For a long while, she lay atop him, listening to his breathing return to normal, enjoying the way his hands slowly stroked over her from shoulder to thigh.

Finally, he drew her face up gently with his hands and looked into her eyes. "Are you all right, darling?"

She saw that the sudden flame of passion had reached him also, for his eyes still hinted of the wildness they'd just experienced. His hair was tossed, and his face slightly flushed. He'd never looked so handsome.

"Again, please," she whispered.

TWENTY-NINE

WES HIT THE ICY WATER LIKE A DEAD MAN TOSSED in to float downstream. He hardly felt the cold surround him and remained underwater until his lungs demanded he surface to breathe.

He'd made love to Allie four times, and it wasn't even dawn yet. In between, she touched him and he touched her. They kissed so often and so deeply, he was sure he scraped her face raw with his stubble.

And each time he finished, Wes felt like he drained his very soul into her, and she only begged for more.

At this rate, he'd be dead within a matter of days. Wes shook the water from his head and laughed. Maybe that was why Miss Victoria had had so many husbands, if Allie was anything like her grandmother. He'd fought all day in battle and not felt this tired, or this close to heaven.

With each of their matings, a wildness grew stronger within Allie. He'd heard that women were told to lie still and endure a husband's needs. Allie had obviously missed such a lecture. She was an active participant, wanting to know and explore. With each loving, a part of her fear vaporized until the strong woman she'd been meant to be shone through.

Wes leaned back and let the cold water rush over him. He'd found in Allie something else besides war to make him feel totally alive. He found an equal inside the frightened creature he'd thought to save. He might have delivered her from terror, but she ransomed him from a life of never feeling anything too deeply. She brought him back to life after layers of war had numbed him.

Thinking about her made a longing grow within him. He climbed from the river and wrapped himself in a blanket, suddenly in a hurry to be back by her side.

Clouds promising rain blackened the night. On his way back to the cave, he checked the animals, making sure they were beneath the cover of trees in case a storm came.

When he reached the chamber deep within, Allie lay curled in a blanket, sound asleep. Wes warmed himself by the fire before lying beside her. It didn't matter that this was probably one of the coldest, dampest, hardest beds he'd ever slept in. Allie made it perfect.

"I love you," he whispered into her hair. "I love you more than I've ever loved anything or anyone in my life." He had to say the words aloud, even if only for his ears. His love for her was greater than he thought himself capable of feeling.

As Allie slept, Wes listened to the distant drum of the rain. Occasionally, a few drops would slip through the crack in the roof of the cave and sizzle into the fire. The wind moved through the cavern in a whisper, chilling whatever part of him didn't face the flames. He pulled another blanket over them both, but sleep eluded him.

Sometime after a gray dawn, Wes came to a conclusion. He wanted Allie as his wife forever. Not until she was safe or until she found a home. He wanted her home to be with him. He wanted to live with her every day of the life he had left. Like Maxwell and Victoria, he wanted to be buried next to her in a family plot their grandchildren would visit.

But he had nothing to offer her other than a dugout on a ranch without cattle. She deserved more. Though the frame of a fine house had been started, the wood would be rotted before he had enough money to finish

building. All he'd ever been a success at in life was
being a soldier, and the war was over.

Wes thought of the map. The Goliad gold. He was
within a day's ride of it. He could leave Allie and be
back before she had time to miss him.

If he told her of his plan, she would want to follow,
and Wes had no idea what he might encounter. She
would be safer here in her cave. He'd bring in enough
firewood to last a week and leave her the supplies.

But he couldn't leave Allie without her knowing he'd
be back. She had to understand that last night was the
beginning, not the end. A note might work, but he
wasn't sure she could read.

Wes reached for his trousers. As he dressed, he pulled
the compass his father had given him from his pocket.
Turning over the largest of her baskets, he placed the
compass on top. She would have no trouble seeing it
when she woke up. She'd know he'd be back. He'd told
her he never left his compass. She would know, and
she'd wait.

He buttoned his coat and slipped from the chamber,
leaving everything he loved deep within the cavern
walls.

The wind seemed stronger as he lifted his saddle and
moved into the rain. "I'll be back soon," he mumbled,
wishing he could have awakened her before he left. But
he knew her. She had a way of talking him into seeing
things her way, even when she didn't speak at all.

Wes was just crossing the river when the wind whispered through the chamber once more, blowing the basket over and sending his compass rolling into the stack
of pelts.

Allie awoke slowly, as if from a long dream. For a few
minutes, she was more in her dream than in reality. The
damp coldness of the cave made her shiver and reach
for Wes. . . . He was gone.

An hour later, she stood and dressed in the shadowy
light of the fire. There was no need to check the cave

entrance. She knew his saddle would not be there. He'd been a man of his word. He said he would take her to the cave if she asked. He never said he would stay.

Allie rolled up the buffalo hide and placed it atop the stack of pelts. Light from the tiny crack in the top of the cavern told her it was day, but clouds prevented any sunbeams. She'd learned years ago to judge the time by the thin sliver of light moving across her room while the day aged.

Walking to the cave opening, she looked out at the rain. Wes hadn't even waited for the storm to clear.

She thought of all the things she'd been called in her life. Wild, savage, creature, a throwaway woman. All names that spoke of her lack of value. But, for a few days, he'd called her darling. He'd held her with cherishing arms. And now his night of lovemaking would have to last her a lifetime.

Part of her wanted to scream, *Let him go*. She didn't need him, she didn't need anyone. She proved that when she walked away from Victoria's ranch. And last night she proved she wasn't afraid.

Her life had come full circle from being alone before her capture to being alone now. Only she had changed. Somehow amidst all the nightmares and loving, she'd grown. She'd learned who she was, and who she wanted.

"Wes," she whispered, as if merely voicing his name could bring him back. She wanted the man who'd risked his life to save her from the cage and who'd married her to keep her from harm's way. She needed the man whose scar added character to his face, whose rough hands could touch her so gently.

Allie lifted her chin. And . . . she would have the man who held her priceless in his eyes.

Her fingers closed into fists. She would have him if she had to track him down and beat sense into him. He was her husband, the only one she would ever have. He might think his worth depended on how much he owned, but she'd prove him wrong. His value lay in the way he kept his word, the way he protected her with his life, the way he loved her with his heart wide open. Words hadn't told her he loved her; his actions had.

Allie lifted the saddle. She knew he'd gone after the gold he thought was at a place called Goliad. And without her, he'd probably get himself killed.

She'd never wanted anything in her life but to survive. Until now. She wanted Wes. She wanted him all the way to her toes, and she planned to fight for what she wanted.

Marching through the mud, half dragging the saddle, Allie formed her plan. Vincent had said the mission was in sight of the river. Well, she'd ride downstream until she saw it. If Wes wasn't there, she'd come back to her cave and think of another plan. But one way or the other, Wes would be her husband.

It took her almost an hour to saddle the horse and move all the supplies back into her chamber. At first she tied the mule, then changed her mind for fear he might be attacked by wolves. The mule would have to go along with her.

She dressed in her leathers, knowing they'd keep her warmer in the rain and be easier to move in. The boots Nichole had given her went well with her leggings. Finally, she braided her hair in one long chain and tied it with a leather strap.

When she left her cave, she looked more Comanche than the only grandchild of Victoria Catlin.

Deep into the night, Allie finally saw the outline of the mission. The tall stone buildings pointed toward the night sky in a silent stand against all time. Several dwellings surrounded it, but the hour was late, and any fires within the houses were low.

She left her horse and the mule at the river and walked slowly toward the mission. Her leather made no sound as she neared. In a few hours it would be dawn. If Wes were here, he'd wait until morning to leave.

Slowly, she recognized the outline of a man leaning against the wall outside the mission. His hat was low, his arms and legs crossed over a slender body with wide shoulders. She felt a sadness, a sense of loss in the way he stood. *Wes*. Whatever he'd found hadn't been a treasure.

She wasn't sure what he'd do when he saw her. Or even if he'd be glad she came, but she had to try. If he didn't want her, he'd have to tell her to her face, not disappear from her life.

Allie moved in front of him and widened her stance, preparing for whatever happened.

Wes raised his head and smiled. "I heard you coming since you left the river."

She tilted her head. Of all the things she'd thought he would say, that wasn't one of them. He didn't reach for her as she hoped he might.

"Why'd you come, Allie? Didn't you know I'd be back as soon as I could?"

He made no sense. How could she have known he'd be back? It was time to say what she planned.

"I came to be with you." She moved a step closer so that she could see his face clearly in the moonlight. "If you don't want me, you'll have to say so face to face. I am of your tribe. I should travel wherever you travel."

Wes pushed away from the wall. "Daniel was right when he said I'm not much of a catch as a husband. I just played my last card inside and didn't win the hand. There is no Goliad gold. A priest told me he has seen a dozen old maps like the one I had. They're all worthless."

"The gold doesn't matter."

"Not to you, but I can't ask you to be my real wife when I have nothing to offer. You deserve more, far more."

Allie couldn't believe what she was hearing. He didn't think himself worthy of her.

A flicker of light blinked above them from the window. The faraway sound of stone scraping against stone creaked through the air.

"Someone's in the church," Allie whispered. "Should we go?"

A thud echoed from inside, then another.

Glancing at the light, Wes shook his head. "No one should be there at this hour."

"Maybe it's the ghosts."

"Maybe." Wes laughed. "Come to get their own gold."

A rattle whispered from the church. A tapping. Someone running.

Wes grabbed Allie's hand and headed toward the entrance. "If the map's worthless, why would anyone be in the church so late? Those aren't ghosts."

They passed huge, hand-carved doors as they entered the almost total darkness of the mission.

Allie pulled at Wes's hand. She didn't want to invade this place. She could feel the sorrow, the sadness, the pain of hundreds who'd once been imprisoned here. Allie knew what it felt like to be locked in when all hope of escape vanished.

"Hello!" he shouted.

The tapping stopped.

Crossing to the lantern sitting on the floor beside a stone that had been pried away, Wes knelt and waited as he drew his Colt.

After a while, the priest he'd given what he thought to be a worthless map crawled from the opening. Dust clung to him like a second skin. "You were right!" he shouted at Wes with an almost wicked laugh. "The map was true. There is a tunnel beneath this stone."

Wes moved closer, not believing the man's words. If the tunnel existed, the gold must also exist.

The priest pulled off his robe and tossed it away. The clothing slid across the floor of the mission. Beneath the robes he wore the clothes of a wrangler, not a man of the cloth. "We've been looking for months and hoping the map hadn't disappeared in that stampede. I've grown weary of wearing those robes every night and pretending. We almost gave up hope that anyone with a true map would show up."

Wes braced himself for a fight. "You laid a trap tonight. You don't belong here at the mission. You're one of the men who tried to kill Vincent."

The accusation did nothing to lesson the man's joy as he pulled a box of tools and explosives from the shadows. "What if I am? Who will you tell? The gold is mine. All you provided was the last key to the puzzle."

Wes raised his gun. "I don't think so."

The man glanced up from his work, as though Wes were no more than a gnat bothering him. "Go ahead, shoot me. But you'll have to watch your lady friend die."

Glancing behind him, Wes saw a short man with massive, hairy arms holding a long knife to Allie's throat. She stared at him, paralyzed in the stranger's grip.

"Choose!" the imposter priest shouted. "The woman or the gold."

Without hesitation, Wes lowered his weapon.

Laughter echoed as the wrangler sneered. "Now get out. I'm too excited to have you both killed tonight. And don't come back, McLain. You see, there's a difference between you and me. I'll do anything, including kill, for this gold. You don't want it that badly. It's not worth your life."

"You're right." Wes pulled Allie beneath his arm. "I've found something far more valuable."

As he walked away, he heard the two men talking as they scrambled to haul dynamite into the opening. One said a section about ten feet down had collapsed, but the map showed it was another five feet to the gold. They had no time to dig. They had to reach the gold and be gone before dawn, when the real priest arrived.

Wes no longer cared if they found the treasure or not. Allie was safe. In a blink of time, he'd made his choice.

They walked down to the river in silence. When they reached the shadows of aging cottonwood trees, he pulled her close and held her against his heart.

"You gave up the gold for me," she whispered when he pulled away.

"It doesn't matter," he answered. "I couldn't allow

any harm to come to you, you're my wife." He caressed her gently. "I didn't want you to come with me tonight because you might be in danger, but you made me realize I already have a treasure."

Allie stared at his chest, unable to look into his eyes. "When I told Jason he was of my tribe," Allie told him, closing her eyes as she remembered the words, "he said, 'I love you too.' "

Wes raised her head. "Are you saying you love me, Mrs. McLain?"

"I am."

Wes kissed her nose and pulled away. "Then there's something that needs doing." He lowered to one knee and held her left hand in both his. "Allie, will you marry me? Will you have me, rich or mostly poor? Will you sleep beneath my blankets for the rest of your life?"

A sudden blast shattered the night. The ground beneath them shook. For a second, Wes thought it was his heart. A light bright as day blinked from inside the mission.

"Stay here!" Wes shouted as he ran across the field.

Allie heard shouts from the buildings around as people emerged in their nightclothes to see what had happened. She couldn't wait. She ran to catch Wes.

When she reached the huge doors, she saw him turn away from the opening in the floor.

"What happened?"

"The dynamite must have gone off before they could get out. The whole tunnel's caved in. If they weren't blown to bits, they're buried ten feet down."

Allie pushed past him and grabbed the loose square of stone that the men had removed. "Help me," she whispered, "before others get here."

Wes lifted the other side of the stone. "Why?"

"Let the gold stay with the ghosts of Goliad. It's wrong for anyone to take it."

Wes helped her slide the stone into place. "So we leave a fortune buried along with the men who tried to take it?"

Allie straightened and nodded. People were already filling the church, asking questions and trying to figure out what caused such an explosion.

She remained silent.

A real priest hurried in, trying to look around as he calmed his flock. Seeing the two strangers, but nothing amiss with the building, he demanded to know why they were in the mission at this hour.

Wes took Allie's hand and said simply, "We want to get married." He glanced in her direction. "If she'll have me? I'd like to do it right this time," he leaned close and whispered, "without you holding a knife."

"But all the ghosts?"

"I don't think they'll mind."

The priest let out a long breath and straightened his robes. Quick weddings and fast funerals were a way of life in this country. "Do you want to marry this man, young lady?"

Allie smiled. "I do."

EPILOGUE

THEY RODE NORTH, AVOIDING TOWNS AS THEY
headed home to Wes's ranch. Even after a few days in
the cave, Wes still didn't want to share Allie with anyone. They could have made the journey in half the time,
but Wes found himself looking for a camp by midafternoon each day. He'd take the time to unload the pack
mule and set up the tent. Then, they'd watch the sun set
and were making love by the time the stars came out
each night. She liked to sleep nude beside him, and Wes
never thought to complain.

When they finally crossed onto his land, he saw it
through her eyes. All that had ever mattered to him was
how many head of cattle he could run on each acre. But
she saw the streams and the rolling hills. To her, his
ranch was beautiful.

As they moved over his land, Wes noticed far more
strays grazing on the property than he remembered leaving before the drive. First a few, then groups of twenty
or thirty head. As they neared, he was surprised to see
they bore his brand.

At first, Wes thought he must have been a fool to miss
so many head, but as he came upon a herd of fifty or
more, he knew something was wrong. No man would
leave so many in the field to winter.

When they cleared the ridge to his dugout, Wes understood. Between his home and the barn was a camp. Wes kicked his horse, ready to demand some answers.

But as he approached, he recognized the men. They were Victoria's Old Guard, and they were milling around as though they'd been there for days.

Wes swung from his saddle. "What's going on?" he asked the first man he saw.

The aging soldier just pointed to the campsite.

Wes saw Colonel Attenbury step from a tent. "Colonel!" Wes called to him. "What's going on?"

The colonel smiled. "We've been sent to deliver Miss Allie's dowry."

"I don't need any—"

Attenbury held up his hand. "I've been told that if you won't take the cattle, we're to take back the bride. It is an insult to refuse a dowry."

Wes heard the sound of several guns clearing leather.

"Which will it be, son? Have no doubt, we'll carry out Miss Victoria's order if we have to make her granddaughter a widow to do so."

Wes smiled. "I guess I'll take the cattle—because I'm not giving up my wife."

He turned in time to see Allie step into the dugout; he felt his heart sink. How could he bring a wife to such a horrible little house that stuck out of the side of a ridge, half underground, half above?

As he walked away, he heard Attenbury invite them to supper, but Wes wasn't thinking of food. She'd probably take one look at the spider web–infested place and run back to Victoria's.

When he stepped into the dugout, it was so black he couldn't even see her. She'd vanished in the shadows.

"It's not so bad once the windows are opened and the lamps are lit," he tried to reassure her. "I never spent much time in here."

He knew she was in the darkness somewhere.

"I'll start on the other house. We'll have it finished in no time." He moved into the blackness.

When he did, her arms slid around his waist. "I love

it," she whispered. "It's half your world and half mine. Half house and half cave."

Her hand moved over his clothes to his hair and pulled his head down to her lips. The kiss was warm and inviting. Cool air surrounded them. Thick walls blocked out all the world but Allie in his arms.

"There's a bed in here somewhere," he mumbled as she unbuttoned his clothes, as if they hadn't made love in days.

"I know," she said, laughing. "I've already stumbled over it." She pulled him along.

"Allie," he whispered as their knees brushed the bed and they tumbled backward. "Are you smiling?"

"Yes," she answered.

"Allie, I love you."

"I take that as a promise."

He kissed her tenderly.

"More, please."

Turn the page for a
preview of Jodi Thomas's
newest romance

To Wed in Texas

Coming soon from Jove Books

ONE

DANIEL MCLAIN WRAPPED HIS ARMS ACROSS HIS chest and fought to keep warm as he stood on the cold, damp dock and watched an ancient trunk being unloaded off the day's only steamboat. Dark, brooding clouds reflected his mood while the boat's whistle echoed to the far bank covered in cypress trees. His massive strength could no more help him now than he could hold back the impending storm. He was alone.

If he were a swearing man, this would be the time for a few carefully chosen words.

Somehow, he'd landed in a Texas town so wild that federal troops were being pulled from along the frontier to handle the riots. Law was almost nonexistent. The worst of men, both Northern and Southern, poured through the streets as though it were the only hole in the dike. Corruption spilled like sewage, fouling even those trying to mend the country's cavernwide rip. Prison corrals, not fit for pigs, held innocent men while the guilty walked free, bragging of their crimes.

Daniel shoved the old trunk, engraved with his late wife's maiden name, into the bed of his wagon. "Hell," he mumbled low enough he hoped heaven wouldn't hear. As if he didn't have enough problems, the trunk from May's aunt had arrived without the old woman attached.

He had his hands full trying to stop war from breaking out. Thanks to one old maid who'd missed the only boat from Shreveport, he had no one to keep his three-year-old daughters out of harm's way.

As rain broke free from above, Daniel closed his eyes and fought back the loneliness that shook from his very core. "Why'd you have to leave me, May?" he whispered for the hundredth time since his wife died. If she'd known how hard his life would be, would she have fought a bit longer to survive? He'd lived through his war injuries to come back to her. Why hadn't she lived through childbirth?

He slapped the horses into action and set his jaw. Somehow, he would do what had to be done. Somehow, he'd make it another day. He'd raise his daughters, he'd do his job, and he'd wait until he could be with May again. He had no doubt there was a heaven, although, except for the twins' smiles, he was living in hell.

Karlee Whitworth fought to stretch her cramped leg amid the scratchy woolens and once-starched cottons that surrounded her like a stagnant tornado. If she'd realized her stay in the trunk would be so long, she would have removed more of the clothing before climbing inside.

"Help," she whispered, knowing no one would hear her. "I'm trapped in here! Help!"

The swaying had stopped hours ago, so she knew she was no longer being transported. She'd recognized the rocking of the ship last night, then felt a shifting when moved to a wagon. The uneven, bumpy ride had seemed endless before she'd felt the trunk lifted and set on solid ground. But where? A night and a day must have passed while she waited.

What if the baggage housing her had been set aside in some storeroom? It might be weeks before her cousin's husband picked it up! Karlee wasn't even sure Aunt Rosy had sent him word she was coming in Rosy's place. The last letter he'd probably received had listed plans for the old aunt to make the trip. Rosy and Violet had hatched up the idea of Karlee going as a surprise. Karlee was packed before the shock had time to wear off. The entire clan seemed in such a hurry to get rid of Karlee, they probably hadn't thought of posting word of her arrival.

What if she had to wait days until someone noticed the shipment? When Reverend Daniel McLain finally opened the chest addressed to him, he'd find nothing but the bones of Karlee Whitworth, an unknown cousin-in-law, amid her wrinkled clothing.

Karlee pounded against the inside of the trunk in earnest. "Help!" she screamed, knowing the fabric around her muffled her cries.

She listened, praying to hear any human sound. Riding in the trunk had seemed such a good idea in Shreveport when she'd run out of money. But now, it was more likely to fall into the category of "half-baked schemes." She always had trouble telling good ideas from half-baked schemes. In the beginning, they were twins. In the end, opposites.

Maybe there *was* something wrong with her brain. Her aunts had whispered often enough that Karlee was "perplexing, at best." They always used the phrase as though talking of an incurable illness to be tolerated. The whole town seemed to agree, for gentlemen callers were as scarce as fleas on a catfish.

Maybe her aunt hadn't sent word of her arrival for fear the good reverend would turn her down. Announcing a "perplexing, at best" cousin-in-law might be rather like wiring ahead of a plague's arrival.

Since her parents' deaths when she was eight, more than one relative had refused to take a turn at raising her. But the matronly aunts had taken precautions this time. They'd provided what they hoped to be enough money to make it to Jefferson, Texas, and not a dime more. No return passage. The reverend would have to take Karlee in.

But she was no penniless child. She was grown, and

she'd come to help. Surely, he'd understand and allow her to earn her keep. That is, if she were ever unpacked.

Hometown headlines flashed through Karlee's imagination: "Crazy old maid dies in box left in warehouse. No kin. No one to care."

She pounded harder.

Her plan had seemed so simple. She knew the codes used by the dock workers, thanks to her father, who'd been a captain. He had explained to her that most of the workers couldn't read, so playing cards were placed on all unaccompanied freight to indicate destination. Jefferson was known all along the waterways as the King of Spades.

Karlee had simply taken a card from the deck in her pocketbook and stuck it on the trunk already addressed to Daniel McLain. Then she climbed inside, planning to sleep the night away and wake at her destination.

But the dockhand had slapped the latch closed when he'd loaded the trunk.

Now, she might sleep forever! Karlee pounded again, then waited, hoping, praying.

After a few seconds, something, or someone, pounded back!

She let out a cry, expecting the lid to open, but nothing happened. The tiny sliver of light between the top boards was too small to see through. She felt like a jack-in-the-box waiting for the tune to end.

Karlee knocked again.

A rapping echoed her cry.

She tried once more with three sharp taps.

Three answered, but nothing more.

Karlee's hopes began to fade as, again and again, the rapping came and she answered, but nothing happened. Whoever was on the other side was toying with her but allowing no freedom.

Pulling into a tight ball, she tried to look at the bright side. If she died in this box, she wouldn't have to worry about all the wild stories she heard of Jefferson. Rumors were told that a man could rape and kill without even

going to jail in this town called the porthole to Texas.
Riverboat trash, outlaws, thieves, carpetbaggers, and angry rebs populated the booming port.

Oh, well, in this coffin she didn't have to worry about
the criminals. She'd simply starve to death in her warm,
dark prison.

She knocked again. She'd rather take her chances
among the outlaws than die in silence.

A devil knocked back without touching the latch.

"Girls, stop knocking on the trunk," Daniel ordered
from the stove, where he was trying to make pancakes.

The twins looked up at their father without the
slightest hint of planning to follow such an order. They
had his blond hair and their mother's brown eyes. As
soon as he returned to the cooking, they returned to
knocking on the tattered old box he'd brought in.

A few minutes passed before Daniel lifted one daughter off the ground with a single hand clamped onto the
back of her overalls. She squealed and wiggled as if on
a carnival ride, but showed no fear of her only parent.

"I said"—Dan couldn't help but smile—"stop
knocking on your great-aunt's trunk."

"But, Daddy," the child on the ground corrected. "It
knocks back."

Daniel raised an eyebrow as he lowered the other girl
to the ground. "It does? Next you'll be telling me it
talks as well."

Both girls nodded, sending their curly hair flying
around their faces.

Daniel pictured May's plump little Aunt Rosy being
stuffed into the trunk and shipped. Impossible.

"Can we open it?" one twin asked as the other
knocked once more on the lid.

"No," Daniel answered. "It belongs to—"

The faint sound of rapping froze his words.

TWO

Daniel flipped open the latch on the old trunk. An explosion of fabric rocked him backward. As he sat on the floor watching, a mass of red hair pushed through the dull-colored clothing, looking more like a huge ball of yarn than a woman's head. Daniel forced his mouth closed as the boxed creature stretched and climbed, none too gracefully, from the trunk. Her arms and legs were long and grew stronger with each movement. The clothes she wore were wrinkled and threadbare.

Bright green eyes glanced at him a moment before the woman yelled, "Clear the decks!" at the top of her lungs. In a mad dash, she ran across the room and out the back door as if her hem were on fire.

Daniel raised to his knees and fought to keep his balance as the twins rushed toward him. He rocked his daughters in strong arms. They all three stared out into the night where she'd vanished. The low howl of the wind and the blackness beyond the door seemed to erase any hint of her passing. She could have been a mythical creature born to full life before them and disappeared just as quickly, if he believed in such things.

"Who was that, Daddy?" the twin on his right knee whispered.

"I'm not sure," he answered honestly, feeling very much as though he'd just opened Pandora's box. "I think it was a woman." *Of course it was a woman*, he corrected mentally. He might have been a widower for years, but he hadn't yet gone blind. "One thing I know, that wasn't your mother's Aunt Rosy."

"Lock the door before she comes back, Daddy!" The other twin stretched and clutched his neck. "I'm afraid."

"No, let's wait and see if she returns. You've nothing to fear." He only hoped he spoke the truth. Women, even normal ones, tended to make him speechless. And he had a strong feeling this one was not within shouting distance of normal.

He lowered his voice to a calming tone. "From the speed she left, she may be halfway to Shreveport by now." He lifted the twins as he stood. "We might as well eat supper. If she's not back by the time we finish, I'll go outside and try to find her. It wouldn't be right not to look after whoever, or whatever, Aunt Rosy shipped us."

The twins dove into their pancakes with zest as Daniel poured himself a cup of coffee and watched the door. A hundred questions drifted through his mind. Answers were way outnumbered, which wasn't all that unusual if May's family was involved.

Quirkiness seemed the only common batter in the mix where the Whitworths were concerned. Even Aunt Rosy, who'd offered to come help, was a woman who liked to do most of the talking and *all* the thinking in a conversation. She not only was free with telling you what she thought, but if given a moment, she'd tell you what you should think also. Her sister, Violet, hadn't ended a sentence in years as far as Daniel could tell. Even when she paused, she began again as soon as possible by starting with an *and* or a *but* or, her favorite, *furthermore*.

One thing he knew, whoever this woman was, she'd been sent by the aunts. But had they packed and shipped the fiery redhead to help him, or to sweep her off their doorstep? From the glance he'd had of her, he guessed her to be mature, midtwenties, maybe. She didn't seem a bad-looking woman. He'd noticed no deformities. Except, of course, her hair. She seemed too thick of body to be stylish, no eighteen-inch waist, he guessed. He'd also noticed an ample chest packed into a properly tight bodice.

Judging from the speed with which she ran, she must be healthy enough.

"Reverend McLain?"

The woman was back, standing just inside the doorway, her dress and hair whirling in the night air.

Daniel stood slowly, forcing himself not to look at the way her clothes clung about her like a second skin. "Yes, I'm Daniel McLain," he answered in his most formal voice.

The stranger leaned her head back and shook her hair as though enjoying the wind's combing. "Good," she said. "I'm in the right place. That's something at least. Sorry about that sudden exit, but sometimes, it's a 'clear the decks,' you know, no time to stop and chat."

Daniel had no idea what she was talking about. Her chatter reminded him of years ago when he and the other seminary students were required to visit the insane wards. One poor man flashed to mind. Daniel had prayed to God with the ill soul for an hour before the man informed Daniel that he *was* God and had grown tired of listening.

The stranger before him glanced at Daniel as if she thought him slow of mind and whispered, "You know, the privy?"

"Oh." Daniel cleared his throat. Men and women weren't supposed to address such subjects. May had made him blush when they first married by simply saying she needed to take a walk outside. He suddenly felt very much older than his twenty-four years.

Changing the subject seemed the safest defense. "And who are you, madam?"

"It's 'miss,' " she answered as she moved into the

room twisting her hair into one thick braid at her shoulder. "I'm the spinster Whitworth, your wife's first cousin. I don't mind being unmarried, but I do get tolerably tired of being called 'miss.' Everyone in town knows I'm an old maid, but they still seem to say the word *miss* a little louder when they introduce me."

"Well, Miss . . . I mean . . ."

"Karlee," she helped. "Call me Karlee. After all, we're almost related."

She walked past him and sat down across the table from the twins. "And these must be your daughters. They do look alike. What are their names?"

Daniel frowned. "I just call them Twin. When I want one, I usually want the other."

The strange woman jumped from her chair once more, and Daniel wouldn't have been surprised to hear her yell "Clear the decks!"

But this time she headed straight toward him like a warrior on the attack. "You mean you haven't named your daughters? They're almost four, by my count, and you still just call them Twin?"

"I've been busy." Daniel forced himself not to step back with her advance.

She was tall; half a head more, and she'd be his height. And she stared directly at him without any respectable fear or feminine shyness.

"How busy does a man have to be to name his children?"

Before he could answer, gunshots rang from just outside, and the sound of horses' hooves gave rhythm to the night.

"Grab the blankets!" Daniel signaled with his head toward a pile of quilts as he tucked a twin beneath each arm. "And run, Spinster Karlee. Trouble's riding in."

She didn't question, but followed as he hurried through the large house almost void of furniture. He not only didn't have time to name his children, he obviously didn't bother with shopping. No chairs, no rugs, no curtains.

They entered the wide entry hall. With one mighty shove of his shoulder, Daniel slid a panel along one side of the foyer. A row of rifles lined the once-hidden wall and a hastily cut trapdoor scarred the floor. For a man of the cloth he seemed ready for anything.

Daniel lifted the lid. "Climb inside! You and the twins will be safe. I made this hiding place yesterday, knowing trouble would come calling."

Karlee glanced down at the hole that looked little more than four feet deep and a coffin's-width across. She was in no hurry to be locked away again.

"What about you?"

"I'll face the men. If they're not too liquored up, I should be able to send them on their way."

"I'll face them with you, Reverend."

"Get in there and be safe, Spinster Karlee!"

"I think not."

As always when emotion rose within him, Daniel's throat closed. He couldn't force the angry words out.

Karlee had no such problem. "I wouldn't climb in there if it were the only way to heaven. And you're not putting your no-name daughters in that hole while I've strength left to fight. We'll face the drunks together, for I'll not be boxed again. And that's my final word."

Daniel almost laughed in amazement. He might be a preacher by calling, but he'd spent most of his life being a blacksmith by necessity. He could easily send her to meet her Maker with one mighty blow, if he were a man given to violence. She might not be a thin woman, but he was well twice her size.

"You have no idea what's going on in this town."

Karlee raised her chin. "Well, if they've come down to murdering women and children, I might as well go now and avoid the dread of dying."

Daniel took a deep breath and reminded himself he was a man of peace as he handed over his daughters to a woman he felt sure could fight off a war party. "Stay out of sight," he ordered.

The spinster nodded once and was wise enough not

to smile at her victory. She hurried back to the kitchen with the twins in tow as Daniel slid the panel closed once more and moved to the front door.

Before Karlee reached the kitchen, she heard boots stomping across what had to be the front porch. She closed the hallway door, but angry shouts rattled it.

She had to think of something fast without frightening the twins. With a forced laugh, she grabbed the corner of the quilt she carried and waved it across the clean end of the table. "Would you like to live in a tent?"

The twins forgot about anyone beyond the kitchen and rushed to crawl beneath the homemade tent.

Karlee arranged the blankets around the table. "Now if you'll both be real quiet, I'll give you a surprise."

She heard them laugh and knew she'd found a game. They'd be safe beneath the table.

A sudden rattling at the back door reminded her that she might not be so secure. Frantically, Karlee searched for something to use as a weapon. She would not go quietly to her death in this nowhere town, and no one would hurt her little cousins as long as she breathed.

Just as the door creaked open, Karlee grabbed a still warm skillet dotted with burned pancake dough. She stepped behind the door as an enormous, hairy man poked his head through the opening like some huge bear checking a new den.

Karlee raised the iron pan and swung with all her might, figuring a skillet was like a gun. She wouldn't have picked it up if she hadn't planned on using it.

The bearded man took the blow to the side of his head without even time for surprise to register on his face. For a moment, he just stood still, like a mighty oak unaware of a final ax cut.

Karlee lifted the skillet, prepared to hit him again. But slowly, he crumbled, open-eyed and out cold.

She moved around him, her weapon ready, pride straightening her shoulders.

Two blond heads popped out from beneath the blanket, their eyes curious at the sound.

''Our surprise!'' they both shouted as they crawled from the blanket tent. ''Uncle Wolf!''

''Uncle Wolf?'' A sickness settled over Karlee thick as cold molasses.

The girls jumped on what they thought was their sleeping uncle.

A fine brew, Karlee thought, another great idea soured into a half-baked scheme. The curse of her life had followed her to Texas.